Hop on Pop

Enjoy reading!
Best wishes,
Susan Gray.

Susan Gray

U K Book Publishing.com

Editing, design, typesetting and publishing by UK Book Publishing

www.ukbookpublishing.com

ISBN: 978-1-917329-53-8

Hope on Hope

To my dad, Eric.

'Rejoice in hope...'

The Bible
Romans chapter 12 verse 12

Prologue

JUNE 1940

'*So, my darling Chantal, it pains me to write these words...but I must be honest with you.*' Chantal gasped, lifted the sheet to read the next page but... found the final paragraph. '*There... I've told you. Now, I must make haste to catch the post. Until we meet again, my beloved girl. Yours forever, Sam xxx*'.

Frantically, Chantal checked the page numbering – sheet number 1, with number 2 on the reverse; sheet number 5, blank on the reverse...but where were sheets 3 and 4? Panicking, she searched – down the side of the armchair, under the chair, on the rug. Along the inside edge of the fender; beneath the table, on the table...no missing sheet!

She ran out into the hallway, her eyes combing the edges of the floor. Arriving at the front door she opened the letterbox, peered inside – nothing. Stepping backwards, she lifted the dusty doormat...but no missing sheet was evident anywhere. Shoulders hunched, she retraced her steps and sat down dejectedly in the armchair, with an audible sigh.

Hanging her head in her hands, she rewound her mind. She had been sitting in this chair drinking her breakfast tea when the letterbox rattled. Placing her cup on the small table, she left the lounge and retrieved the solitary envelope from the hessian doormat. Her heart quickened. The postmark was undecipherable, but the handwriting was unmistakable. The once white envelope was muddied with someone's partial footprint, but not to worry... it had reached its destination.

She shivered, not with the cold on that warm June morning, but with anticipation. She ran her slender fingers over the characteristic symbol Sam drew on the envelope point. It was a tiny heart shape with a line curling away to an arrow point. '*Know this, my darling,*' Sam explained once, 'a*s I seal this envelope with my lips, my love travels to where you are*'. Gently, she slid her finger into the corner, ripped the edge and pulled out the contents. Unfolding the sheets, she began to read Sam's distinctive script. It was less than ten minutes since she had performed these actions.

Chantal removed her hands from her face and looked up. Her long-awaited letter from Sam... was a letter with a missing page! Did Sam forget to include it? Did it fall out as he put the sheets in the envelope? The seal was intact, so no one removed it. Oh, Sam...what did you want to tell me? She picked up the partial letter with a heavy heart and re-read the contents.

'My darling Chantal,

Apologies in advance for the splodges on this writing paper. Tears stream down my face as I pen these words. Tomorrow, we leave – you understand I can say no more. This may be our last communication, my darling…we may never meet again on this earth. Yet I carry a hope, a steadfast hope – that whatever lies before me, I will survive. So, I must impart something of immense importance. I love you deeply, Chantal, every day without you is torture. I re-live that wonderful weekend at The Bungalow constantly – it was so special. My memories of you and our love, keep me going. They make me determined to help fight this wretched war to hasten our reunion. I adore you, my precious girl. You are my 'raison d'etre'. So, my darling Chantal, it pains me to write these words…but I must be honest with you…

Chantal lifted the sheet…but as before… she read page 5 – the final page. *'There I've told you. I must make haste to catch the post. Until we meet again, my beloved girl. Yours forever, Sam xxx'.*

She glanced at the clock. She was running late for her first appointment. Chantal brought her lips to Sam's signature and kissed it. Then folding the letter, returned it to the envelope and placed it on the table. Her mind was troubled as she navigated her bicycle along the narrow country lanes of the French countryside.

Chapter 1

AUGUST 1946
ENGLAND

"Deal with her, Tom, she's your daughter," called Rachel with agitation. She was standing in the hallway with her hands on her hips. Tom sauntered through from the rear lounge to discover the cause of his wife's angst. Rachel eyeballed him.

"Tell her, in no uncertain terms, she *must* be ready, and by that, I mean, appropriately dressed, in twenty minutes!" Rachel's voice was almost at fever pitch.

Tom shook his head and addressed his irate wife. "Rachel, calm down. You'll give yourself a heart attack," he remarked, placing his hands on her shoulders. As always, his gentle words and soothing touch worked their magic. Rachel sunk her head onto her husband's broad chest, as he embraced her fondly.

Pulling back, he walked over to the foot of the wood-panelled stairs and shouted sternly. "Darcy Smallwood,

5

you have fifteen minutes to be dressed smartly and down here – do you understand me?"

There was a brief pause, during which a door slammed. Then a tall young man descended the creaky stairs, leading to the spacious, square hallway. Tom looked up at his blond-haired son and smiled.

"What is she doing?" he asked with a hint of exasperation.

"Search me, she's in a right fettle and has been in the bathroom for ages. She's used all the hot water – *again*," he emphasised. "I had to wash in cold water."

"Is she dressed, Josh?" enquired his fractious mother.

Josh shrugged his shoulders, rolled his eyes and walked towards the front door. The actions of his older sister usually annoyed him, exasperated his father and irritated his mother. He was not about to spring to her defence, so remained silent. Josh opened the front door.

"And where are you going?" asked his father.

Josh sighed. "To get some fresh air, peace and quiet before we must spend ages sitting in that stuffy conservatory," he replied wearily, then stepped out onto the driveway.

Tom turned to face his petite wife.

"Don't fret, Rachel. I imagine Peg and Pierre have the same problems with their offspring and will understand." He placed a gentle kiss on Rachel's forehead. "Come on, darling, cheer up – go and take a seat in the conservatory and I'll fetch you a glass of lemonade. Take a few minutes to relax before our guests arrive." He gazed lovingly into the frazzled, red face of his beautiful wife, then giggled.

"Your face is the colour of beetroot," he declared. Rachel dashed over to the hall mirror. Tom ambled up behind her and grinned, narrowly avoiding a pointed elbow in his side. "Go and sit down," he commanded, disappearing into the rear lounge.

Amazingly, by the time the French visitors arrived at Meckleridge House, all the Smallwood family were ready and waiting. Hugs, kisses, embraces, hand shaking and backslapping ensued as Tom, Rachel, Darcy and Josh welcomed their relatives... the Thibault family. Luggage and jackets were strewn across the floor, but the joy experienced by all was infectious, and with loud voices, roars of laughter, calls of ooos and ahhhs, Peg, Pierre, Jonty and Sylvie Thibault were welcomed exuberantly to Meckleridge House.

"I can't believe we are actually here," declared Tom's sister, Peg, as she sat down in the conservatory. Tom was handing round glasses of lemonade.

"This visit is long overdue," he remarked, smiling broadly at her. "How long has it been?"

His French brother-in-law answered. "Seven years, mon frère. Jonty was eleven years old, and Sylvie was eight...and just look at them now!" he commented, gazing adoringly at his two children, who were sitting, side by side, rather stiffly, on the edge of one of the settees.

On the other side of the large room, sitting equally stiffly, were Tom and Rachel's family. They sat staring at their French cousins...they were strangers.

On their last visit the four youngsters were close pals, roaming the extensive grounds around the then Meckleridge House Hotel; camping in the woods on the adjoining farmlands; swimming in the nearby river; playing competitive sports and sharing endless jokes. But seven years in adolescent life was a long time. Although the families had kept in touch with letters and telephone calls, the rapport between the young people appeared to be yet another casualty of the world war, which had prevented the two families from enjoying this annual visit.

"Have you seen Chantal?" Rachel asked Peg, with anxiety written across her face.

Peg shook her head. "We last spoke on the telephone at Easter, but we have been unable to meet her."

Rachel looked dejected. Her younger sister also lived in France in Bordeaux, some three hundred kilometres from Lyon, where the Thibaults resided.

"Have you heard much from her?" Peg enquired.

Rachel sighed. "Only an occasional letter. I've begged her to come here, now the war is over, but she is always evasive. At least the post is more regular, but the last time I tried to telephone her, the number was unobtainable. I keep telling Tom...if she won't come here, then we must go to France to see how she is coping. There are so many things I want to know about her."

A pause followed, then Peg spoke.

"Do you think we can go to our rooms and unpack?"

Tom sprang to his feet. "Of course, of course...how remiss of me, I must be losing my touch," he replied, leading the way out of the conservatory.

For almost twenty years, Tom Smallwood had been the proprietor of Meckleridge House Hotel – a small establishment located in the town of Malhaven, in northwest Durham. He, along with his deceased brother, had inherited the property and adjacent farmlands from their aunt as young men. The hotel had been Tom's 'pride and joy' and was a successful enterprise, until the advent of the Second World War. At that point, just like his aunt, the previous owner, had done, he offered the accommodation for wartime requirements. Ultimately, the hotel became a convalescent home for wounded and incapacitated military personnel. When its facilities were no longer required, and the remaining patients were transferred elsewhere, Tom and Rachel's home was returned to them in the summer of 1945. However, they decided to take a break and consider their options before reinstating the hotel.

Subsequently, the French visitors had plenty of accommodation at their disposal. In previous years they'd slept in the attic rooms. When Meckleridge House was a hotel, it boasted ten bedrooms plus a stable block annexe. The latter was currently housing Polish refugees. The land surrounding the hotel grounds was utilised during the war to provide an extensive market garden, overseen by Tom, to assist the war effort. The refugees were grateful for the work it provided, and the accompanying accommodation.

* * *

Tom glanced around the supper table, a few hours later. It was so satisfying to see the dining room being used for a family occasion again. Rachel had worked hard preparing things for their guests. Many items from the hotel days had been stored away in the attics during the war years. Restoring the place had proved a demanding task. A crisp white tablecloth overlaid with silver cutlery and a china dinner service graced the table, accompanied by white embroidered napkins – her attention to detail was praiseworthy.

"Rachel, the place looks splendid…just as I remembered it!" declared Peg, admiring her sister-in-law's handiwork.

Rachel beamed. "Thank you, Peg. It's so good to see things restored to their rightful place."

Tom was distracted and grinned as he observed his nephew Jonty, engaging his sixteen-year-old daughter, Darcy, in conversation. He tried to eavesdrop without success but did detect a brightness in Darcy's normally solemn visage. It was something he'd missed in recent times. His bright, bubbly effervescent child had morphed into a moody, sullen teenager, who seemed to thrive in picking faults with everyone around her. Whatever the handsome young Frenchman was relaying to his English cousin – it was certainly making her eyes sparkle!

"Who's for a game of Monopoly?" asked Peg enthusiastically, as the dishes were being collected.

"Peg…seriously? Surely you are exhausted after your long journey?" remarked Rachel in astonishment.

"Certainly not," replied Peg indignantly. "I've been anticipating playing competitively with you all. Back home, I have great difficulty organising a straightforward game, so I'm relishing the idea of a tournament while we are here," she declared.

Tom laughed – oh, it was good to have his sister back home. Playing board games had always been a regular evening pursuit in the Smallwood household years ago and during Peg's summer visits. The competitive spirit she brought was a bonus. Yes, Tom had missed these simple pleasures of family life, cruelly snatched from them due to the war.

* * *

Darcy brushed her blonde, bouncy curls, sitting at her dressing table. Using grips, she swept her hair upwards into a style she'd observed in a magazine recently. She turned using her hand mirror to see the back view and sighed. "Bother!" she exclaimed, undid the grips and started again, brushing frantically. Several attempts later she stood and walked over to the full-length vanity mirror.

She viewed herself from various angles. Self-image was paramount to Darcy Smallwood. She needed to look good, whatever she was doing. She was attired in cream trousers and a primrose yellow cotton shirt. Her outfit was slightly subdued today in honour of their guests. 'Just wait,' she whispered to herself, smirking.

She grinned as she recalled the handsome young Frenchman, who'd engaged her in lively conversation at the supper table the previous evening. Jonty Thibault was a surprise…a total surprise! Learning of their visit several weeks ago, she'd pictured her cousin as she remembered him – tall, lanky with a pimply face and a mop of dark brown hair. But seven years had transformed him. Now he was a tall, handsome, well-built eighteen-year-old complete with an endearing manner and a seducing accent.

'Wish he wasn't my cousin,' thought Darcy, envisaging running her fingers through his dark hair. He towered above her and she felt a fluttering sensation just thinking about him. Slipping her feet into her canvas shoes, she rebuked herself… 'maybe he has some equally handsome friends' she thought. Then with one final check in the mirror, she went down to breakfast.

* * *

The initial awkwardness between the four young cousins gradually ebbed away. Jonty's mother Peg was a born organiser and made sure each day was filled with a variety of pursuits which the young people found engaging. Peg Thibault had moved to France when she was twenty-one years old, first for work as a lady's companion, returning to northeast England intermittently. But when she captured the heart of a dashing French detective, Pierre Thibault, she soon married and moved permanently to live in Lyon.

The three-week holiday saw the families travelling to various parts of the northeast region – coast, country and cities. This year Peg was determined to pack in as much sightseeing as possible. Tom and Rachel were able to accompany them, unlike past years when they were restrained by their hotel duties. But the highlight of the holiday was to be a visit to a local beauty spot – a waterfall called Lasham Cragg in the Pennine hills.

"You are not wearing that outfit," shrieked Rachel to her daughter, as she entered the dining room where Rachel was laying the breakfast table on the morning of the visit. As usual, Darcy was being controversial in her choice of attire. She stood in the doorway with her hand on the doorknob.

"Why not?" she retaliated. "I'm comfortable; the weather looks set to be warm, if not hot. At least dressed like this, I'll be cool with all the trekking."

Rachel glowered at her cantankerous daughter dressed in skimpy, pale green shorts and a floral, wide necked blouse. In Rachel's opinion the outfit was unsuitable for the occasion.

Tom entered the room carrying a tray laden with bread rolls, toast and butter.

"Your father will agree with me," continued Rachel, wiping her brow.

"I will, will I? Over what exactly?" he queried, placing the food items on the table. He was totally unaware of the topic under discussion.

Darcy flounced down onto the nearest chair.

"If I can't go dressed like this…then I won't go…so there!" she exclaimed loudly.

Sensing he was needed to act as an adjudicator, Tom quickly assessed the situation.

"Why don't you pack some trousers and a cardigan in your rucksack – just in case the temperatures plummet," suggested Tom.

Darcy pulled a face and stood up. "Ugh! She wins… again!" she retaliated, storming out of the room, almost colliding with her Aunt Peg.

Tom breezed past his sister en route to the kitchen. "Excuse our family disagreements, Peg," he chortled.

Peg walked over to her sister-in-law.

"It's just a passing phase, Rachel, she'll grow out of it. Try to be diplomatic and avoid face-to-face confrontations. No doubt I've yet to face all this with Sylvie," she commented, as Rachel finished setting the table. Peg noted her sister-in-law's pristine blue and white cotton dress and white cardigan – as usual, a picture of elegance…not conducive to the day's demands, in Peg's humble opinion.

After breakfast the families assembled in the hallway, all except Darcy who could be heard stomping around upstairs. Tom and Pierre collected the bags and went out to the cars. Rachel picked up her straw hat from the hall table, then called up the stairwell. "Remember to bring your sunhat, Darcy." Turning to Peg she muttered, "May as well save my breath – she won't be seen dead wearing a head covering – it might spoil her hair."

Peg reached out and hugged Rachel, sensing her exasperation. "Come on, it's a splendid day – don't let these petty squabbles distract you."

Rachel sighed and followed Peg outside.

"Are we ready?" asked Tom, looking at his wife.

Feeling close to tears, Rachel just shook her head and raised her hands questioningly.

"In my opinion you should just leave her," mumbled Josh, climbing into the back seat of his dad's car to sit beside his cousin Jonty. Moments later, Darcy flew out of the house and clambered into the rear seat of her uncle's car, kindly loaned by the farm manager, for the duration of their stay. Tom walked over and locked the front door. How typical of his daughter, he mused, causing a fracas at the last minute – where, oh where had his delightful little girl gone to? She'd always been headstrong, but in an adoring way – now she was just plain awkward and constantly causing friction.

But Darcy's choice of clothing proved perfect for the weather conditions that day. The two cars travelled for over an hour to the famous beauty spot – a stunning waterfall on the borders of County Durham. The venue was poignant. Twenty years ago, Tom and Peg's older brother Jonathan had fallen at the Cragg. The injuries he received that day had resulted in his death three months later. For years the anniversary of his accident was an annual pilgrimage for Tom, but with the passage of time and the war years, the event was only alluded to in the individual minds of those present on the day. Now they deemed it wise to let the younger generation enjoy the beauty of the place, without it being tinged with sad memories for the uncle they never knew.

The French family's holiday was ending and as was a tradition in the Smallwood family, a special meal was arranged to mark the occasion.

"Do you remember Mother's celebration meals?" recalled Peg to her brother and Rachel as they tidied up later.

Tom smiled. "Indeed, I do. Mother certainly knew how to put on a lavish spread to mark special events. But, Peg, you have inherited her passion for cooking and entertaining," Tom remarked.

Peg looked embarrassed. "Oh, it just seems to come naturally, born out of necessity. But changing the subject, would you," she paused and looked at her brother and sister-in-law, "the four of you, I mean, like to visit us in France this Christmas? It's a unique opportunity for you – no hotel business to keep you here, at least for this year."

Tom and Rachel shared a knowing look. Being able to visit France for the festive season would be such a treat.

Before the war they'd visited Lyon, but it was during the hotel's winter break in January. Darcy and Josh were unable to accompany them on those occasions due to their schooling, So, it was an appealing prospect.

"That's a cracking idea, Peg. The children have a two-week break from school and maybe we could go to Bordeaux and visit Chantal as well."

Peg looked excited. "I'll invite Chantal to join us for Noël," she suggested.

Rachel looked surprised. "But, Peg, where will we all sleep?" she asked, knowing the size of the Thibault's apartment.

True to form Peg was not about to let a small detail like accommodation cut across her proposal.

"No problem – I'll sort it," she declared. "Now, what are your plans about re-opening the hotel?" she enquired. She'd sensed it was an underlying issue in the time they'd been in Malhaven.

Tom ran his hand across his brow. "The more time passes, Peg, the less inclined I feel to restart the hotel business. It was so tying. Christmas, New Year and Easter were always highlights for us…but the war seems to have changed things. The market garden provides extra income and along with the farm…well, we are amply provided for…so," his voice trailed off and Rachel spoke up. Tom placed his arm around Rachel's shoulders.

"No definite decisions yet, Peg. We felt so drained after the last of the patients left. We took a couple of months and re-decorated the place, repaired various things which had suffered and made it our home again. We said we'd give it a year and maybe Tom might follow a different direction," she added, smiling at her husband."

Peg raised her eyebrows in surprise as Jonty bounced into the kitchen, closely followed by Darcy.

"Can we have a snack please?" he asked, heading for the biscuit tin.

"Jonty Thibault, I declare you have hollow legs…it's only an hour since you finished your meal!" exclaimed his mother. "Now, Jonty…we are going to have guests for Noël…English guests."

Jonty raised his eyebrows. "Really? That's splendid," he remarked.

Darcy looked at her mother. "Yippee! Will we be able to visit Tante Tallie as well?" she asked.

Tom squeezed his wife's shoulder. "Yes, Darcy. Your mother will write to her about our impending visit. Aunt Peg is inviting Chantal to join us. She will have plenty of notice, so no chance for her to make other arrangements."

Darcy looked happy; she held fond memories for her mother's sister.

The following day the French family departed. It was nostalgic saying goodbye, but the summer holiday had restored the tight family bond and with the proposed return visit to France, it would only be a few months before they were reunited again.

Rachel was longing to see her sister. Chantal was fourteen years younger than Rachel. Before the war, Chantal lived with them for almost six years, while training to be a midwife in Newcastle. Darcy became very attached to Chantal during those years and missed her when she returned to France...would her bond with Tante Tallie be rekindled easily? Rachel's thoughts were mixed as she anticipated spending Christmas on French soil.

Chapter 2

SEPTEMBER 1946

"All done," remarked Rachel, sealing the envelope. She twisted her fingers in her shoulder length hair – once blonde but now tweaked with grey. "I've told Chantal about our visit and how Peg expects her to join us." She swivelled on her chair and beamed at Tom.

Her husband looked up from reading his newspaper, in the armchair beside the fireplace. He nodded. "Good, I'll pop along into town and post it for you," he commented, standing and taking the letter from her outstretched hand.

Meckleridge House was surrounded by extensive gardens. It lay about half a mile outside the local town of Malhaven. Tom sauntered down the sweeping driveway. It was a beautiful September morning – a hint of early morning chill still hung in the air and touches of autumn tinged the trees. Malhaven was a large village rather than a town, but it possessed all the required facilities to bear the title. It boasted a resplendent Town Hall, gas works and shops to meet the needs of the residents. A railway station could be accessed after climbing a hill, as Malhaven lay in in a valley on the banks of the river Meckle.

The river was the attraction for the establishment of light industries – sword making and a papermill in years gone by – but Malhaven's main claim to fame was its spa waters. During the Victorian era it became a popular venue for wealthy visitors, staying in local hotels to 'take the waters' as a health benefit. Many grand houses were built in the town in the late nineteenth century and Meckleridge House was among them. Tom's aunt and uncle had acquired the house before the onset of the First World War and turned it into a profitable hotel afterwards. Dora's untimely death, two years after her husband, saw her two nephews take up the reins in the early 1920s.

A bell jingled, signalling Tom's entry into the Post Office.

"Good morning, Freda," he greeted the postmistress cheerily. "A letter for France please," he added, handing over the envelope.

"Ee, it was grand to see your Peggy again, Tom," remarked Freda. "She doesn't change that one, still full of life and perky with it. It must have been great to see her and the family after so long," she added, attending to the mail.

Tom grinned. "Yes, Peg hasn't changed, thankfully. We're so grateful we were all spared – so many families lost loved ones during the war...we are the fortunate ones. Peg was quite taken how Malhaven has remained untouched by the ravages of war. France did not fare well – a lot of bombing with the Occupation, but she says it's amazing how the communities are bouncing back."

Freda Dawson and Peg Smallwood had attended school at the same time.

Taking payment for the postage, Freda added, "I guess Peg's more French than English now... how long has she lived over there?"

Tom took his change, thanked her and rubbed his brow. "Oh, gosh, now you're asking, Freda. Let's see – it must be nigh on twenty-five years. She first went to France when she was in her early twenties and she's in her mid-forties now!"

Freda nodded. "Yes, the years have flown by. Will you be re-opening the hotel soon, Tom, now the house is no longer needed for the war effort? The hotel brings good trade into the town, you know."

The bell jingled, indicating the arrival of a customer. Tom stood back.

"No plans yet, Freda. Well, I'll be on my way. Cheerio," he added, and left the Post Office.

After attending to several errands, Tom walked back along the main road towards his home. As he walked, he pondered Freda's questioning about re-opening the hotel. Why not? It was all he knew, but Tom had never intended to have a career in hotel management. He'd studied to be a botanist as a young man, but it was short-lived, and he'd been a hotel owner for as long as his sister had lived in France. Yet, something was tugging at Tom's mind to change direction. He was fortunate finance was not a problem. The farmlands adjacent to Meckleridge House, plus the steady income from the market garden, kept his family well provided. His management of these two reserved occupations had prevented him from seeing active service during the war... yet he knew he must 'do' something.

In two years, he would turn fifty years of age – still a young man in his mind! Rachel was already putting her skills to good use, giving private tuition to young students – she'd been a governess before they married. But Tom was restless. He was drawn to the idea of cultivating roses... creating a new species perhaps. The thought excited and motivated him...maybe he should investigate developing hardy flowering plants alongside the market garden?

* * *

With his thoughts still hankering after flower cultivation, Tom stepped out into the garden later that day. Their faithful golden retriever, Jess, at his heels. He ambled along the gravel driveway in the direction of the kitchen garden. Although it was late afternoon, there was still a warmth in the golden sunshine. He spotted his daughter stretched out on a blanket sunbathing and smiled. Stepping onto the grass to dull the sound of his approach, he slowly crept up behind her. "Boo!" he exclaimed, bending over and tickling his young daughter.

Darcy sat up startled and pushed her sunglasses on the top of her head. "Dad, you idiot...you gave me such a fright," she responded.

Tom sat down beside her as Jess wandered across to greet Darcy, wagging her tail.

"Did you have a good day?" Tom enquired.

Both Darcy and Josh attended the local Grammar School in nearby Malsett. The new academic year was in its second week. Darcy stroked the dog who lay down at her side.

"It was okay, I suppose," she responded. "I got a merit for my French homework."

Tom smiled. Darcy was studying languages for her Highers.

"Well, so you should – you could speak the language fluently before you were ten years old!" he chuckled. Rachel's French sister had lived with them when Darcy was small and Darcy idolised her Tante Tallie, becoming her shadow. Chantal had taught her little niece to speak her native language, as her mother had taught her to speak English, resulting in Darcy being bilingual.

Crunching on the gravel path caused Tom to turn. Rachel was approaching with a worried look on her face. "Have either of you seen Josh?" she asked.

Tom pursed his lips and shook his head. Darcy lay back on the rug and replaced her sunglasses. Her mother stiffened.

"Did you see him after school?" she asked anxiously, and Tom noticed.

"No, Mother, I didn't...he's fourteen years old... he doesn't need babysitting," Darcy responded curtly.

Tom sensed his wife's distress and jumped up.

"It's about time you left him to grow up. He's probably gone down to the river with some raving beauty in his class," added Darcy, deliberately taunting her mother.

Rachel stared wide-eyed at her daughter in disbelief. "Don't be ridiculous," she chided. "He always comes straight home from school."

Darcy rolled over and propped herself up on her elbows.

"Do you seriously think he would inform you if he's chasing a girl?" she mocked.

Tom had developed a nose for mother and daughter friction. He walked over to his wife and placed his arm around her shoulders, steering her back towards the house.

"It's so unlike him, Tom, he's a creature of habit. He always comes straight home from school and gets his homework done so he has free time later."

Tom sighed – it was true. Josh was unlike his rebellious sister and even if he did have a change of plan, he would have passed a message via Darcy. Yet, Tom knew from his own experience at that age – once the pull of romance tugged at your heart all 'sense' vanished.

"Darcy might be right, Rachel. There could be a girl involved. Don't fret...his stomach will bring him home."

He stopped and looked into his wife's eyes, then pulling her close, whispered, "Try to stop worrying, Rachel." But Tom was concerned about his wife – she wasn't coping well with their teenage children's behaviour.

It was after seven o'clock when Josh returned. By then Rachel was frantic and urging Tom to contact the police. Tom had telephoned two of Josh's friends' parents but drew a blank as to his son's whereabouts. When Josh eventually walked into the house, Rachel opened her mouth to speak but Tom signalled for her to remain quiet.

The young lad devoured his plate of food. "I've got loads of homework, so I'll say goodnight," he commented and after putting his dishes in the sink, left the kitchen. Rachel stared at his retreating figure.

"He'll talk when he's ready," remarked Tom.

Rachel sat at the kitchen table, hung her head and began to sob.

* * *

Sleep evaded Tom that night. Tossing and turning, his mind churned over his concerns from earlier. What was it about the deep, dark hours of the night which caused your problems to grow legs, wear boots and thud all over your brain as you tried to rest? Rachel's constant worrying was hard to ignore. Her former bright, bubbly personality and positive outlook on life seemed to have eroded. The early years of their marriage were blessed with Rachel's optimistic attitude – even under the heavy cloud of the war days, she always found something to be cheerful about. But now she was fraught with anxiety about handling their daughter's awkwardness; the concern for the welfare of her sister in France...and now Josh – what was troubling him? He was a sensitive lad, always had been, choosing to bottle things up. Whereas with Darcy you got 'it', whatever 'it' might be. She was in your face, giving you the guts of the issue and invariably blaming you!

Yet, underneath this hostile façade was a girl with a heart of gold. She possessed a loving nature and just wanted others to see things from her viewpoint and do things the way she wanted them done...as if life was that easy. Darcy was impulsive and acted before she thought things through. He recalled the day they had visited a stately house before the war, she would have been about six years old. She saw a path with an archway at the top and no amount of persuasion could prevent her from exploring. Tom decided to let her discover the error of her ways. He knew where the path would take her … into a maze. Half an hour later Tom found a distressed little girl crouching in a corner breaking her heart. "But daddy it...it...looked so exciting and it just went on and on and on and I couldn't find the way out!" she sobbed. He tried to explain to her how serious her decision could have been – she could have walked into danger.

As a toddler she was fearless, as a young child she was adventurous, and now on the cusp of adulthood...well he didn't want to imagine. He hoped her impetuous nature could be tamed; hoped she would learn to think 'things through' before acting. In the meantime, he must give Josh the space he needed...he would talk in his own time ...when he was ready.

* * *

"I need food supplies for tomorrow," Darcy informed her mother on Friday evening.

"Where are you off to?" queried Rachel, knowing her adventurous daughter spent most of her Saturdays cycling around the local countryside.

"There's about ten of us from the Cycling Club heading up onto the moors... we're hoping to make it to Blyhope," answered Darcy, munching an apple.

"Gosh, that's a trek, make sure you stay with the group," urged her mother. "I'll pack some provisions in the morning. What time are you leaving?" Darcy wandered over to the bin to dispose of her apple core.

"We're meeting at the Fountain at ten o'clock and aim to be back home before six and yes, Mother...I have checked my bike."

Darcy was passionate about cycling. Her Raleigh bicycle was a treasured possession. She'd learned to cycle as a young girl, following her Tante Tallie around the hotel grounds then advancing to the country lanes surrounding Malhaven. Aunt and niece enjoyed many cycling adventures in those pre-war days.

The name 'Tante Tallie' was Darcy's attempt to articulate Tante or Aunt Chantal when she was learning to talk and somehow the name stuck. Chantal was fourteen years older than Darcy and fourteen years younger than Rachel...she sat plumb in the middle! Darcy and her aunt were great pals when Chantal lived in Malhaven, but the bond was severed when she returned to France to care for her invalid mother.

It was a wrench for Rachel to 'lose' her sister again. She had only learned of Chantal's existence after her marriage to Tom. Rachel had been brought up by her aunt and grandfather in Devon, believing her parents were dead, when they abandoned her as a young teenager. Rachel struggled to form a meaningful relationship with her widowed mother, Yvette, after their reunion, but welcomed the discovery of a younger sister and they became close.

Darcy had joined the local Cycling Club after the war. She loved to cycle, and her parents encouraged her to channel her energies into the sport. Each Saturday, as weather permitted, the local group planned an outing. There was a twenty-strong membership, and the leaders were known to Tom and Rachel. The club originated as a men's cycling group, but during the war years women were accepted into their ranks, resulting in an even gender balance. Josh also belonged to the Cycling Club but was not quite so enthusiastic as his sister.

"Is Josh joining you?" asked Tom, entering the kitchen, having overheard the conversation.

Darcy shrugged her shoulders. "No idea...Mr Moody isn't communicating at present, so I don't know!" she retorted.

The next morning dawned rich and mellow with the promise of a fine day. Darcy wore long trousers, knowing the temperature could change on the top of the moors. She carefully packed her gear in the saddle bag and was soon at the meeting point in Malhaven. Her usual cycling buddy, Chrissie, was unable to attend due to a family wedding, but Darcy wasn't fazed, knowing others, so joined in with the group as they began their journey.

Their route took them over the River Meckle and up onto the country lanes. The terrain was challenging, as usual. Any direction surrounding Malhaven encountered hills and valleys. Charlie Simpson was their leader today. He and his wife were avid cyclists and Charlie was the president of their club. His manner was easy going and he preferred to be one of the crowd.

Half an hour into the ride, Darcy became aware of a young man keeping pace alongside.

"Great day," he called.

"Smashing," replied Darcy, not really wanting to engage in any conversation. The collective speed of the group was moderate, so communication was possible, but

Darcy preferred to lose herself in her own thoughts. The route proved demanding, involving a significant climb on a winding road. Soon the open expanse of heather-clad moorland took over from walled fields, as they dismounted and pushed through a gate to negotiate a cattle grid.

She recognised the young man. Grady Forrester was a year ahead of her at school. His family were 'incomers' into the area, having moved from the south prior to the war. His father was a 'big knob' at the local Iron Works in Malsett, and his mother was an American lady. She was aware of this information because her friend Chrissie had a crush on him. He was a tall, well-built athletic type and his accent was different – certainly not a Durham accent, more a mix of south of England and an American twang. She'd only observed him from afar, as Chrissie endeavoured to attract his attention.

The group stopped to take their first break. Darcy was rummaging in her saddle bag, relishing her well-earned apple and cup of water from her provisions, when a voice from behind spoke.

"Where's Chrissie today?" asked Grady.

Darcy turned and gave a brief explanation.

"You're Josh Smallwood's sister, aren't you?" he continued.

Darcy was taken aback. "How do you know my brother?" she asked warily, as Grady took a drink from his flask.

The brown-haired youngster wiped the sweat from his brow with his sleeve. "Cricket Club," came the reply. Josh was a member of the Junior Boy's Cricket Club in Malhaven. "He's a cracking bowler for a young lad," Grady continued.

Darcy pulled a face and looked cautiously at the confident young man. "And I suppose you say that from a senior perspective?" she quipped.

Grady grinned broadly. "No, not for another year, but I've observed your young brother's talent," he answered. Then raising his eyebrows added, "I was being complimentary." He took another drink. "I'm Grady, Grady Forrester, I don't think we've been formally introduced." He held out his hand.

Darcy burst out laughing, then looking up their eyes met. She felt embarrassed.

"Sorry, that was rude of me. We've both been in this Cycling Club for ages, and it seems a trifle late for formal introductions. Anyway, I'm Darcy Smallwood," she replied and took hold of his outstretched hand.

As he shook her hand, Darcy felt his eyes sweeping over her features. She clasped her blonde ponytail in her other hand and raised her head, enjoying the scrutiny of this rather attractive young man.

"There...that wasn't so bad...was it?" he remarked, releasing her hand and continuing to gaze into her pale blue eyes. Grady Forrester was quite endearing. Until now she'd only listened passively to Chrissie's admiring comments. "Do you mind if I cycle alongside as we both seem to have been deserted by our cycling buddies – my mate Frank is also otherwise engaged today."

Before she could reply, Charlie called the cycling group to attention.

"Okay, folks – a bit of information about our route. We're almost at the peak of our ascent. We'll pass three small reservoirs. On the right is Taskerly – where our water supply comes from in Malhaven. Further along on the left are two smaller reservoirs – Stadley Shaw and Lishop. The road follows closely to the rail track, in some places." He paused as someone asked a question then resumed. "We are about halfway to Blyhope, so should be there by one o'clock."

The next leg of the journey was less demanding, following the open moorland. Grady rode alongside Darcy, passing occasional comments and swerving to avoid meandering sheep. Eventually, they reached the long slow descent down Fowleyside Bank to their destination, Blyhope.

"Hope your brakes are in good shape," called Grady. "See you at the bottom!" he yelled, taking off down the hill.

Darcy followed, enjoying the exhilarating experience. The breeze rushed past her as she coasted down the steep road. She loved the speed and the freedom. Reaching the bottom safely, she waited beside Grady as the more hesitant participants of the group made their way cautiously. Grady straddled his bike.

"You're fearless for a girl," he commented, with a twinkle in his eye, recalling how skilfully Darcy had tackled the steep hill.

"Of course," she quipped, "being a girl has nothing to do with it. I'll have you know this girl is made of strong stuff!" she responded, silently praising herself.

"Mmmm – a right little 'clever clogs', aren't you?" Grady remarked.

Before Darcy could reply, their leader explained they were going to sit by the river to eat their well-deserved lunch.

Darcy was tired and aching but floating on air, as she snuggled under the covers in her bed later that night. She felt euphoric. Today was a satisfying day...very satisfying. The cycle ride was demanding, but she had tackled it with no problems and her trusty bicycle behaved splendidly. The weather was spectacular for mid-September, but the cause of her euphoria lay not in her cycling expertise, but in the knowledge she had attracted the attention of a certain Grady Forrester!

He proved to be most attentive and thanked her profusely for being his cycling buddy, as they returned to Malhaven. When the group gathered around to listen to Charlie's parting comments, Darcy looked dejected, hearing it would be two weeks before the next Cycling Club outing.

"Awww," she moaned.

Grady looked across at her. "We could always do our own cycle ride – how about it? You can ask Chrissie, and

I'll ask Frank. Not too far ...about a three hour round trip next Saturday. A foursome – does that appeal?" he queried.

Darcy was thoughtful, anticipating her friend Chrissie's reaction.

"Maybe," she'd replied, not wanting to sound too enthusiastic. But the suggestion interested her...greatly!

Chapter 3

BORDEAUX FRANCE,
SEPTEMBER 1946

There was a deep mellowness to the morning vibe. A richness associated with the season of fruitfulness and harvest. Yet, a faint chill penetrated Chantal Martin's face as she wound her way along the tree-lined rugged lane. She praised her forethought in attiring herself with a tweed jacket over her uniform. Maybe her years of residing in northeast England bore testament to overthinking her outdoor wear, but it frequently proved superfluous in the milder French climate. This morning, however, she was thankful for the extra layer.

She greeted various residents as she cycled past, making her way through the suburbs of Bordeaux to a farmstead some three kilometres from the town centre. Her patient today was a well-seasoned mother of four healthy children. Chantal had attended to each of the births in quick succession during the war. This newly expected addition was being regarded as an oversight – but no matter how inconvenient the new bébé appeared to be anticipated, Chantal knew he or she would be welcomed and adored in the same manner as its older siblings.

She slowed and turned off the lane onto a farm track as the 'boulangère' in his rusty Citroen truck rumbled along the track towards her. She pulled over, stopped and waved enthusiastically.

"Bonjour, Claude," she called.

The old baker returned her greeting.

Propping her bike up against the gable wall of the farmhouse, Chantal unleashed her midwifery bag from its restraints and walked over to the open door.

"Bonjour, Bonjour," called Cécile Bernard as two excitable young children chased around the large, rectangular kitchen table. After exchanging greetings and a few snippets of local news, courtesy of the recently departed baker, Chantal attended to her patient's routine examination. Oh, that all mothers were as sensible as Cécile, Chantal mused. In fairness, the Frenchwoman's pregnancies had been textbook, and she saw no reason to suspect *bébé numero cinq* would be any different.

"You look concerned *ce matin*, Chantal," remarked the expectant mother as the examination ended.

Chantal was washing her hands at the sink. She paused before replying.

"*Oui*, Cécile…I am. I have received notification telling me I must vacate my home by the end of the month. I knew it would happen one day. The property was left for my mother's use, and it is six years since she passed away, but with the war I was allowed to stay." She began to pack her bag. "I was naïve to think the arrangement would continue, but I was hopeful. It has always been my home – I was born there." She sat at the table as Cécile made *une tasse de café*. She sighed. "Now I must look for new accommodation to rent in Bordeaux, as this is where I work."

Cécile handed the beverage to the young *sage femme*. "I am pleased you are not moving away, Chantal; you are a great asset to our community."

Chantal smiled, finished her beverage and chatted about Cécile's children, then she glanced at her watch. The younger woman stood and picked up her bag. As she did, Cécile reached out and tapped Chantal's midwifery bag, "If this bag could talk, Chantal..." she added, smiling. "You proved yourself to be a loyal, brave citizen and I'm sure you will find suitable lodgings."

Chantal bade Cécile and her two young children *au revoir*, then mounting her cycle she left the farmstead.

Chantal loved her job and could not imagine working elsewhere now. When she returned to France in early 1939 her objective was to go back to England at the earliest opportunity. But circumstances overtook her. Yvette Martin's illness had proved terminal and while caring for her mother she was called upon to assist at the local midwifery clinic. Yvette Martin was a retired midwife, and she had persuaded her daughter to offer her skills during a time of staff shortage. When her mother passed away in Spring 1940, Chantal was unable to return to England because of the war.

Cycling back towards Bordeaux she admired the rural scenery. Bordeaux was a beautiful Atlantic port city. It was situated on the Gironde estuary, at the confluence of the Dordogne and Garonne rivers. A rich golden hue was in evidence in the surrounding vineyards, enhancing the beauty of the area. She loved traversing these country lanes and relished mornings when her duties took her to the outskirts of the city.

But it was not so long ago, travelling these routes was far from pleasurable. As Cécile Bernard had reminded her, the midwifery bag attached to her bicycle could tell many tales – both scary and daring. The breeze lifted her mound of blonde curls as she pressed forward, refusing to let her mind drift back to those dark days of the Occupation of France.

Arriving home later that day, she picked up the post from the doormat, delivered in her absence. Quickly she scanned the envelopes, ever hopeful for the familiar handwriting she longed to see. But like the six disappointing years which had intervened … no letter bearing Sam Carter's handwriting was in evidence. Among the delivery though, was a letter from her sister Rachel.

Before allowing herself the luxury of reading Rachel's news, she attended to her early evening tasks – sterilising her instruments and repacking her bag. Then she made her evening meal. Chantal lived her life with strict routines. She could be called upon at short notice to attend an emergency, so she needed to be prepared. Her chores completed; she opened her letter from England.

'Dear Chantal,

I trust this finds you well. I have tried repeatedly to telephone you without success and my last two letters have been unanswered – did you receive them? Surely things are returning to normality now the wretched war has ended.'

Chantal sighed. Rachel lived in a 'bubble' with her adorable husband and children. The war seemed to have passed them by without any major interruption to their lives – apart from the hotel occupancy. Even then, they were probably compensated financially. But yes… she had been remiss in keeping her sister informed of her welfare. The correspondence from England had arrived safely but knowing how to phrase a reply proved challenging. She still lived in fear of inadvertently disclosing some minor detail of her former activities, so in the end she put off replying to Rachel, only sending an occasional general letter, bland in its content.

Telephone calls were a luxury she could no longer receive. For the last year her number had been 'cut off', which was extremely inconvenient in her line of work. Thankfully, the local postmaster took messages on her behalf, which were speedily delivered by his teenage son. The termination of her telephone line was the first indication that her tenancy in the beautiful four bedroomed detached house was nearing its end. '*A necessary curtailment in our resources*', she was informed – but it was the beginning of the end. The house needed repairs – like so many after the war, and her long list was unlikely to be addressed, due to pressing demands on the company finances. And now the final notification had been received – her home on the Rue de Arbes would not be hers after the end of the month.

Chantal returned to reading her sister's letter. It was packed with details of Tom's sister's family's summer visit. Oh, how Chantal longed to visit Malhaven again. She loved the Thibaults' visits during her years in England. All the children – the Smallwoods and the Thibaults... they would be young people now, she mused – the years stolen from them, because of the war. She picked up the letter again.

> '*And now some exciting news, Chantal. We – Tom, Darcy, Josh and I – are to visit Lyon for Christmas! How exciting is that? We are not reopening the hotel for the foreseeable future. It means, dear Chantal, we can see you – in the flesh, for real... after all these long, long years. Peg has invited you to join*

us…please, please, please say you can be in Lyon for Christmas! No excuses, Chantal – we must be reunited. Accommodation will be sorted, you know how organised my sister-in law can be, so we expect to see you on 23rd December.

Your loving sister, Rachel.

PS The family send their love xxx'

Chantal folded the letter. She relished the prospect of a family Noël. Peg Thibault had been a good friend to Chantal over the years and she fully intended to make the long train journey to be with them all. But first she must attend to the urgent need of finding a new home.

* * *

"Bonjour, Margot," Chantal greeted the elderly French lady as she opened the door. It was a week since she'd received her sister's letter, and she still needed to reply but had been distracted trying to find alternative accommodation. Most properties available to rent were in a dilapidated condition due to the Occupation. Chantal had viewed several, each in varying degrees of disrepair. She was now resigned to renting a 'room' instead – this option pained her. Her home contained many beautiful items of furniture, which she was reluctant to leave behind…but she rebuked herself – they were only possessions. People lost so much during the war; she must put things into perspective.

"Now, Chantal, where do you want me to start?" asked Margot Picardi.

Chantal led the elderly lady into the lounge.

"If you can start with the cabinet and the dresser, please, Margot," she instructed.

Margot placed a pile of newspapers on a chair.

"I'll empty and wrap the contents," she remarked.

Chantal returned to the kitchen to continue her dissembling of the kitchen cupboards. Margot Picardi had been a friend of her mother Yvette. She was a spinster and lived with her bachelor brother in the next road, their house was a similar size and style to the one Chantal was about to vacate.

Quite by chance as Chantal was in the Post office two days earlier, she met Margot. After a brief conversation, Chantal's housing predicament was resolved. Margot offered the young woman a spacious downstairs room and a large bedroom as a paying guest. "It won't house all your mother's furniture, Chantal, but it means you can retain some valuable items. And there will be room to store boxes and crates." Margot also offered to help pack the beautiful ornaments and antiques Yvette Martin had acquired.

"Your mother possessed an eye for collecting beautiful objects, Chantal," Margot commented a while later.

Chantal sighed. "Honestly, Margot, I wondered why I am storing them. I am unlikely to ever own a house big enough to display them."

"Nonsense, dear girl. You are young and attractive. Soon you will meet a handsome young man and set up a home; he will be delighted to see all these beautiful items."

Chantal swallowed and returned to the kitchen before tears erupted from her eyes. The only young man she wanted to meet was Sam Carter, and after all these years the possibility of that eventuality seemed remote...but she continued to hope he had survived the war.

Moving day arrived. A truck pulled up outside the house. "This is it!" Chantal remarked to herself, as she watched the furniture, boxes and crates being loaded onto the lorry. She surveyed the house she had regarded as 'home' all her life. Even during her years of training in northeast England, she always regarded this house in Bordeaux as 'home'. But now it was time to leave it behind. She walked from room to room, memories springing to mind.

The bedroom where she had nursed her sick mother during her illness; her own bedroom always swathed in beautiful morning sunshine; the lounge where she was introduced to her previously unknown sister Rachel and brother-in-law Tom; the dining room where her father always insisted on punctuality and adherence to etiquette and good manners. This was the house where she was born and now, she was leaving. Memories...memories – all stored away in the recesses of her mind. She made her way to the front door and noted the hessian doormat. A final memory before she closed the door...the doormat where her last communication from Sam Carter had landed. A tear escaped from her eye, but she quickly wiped it away. She was strong; she had hope. She closed and locked the door.

* * *

For over six years Chantal Martin had trained herself to never lose hope. Hope was her anchor. It helped her to push through setbacks...push through negativity... and crucially to never, ever give up on the possibility of finding Sam. Each new day heralded a new day of hope. She'd convinced herself that once the war ended, a letter would arrive explaining how he, Sam, was unable to communicate during the war. But over a year had passed now...and still no communication.

On some bright mornings, if she was visiting a patient in the countryside, she would stop and look across the fields. She would *sense* rather than *see* a glimmer...a tiny flicker on the horizon. To Chantal it wasn't just light... it signified hope. Hope that her soulmate, her one true love, was still breathing... somewhere...out there. She felt she would know Sam's departure from this world. But days turned to weeks; weeks turned to months; months turned to years... and now it was six long years since she'd received his last letter...the letter with the missing page.

Frequently, she would take the letter – now faded and crumpled with incessant handling. She would read his words of endearment. It was all she had – her memories, her letters and the boy with the fish. This latter item was an ornament – given to her on a special occasion.

With hindsight Chantal sensed how her sister seemed to anticipate the poignancy of that special occasion at The Bungalow. It should have been a family outing. The Bungalow was a retreat for Tom and Rachel's family. It was situated about seven miles from Malhaven – a wooden structure in a field, close to a river. The place was called Trespershields. It provided a bolt hole for the Smallwoods to escape to, from the hotel, with their young family.

But a last-minute change of plan had seen Rachel urging Chantal and Sam to go by themselves. It was such a rare event for Sam, as a doctor, and Chantal, as a nurse, to find themselves with a weekend off together. "You two go and enjoy yourselves," Rachel commented. "Don't let our changed circumstances spoil your precious time together… and don't hurry back," she said, loading the car with enough food to last a week.

Chantal allowed herself to luxuriate, reliving those precious hours. Feeling Sam's arms around her holding her tight, his lips on hers. The pleasure of love given, and love returned. Sam's declaration of his love and her reciprocated response. That was the day he had given her the ornament – the boy with the fish. "I've bought you a present," he said, rummaging in his rucksack. "I was passing an antique shop in town and spotted it in the window." He had pulled out an item wrapped in brown paper and given it to her. It was a ceramic creation of a boy holding a fish in his hand. It was about six inches tall, resting on a rectangular, marble base.

"Remember when I told you how my grandfather taught me to catch a fish with my hands? I would tickle it, by caressing and rubbing the underside of the fish until it went into a kind of trance, then I could grab hold of its head." Chantal recalled the day he had told her that story, as they sat by the river at Trespershields. "I know it's a strange gift, but it reminded me of this place," he added. Chantal read the name on the base of the ornament...it was called 'Conrad'. "I guess that was the boy's name," Sam chuckled.

When Chantal had shown Rachel the ornament, she looked perplexed. "What a peculiar gift to give to a sweetheart – an item of jewellery perhaps, but an ornament?" Yet, to Chantal the gift was precious. It signified a gift given in more than one sense, on that precious occasion at The Bungalow.

Chantal Martin made her way to Margot's house. Tomorrow she would write to Rachel, informing her of the new address and telephone number. She would write to Peg Thibault, accepting her kind invitation to spend Noël in Lyon. She would also ask the postmaster to redirect any mail to her new address. She was ready to begin a new chapter in her life.

Chapter 4

ENGLAND,
OCTOBER 1946

"Something to cheer you up," remarked Tom, kissing the top of his wife's head, as she sat in the rear lounge. She turned and looked up at her husband expectantly. A mischievous grin spread across his face. He cupped her chin with one hand and held a letter, tantalisingly high above her head, in the other hand. "Smile, Rachel…otherwise I won't give you this," he chuckled. Rachel grinned, reached up and tried to grab the letter, but Tom bent forward and kissed her. "That's better, here you are," he commented, lowering the envelope into her hands. "Now, cheer up – your sister has replied."

Rachel was so relieved. It was weeks since she'd written to Chantal, informing her about the proposed Christmas holiday. She ripped open the letter.

'Dear Family,

Apologies for my lack of communication but at long last I can share some news. I have moved house! As you know, use of the house in Rue de Arbes, should have ended when mother passed away. I was able to continue to reside there because of the war but was asked to vacate the premises last month. I am renting rooms in the home of mother's friend Margot, just around the corner from my old house. I am excited about meeting you all at Christmas – I probably won't recognise my niece and nephew. My new address and telephone number are included. I will write to Peg, accepting her kind invitation. Counting the days until December.

Love Chantal.'

A wave of peace enveloped Rachel, as she passed the letter to Tom. After reading the short account he looked up. "Happy?" he asked, Rachel nodded.

"She's moved house...she knew it would happen one day. It was kind of Father's employers to allow her to continue to live there all this time. But she makes no mention of Sam...has she heard from him?"

"Not long now, my darling. Only a few more weeks until you will see your dear sister...then all your questions will be answered."

A noise from the hallway caused the dog to jump up. "What is it, Jess?" asked Tom, rising to let the dog through the door. The sight which greeted Tom was alarming. "What on earth…" he began, then quickening his step bounded into the hallway, Rachel in hot pursuit.

Josh was kneeling on the floor, burying his head in the dog's fur. His rucksack and jacket were strewn behind him. Tom could see blood smeared across his teenage son's face and as he lifted his head, he noticed a bright red blotch under his left eye, heralding the formation of a bruise. By now, Rachel was kneeling beside her son, trying to comfort him. "Have you been fighting?" Tom enquired.

Tears rolled down the young lad's face as he attempted to speak.

"He…he…asked for it," spluttered Josh.

Tom was in disbelief – not for a moment did he imagine his son could be the instigator of this mess.

"Who?" asked his father, glancing at the hall clock. It was only ten o'clock – one hour after the school day began…just where had Josh been? The lad pulled away from his mother's protective arms and stumbled to his feet. "Explain yourself, Josh," demanded Tom, but Josh pushed past his father, retrieved his belongings and headed for the stairs.

"I don't want to talk about it," he muttered. "I'll get changed and go back to school," he announced.

Tom watched as his teenage son climbed the stairs... something was wrong, and he was determined to get to the bottom of it.

* * *

"Darcy...Darcy...telephone for you," called Tom, then speaking into the receiver asked, "Who is calling please?" Tom's curiosity was piqued. The caller was obviously a young man and Tom reasoned as her father, he had every right to know who was telephoning to speak to his beautiful young daughter.

"Grady Forrester, sir," answered a cultured voice. "I guess I am speaking to Mr Smallwood – would that be correct?"

Tom pursed his lips; it was an unfamiliar name and an unfamiliar accent – certainly not local. Darcy appeared on the staircase just as Tom replied.

"Grady Forrester for you, Darcy," said Tom, passing the receiver to his starry-eyed daughter. He tried to loiter in the hope of hearing some snippets of conversation, but it seemed rather obvious, so he slunk away into the conservatory, where Rachel was darning some socks.

"Stop eavesdropping, Tom Smallwood," Rachel rebuked her husband. "She's sixteen years old – she is bound to have gentleman callers at her age."

Tom sat down and stared at his wife.

"How do we know he's a gentleman?" asked Tom. "Do you know who he is...this Grady Forrester? He's not from around here, judging by his accent and calling me 'sir'."

Rachel laid her sewing on the stool.

"He's the son of the assistant manager of the Iron Works, Tom. You must remember, they arrived about a year before the war began. According to local gossip, he's made quite an impression and is tipped for the top job when the manager, Arthur Batey, retires."

Tom nodded, vague memories resurfacing in his mind.

"Where did they live previously before coming to Malsett?" Tom asked.

Rachel shrugged her shoulders. "Down south somewhere, but the wife is an American."

Tom looked thoughtful. "Ahh, that would explain the name Grady and the boy's manners." He stood and walked over to look out of the window, noting the signs of autumn in the grounds. "Changing the subject, Rachel, we'll be needing to light a fire in here now the nights are turning cooler. We may as well use this room on an evening, so I'll lay a fire in a morning, and we can set it away before supper." It was strange to be using the conservatory as a family room. This had always been a guest room, along with the large adjacent lounge in the hotel era. Beds had occupied both rooms during the convalescent home days.

Tom spun around and walked over to his wife, who had resumed her darning. "Are we doing the right thing, Rachel, by not reopening the hotel?"

Rachel sensed a tone of anxiety in Tom's voice. He was normally a placid, easy-going man and it was unlike him to raise concerns. He'd aged during the war years – his hair was turning grey.

"Tom, we said we'd give it a year. The year isn't up until the Spring. We've got Christmas in France to look forward to before then. If we'd reopened the hotel, we'd have been unable to visit France, so there's a benefit…agree?"

"Yes, my dear, spoken with wisdom, we'll think about it in the new year," he acknowledged, as Darcy bounced into the large room, her excitement tangible.

"I've been invited to a posh dinner," she announced, her delight obvious.

Tom's hackles rose. "And am I being consulted?" he asked, rather sternly.

Darcy stood with her hands on her hips.

"Dad, you are so old fashioned. Young men do not need to seek approval from a girl's father to invite them on a date. Anyway, I'm going regardless of your stuffiness!"

Tom opened his mouth to retaliate. "Now, listen to me young lady…" he began, as Rachel interjected.

"Oh, this sounds exciting. Tell us where and when, Darcy."

The bright-eyed girl sat down cross-legged on the hearth rug, beside the dog.

"It's the Works Annual Dinner Dance to be held on the last Saturday in November, so I have about six weeks to sort my outfit."

Rachel appeared as elated as Darcy, so Tom bit back his comment. The world was changing. Former protocols seemed to have vanished. Young people did not seek their parents' approval over such matters anymore. But Tom wanted to meet this young man.

"I think it would be appropriate if we met this Grady before the event – don't you agree?"

Darcy twisted her face. "Did you say you were going up to The Bungalow before the end of the month?" she asked.

Tom looked surprised at the question. "Well... I must check for leaks and try to prepare it for the winter. We've not used The Bungalow for some time...why do you ask?"

Darcy looked up from stroking Jess. "Just a thought... if you were going up to Trespershields, Grady and I could cycle up. That way you'd get to meet him."

Tom smiled...an opportunity to check the Bungalow and meet Grady Forrester. "Good idea, Darcy. How about a week on Saturday?"

Darcy grinned and agreed.

"Now, Mother...you and I have some serious shopping to do... is this Saturday any good?"

* * *

Darcy and Grady set off to cycle up to Trespershields the following week.

"Why do your parents have a bungalow in the country?" asked Grady as they cycled.

Darcy began to laugh. "Don't hold your breath, Grady. It's only a wooden shack on stilts. In fact, it's probably in such a state of disrepair I doubt we'll be able to have a cup of tea!"

Darcy negotiated a bend then spoke again.

"No, I'm being unfair. It's in a beautiful spot – a two bedroomed wooden building in a lovely meadow, with a river nearby. Josh and I spent hours there as children – hunting for insects; fishing; paddling; building dams and camps. We walked up to the farm to collect milk and eggs, and the old farmer would let us see the animals. Mother and Dad used it as a country retreat because our house was a hotel, before the war. It's called 'Green Pastures'. They couldn't take us away on a holiday because summer was the hotel's busy season. The Bungalow gave them a few hours away from their workplace. Sometimes Josh, Mother and I stayed there – if the weather was fine, and Dad came up each day. The housekeeper and cook saw to the guests' requirements during the daytime."

"Sounds like you had a perfect childhood," Grady commented.

Josh wasn't relishing spending time at The Bungalow that Saturday afternoon, but the cricket season was over, and he had no other plans. He chose not to accompany his sister and Grady Forrester on his bike. "I'm not playing 'gooseberry'," he objected, when Tom suggested it. Tom chuckled – his parenting was entering a new phase; he must learn to pre-think these situations. But as Josh spoke an idea formed in Tom's mind and he ran it past Rachel before lunch.

"This afternoon when we go up to The Bungalow can you make a thing about wanting us out of the way, so you can tidy something?"

Rachel looked questioningly at Tom.

"It might give me that opportunity to have a 'heart to heart' conversation with our son to see what's been bothering him."

Rachel agreed.

Arriving at the country location, Rachel headed into the small bungalow.

"Now, you two…take the dog and go for a long walk. I want to empty and clean these cupboards. I need space without anyone hanging around."

Tom looked at his son. "Guess that's your mother's way of saying – 'get lost'!" Tom chuckled and whistled for Jess.

Father and son walked across to the river. After discussing various current topics, Tom turned to face Josh.

"Have you sorted your problems yet?" he asked.

The young lad shrugged his shoulders. He was tall, like Tom, and looked set to develop a similar broad build.

Tom stood, hands in his pockets, looking across the river. "It does no good to bottle things up, Josh. Remember, a problem shared is a problem halved. I may be able to offer some advice or give a different perspective on an issue."

Josh crouched down beside the edge of the river and selected a few flat pebbles, then proceeded to skim them across the water – a skill he learned from his dad years ago. Josh's reply, when it came, was totally unexpected.

"I doubt if you can help, Dad, seeing as you are the cause of the problem," he blurted out.

Tom was momentarily stunned. "Pardon?" he asked, unsure he had heard correctly. "How?"

Josh remained silent for a few minutes. "How, Josh... how am I the cause of the problem?" Tom's patience was being tested. Josh picked up more pebbles... as Tom waited.

"It doesn't matter anymore. I told him to stop harassing me, or I would deal with him. He didn't... so I dealt with him. He hasn't bothered me since." Josh turned and walked away, back along the riverside and up onto the bridge.

Tom was annoyed. "Josh, stop there," he commanded.

Josh stopped and rested his arms on the metal rails of the bridge. Tom was beside him in seconds.

"Why didn't you tell us?" mumbled Josh, looking off into the distance. Tom was even more perplexed as he stood beside him.

"Tell you what, Josh?" Tom asked the sullen young man.

"About the trial."

A tight knot clutched at Tom's stomach. He'd always dreaded his children discovering about the trial.

"What did you hear?" Tom asked, trying to remain calm.

Josh bent down and stroked the dog. "A boy at school said he knew something *juicy* about my parents."

Tom was in disbelief. *Juicy* was hardly the word to describe the ordeal he had endured nearly twenty years ago.

"Was this the same boy you punched?" asked Tom.

Josh nodded. "He kept going on about it, so that morning, a few weeks ago, I cornered him. Asked him to 'cough up' and if he didn't, I'd punch him. He told me... but I punched him in any case. He said you were put on trial for killing your brother and it was my mother who accused you...was it true?"

Tom froze. He'd been a fool to think their children could live in a town like Malhaven and not hear gossip from the past. He sighed.

"Yes, Josh...it's true... but the important thing is...I was found not guilty."

A shout distracted them. Darcy and Grady were cycling towards them. "You made good time," he called to them, then under his breath spoke to Josh. "Stay out of your mother's way, she's busy, I'll go to help her."

Darcy and Grady dismounted their cycles.

"Dad, this is Grady Forrester," Darcy commented, introducing her friend.

"Pleased to meet you, Mr Smallwood," said Grady, smiling.

"Yes, good to meet you too," added Tom, shaking the young man's hand.

Grady surveyed the landscape. "This is a fantastic spot," he declared.

"Have you been skimming pebbles?" Darcy asked her brother. Not waiting for his reply, she started to run down to the river. "Come on you two…let's have a skimming competition," she shouted gleefully.

Grady, Josh and Jess followed her as Tom walked back to The Bungalow with a heavy heart.

* * *

FRANCE

Chantal unlocked the front door. For the next few days, she had the house to herself, as Margot and her brother were attending a funeral in Paris. It was four weeks since she'd moved and so far, barring a few essential items, the crates remained unpacked. Tonight, she decided, in the absence of her hosts, she would tackle the task.

Her mother's beautiful sideboard was standing empty along a wall in the room she was using as a lounge. It was calling out to be utilised and Chantal knew filling the space with her mother's possessions would help her to feel more settled.

Margot and her brother were so welcoming. Each evening, they invited her to share their meal, but she wanted to establish her own routine. After eating a light supper, she began her task. Placing a cloth on the table, she pulled out a crate and began unwrapping. Soon the large sideboard filled up. She placed figurines and a clock on the broad mantel shelf. She found 'the boy with the fish' and stared at it nostalgically. She gave it pride of place on the top of the sideboard, alongside photographs of her parents, Rachel and her family and one very special image…a slightly blurred snapshot of Sam with Josh and Darcy, taken at The Bungalow.

She possessed two other photographs of Sam, both in position on her bedside table. They were the first thing she saw in a morning and the last thing she saw before she extinguished her bedside lamp. On impulse, she ran up the stairs to her room and picked up one of the precious items.

The photograph showed Sam with his arm around her, standing in the garden at Meckleridge House. It was taken on one of Sam's visits to Malhaven during the summer of 1938. They looked so happy. She ran her fingers over Sam's face. He was tall, clean shaven, with dark brown wavy hair. Her heart leapt within her...where was he? She sat down on the bed.

She'd tried to make enquiries the previous year. She'd written to the hospital in Newcastle where they both worked – without success. She asked if he had returned to his work as an orthopaedic surgeon after the war, and if not, did they have any information regarding his present whereabouts. She knew it was a 'long shot', but it was her only line of enquiry. She received a brief reply to her letter months later... *Doctor Samuel Carter left our employ in early 1940.* This was disappointing.

Chantal had returned to France in the January of 1939, eight months before the outbreak of the Second World War. She was in regular correspondence with Sam for eighteen months until she received his final letter...the one with the missing page. She knew he intended to 'join up', but she continued to write to him at his lodgings in Newcastle. She was aware he could not give any details of his war involvement, but it all seemed so 'vague'. Did he receive her letters after leaving Newcastle? She wrote to his lodgings after the war, addressing the communication to The Proprietor...but no reply was received.

She felt helpless. How could she further her inquiries? Perhaps Tom could suggest something. She determined to speak to him and Pierre Thibault when she visited Lyon for Noël. With that in mind she took some paper and a pen and wrote down everything she knew which may assist enquiries… but it wasn't much.

She'd moved from her home in France to begin her nurses training in Autumn 1935, aged nineteen years old. She had lived with Rachel and Tom at weekends and stayed in the Nurses Home in Newcastle, during the week. Changes to this routine took place when she began working shifts, but she always spent her free time with the family in Malhaven. She lay back on her bed, reliving her memories.

She had first met Sam Carter when she was working on an orthopaedic ward, during her training. By this stage she knew she wanted to specialise in midwifery. She found him attentive as he made his daily rounds. He noticed her accent and asked where she belonged. He often lingered, chatting to her longer than was necessary, regarding a patient's care. When she finished her training, she knew it was unlikely their paths would cross again.

However, attending a 'leaving do' for the formidable Sister Manson, Chantal heard a voice behind her. "Bonjour," he crooned.

"Oh, Dr Carter, how pleasant to meet you again," she replied.

He'd looked at her with an admiring smile. "Call me Sam, please, we are not on duty…and what is your name, Nurse Martin?"

She blushed. He'd remembered her name and he pronounced it the French way, rolling the 'r', unlike most of her colleagues who said it the English way.

"It's Chantal," she replied, feeling awesome.

"Chantal Martin," he proclaimed, pronouncing the sounds in a very French manner. "Allow me to replenish your drink, mademoiselle," he offered, noting her almost empty glass. He returned with her drink and asked about her training, her family, her thoughts on living in England. She was mesmerised by him. They conversed easily. She discovered he was now a fully qualified surgeon.

"Oh, pardon, monsieur," she apologised. "Congratulations, it means I must address you as 'Mr Carter'," she added.

Sam had raised his eyebrows, looked adoringly into her eyes and remarked, "Non, non, ma chérie…you can call me Sam." And that was it. A chance meeting and a definite connection. At the end of the evening, he escorted Chantal back to the Nurses Home.

Over the next few weeks, they met whenever their shift patterns allowed. They visited the cinema; the theatre; an evening concert in The City Hall; and various museums and parks in the historic city of Newcastle. He took her to expensive restaurants and one day they visited a tearoom and enjoyed an English afternoon tea, laughing when Sam coiled his little finger, as he held the dainty china cup decorated with tiny rosebuds. He was always a gentleman – opening doors, lifting out her seat and kissing her lovingly, each time they parted.

Chantal wanted to introduce Sam to her family and hoped she could arrange it over the Christmas holidays. She was disappointed when Sam indicated he was going to be away visiting his family in Edinburgh.

It was Easter before another suitable opportunity arose. She invited him to Malhaven to meet her sister and family. Sam owned a car, and they visited Trespershields with the Smallwoods. Rachel and Tom were delighted to make his acquaintance and over the summer of 1938 he became a regular visitor to their home, whenever they could match their free time.

However, in early August Sam informed Chantal he was spending two weeks with his family in Edinburgh. She asked about his family – were his parents still alive? Did he have any brothers or sisters? His answers were clipped – yes, his parents were alive, and his twin brother had died as an infant. He quickly turned the conversation to other matters.

When he returned, she enquired about his holiday. "Did you have a pleasant time with your family, Sam? It must have been good to see them. Did you take them out and about?"

Chantal recalled Sam's offhand response.

"I did my duty. Now, if you don't mind, I'd rather not talk about it, I'm much more interested in what you've been up to while I've been away."

Chantal thought no more about it until Rachel raised the subject.

"I think Sam is more than just a friend, Chantal...am I correct?" her perceptive sister asked.

Chantal blushed. "Is it that obvious?" she asked.

Rachel smiled and hugged her young sister.

"Rather...and for what it's worth, Tom and I approve, wholeheartedly. Has he talked about taking you to meet his family yet?"

Chantal shook her head. "No, he's rather vague about his family. All I know is they live in Edinburgh."

Chantal sighed, gazing at Sam's photograph – she felt so sad. At the time it didn't seem important, but now... she wished she'd known the whereabouts of his parents, then she could have contacted them regarding Sam's welfare.

She was roused from her reminiscences by the shrill ringing of the telephone. "*Bonsoir*," she answered. Ten minutes later, the young *sage femme* was cycling to the home of one of her patients whose waters had broken. Thankfully, it was only a short ride. All thoughts of Sam Carter were forgotten, as she applied herself to the task of helping to bring a new life into the world.

Chapter 5

ENGLAND

A roaring log fire and the residual heat of the earlier sunshine brought a cosiness to the conservatory as Rachel and Tom relaxed after their supper. Both were tired but satisfied with the work they'd accomplished at The Bungalow. Rachel had cleaned out all the crockery cupboards, cutlery and linen drawers. Tom had carried out a small repair on the corner of the roof.

"Good day's work," remarked Tom. "We must pay more attention to small repairs next year – hope we have a storm-free winter."

Rachel laid her head on Tom's chest as he placed his arm around her.

"By the time we visit The Bungalow next Spring – we'll have made our decision about the hotel," mused Rachel.

Tom was thoughtful.

"Would you consider taking on more students for tutoring…if we didn't re-open?" Tom asked.

Rachel's reply was instant. "Yes, I'd be happy to do that, if it meant you could develop your horticulture plans. Until now, I've acquired my students through 'word of mouth', but I guess I could put an advert in the Post Office."

The light from the glowing fire was mesmerising as they watched the dancing flames in the grate.

Tom broke the silence. "Rachel...we have a problem," Tom began. He felt her tense.

"Problem? What kind of a problem?"

Tom had refrained from disclosing the details of his earlier conversation with Josh.

"It appears our son's recent problems stem from some comments passed to him by a boy in his class at school."

Rachel sat up and looked at her husband. "What comments?"

Tom exhaled slowly. The problems he and Rachel had experienced, nearly twenty years ago, were rarely, if ever, spoken about.

"About the trial," Tom replied.

Rachel froze, staring at Tom in disbelief. "Surely not...I mean how...and why?"

Tom looked pensive.

"Honestly, Rachel...I don't know any more details. Apparently, this boy taunted him for weeks, saying he knew something *juicy* about his parents. Eventually, Josh cornered him, asking him to explain. The lad told him I was put on trial for trying to kill my brother and the accuser was you."

Rachel leapt off the settee. "Juicy," she shrieked incredulously, clenching her fists.

"Calm down, Rachel," Tom urged, as she began to pace the floor in front of the fireplace, the dog moving out of her way.

"How on earth does a fourteen-year-old boy know about events which took place twenty years ago?" she demanded.

Tom rubbed his brow. "Probably some parent, or grandparent remembered the name Smallwood and passed on some old gossip. This lad saw it as an opportunity to use it against Josh. Remember that day a few weeks ago when he came home with a bruised and bloodied face?"

Rachel nodded.

"Well, that was the day Josh confronted him and asked him to explain. Josh threatened to punch him if he didn't. The lad told him…and Josh thumped him in any case, as a warning to keep his mouth shut!" Tom sat forward and stretched. "As far as I'm aware, that's the extent of what Josh knows."

Rachel was seething. "Busybodies…gossip mongers, who cannot mind their own business. It's all in the past and is of no relevance to our children." Rachel placed her hands on the mantelshelf and stared into the glowing embers of the fire. "Do you think we should tell them what happened, Tom?"

"No, Rachel. I don't, it will just stir things up. I think Josh handled the situation in the way a young lad would…

with his fists. Secretly…I'm proud of him, shutting the boy up in that way."

Rachel returned to her seat. "But what else did he tell him, I wonder…" Rachel's voice tailed off.

"I think we leave the situation alone. He knows the basic facts – and I told him I was found 'not guilty'. The least he knows the better. If he asks about it again…then I'll explain. If he raises the subject with you, tell him to speak to me. Otherwise, we keep quiet…agreed?"

Rachel nodded. It was all water under the bridge.

"It proves the adage 'the sins of the father are to be laid upon the children.' Only in this case the sins stemmed from the mother," Rachel remarked wearily. "It's a quotation from Shakespeare in 'The Merchant of Venice'. It's also referenced in the Bible," she added.

Tom turned to face her. "Rachel… let's leave it!" Tom admonished his wife, sternly.

* * *

NOVEMBER 1946

"No, no, no…I'll do it myself," objected Darcy, pulling at the hairpins in her blonde, curly hair.

Rachel stood back, raised her hands and shook her head. "As you wish!" she conceded and left her daughter's bedroom. "Call me when you want zipping up," she added.

It was the day of the eagerly anticipated Works Dinner Dance. Rachel was astounded, but at the same time delighted, when her tempestuous offspring had asked for her assistance with her hair styling. However, true to form it had backfired!

In less than an hour Grady Forrester would be arriving to collect Darcy and escort her to the venue. She'd fretted over her hairstyle for the last week and was determined to wear it naturally, cascading over her shoulders. Her mother suggested pinning the top, to add height and elegance, but Darcy disliked the style. Then they tried a chignon, which Darcy also dismissed.

Eventually, with the aid of a few pins she managed to lift her hair from her face, and applied some simple make up, to enhance her natural look. "Good," she declared to herself and walked over to the ballgown draped on a hanger on the wardrobe door. Carefully, she slid it off and stepped into the satin dress – a turquoise blue creation, straight with a wide neckline and short sleeves. Her mother was summonsed to secure the fastening. The style was fitted and flattered Darcy's youthful figure. She attached a pearl drop necklace and tiny 'clip on' pearl earrings, then slipped into her low-heeled shoes. A final touch was added – elbow length evening gloves. Rachel smiled, with approval.

Darcy viewed the finished ensemble in the full-length vanity mirror with satisfaction. The dress had been purchased from Fenwick's in Newcastle, a few weeks earlier.

She picked up her lightweight stole and black clutch bag and made her way downstairs, with five minutes to spare.

Tom was waiting in the hallway. He gasped with delight as his beguiling daughter, followed by her mother, descended the stairs. "Oh, gosh...you are so beautiful... my Darcy Rose," he declared, a lump forming in his throat. He reached out to embrace her, but jumped back as she called out.

"Dad, don't...you'll smudge something!"

Instead, Tom lifted her gloved hand and brought it to his lips as Josh appeared from the back lounge.

"My, my, big sis...you scrub up well!" Josh remarked jovially, as a crunching on the driveway outside heralded the arrival of a car.

The tall dark-haired Grady Forrester looked dapper, attired in a black dinner suit. Rachel invited him inside. After shaking hands with his daughter's escort, Tom picked up his new camera, complete with flash equipment from the hall table. Darcy pulled a face at the sight.

"Oh, no, Dad...do we have to?" she exclaimed, but happily posed with her handsome beau beside the hall table.

"One for the family album," remarked Rachel as they waved the young couple on their way.

"Oh, I guess there will be many admirers before she settles down," chuckled Tom. "It's very early days."

* * *

Darcy Smallwood oozed confidence. The word 'shy' and 'Darcy' did not fit in the same sentence. From being a tiny tot, she'd developed an outgoing personality and never failed to make an impression on everyone she met. Over the years hotel guests fell for her charms, with her winsome smiles and perky comments. Even when the hotel became a convalescent home, during the war, Darcy continued to befriend many of the patients and could often be found reading to them or playing various board games. She possessed a caring nature and at one stage Rachel suspected she might follow her Tante Tallie into the nursing profession, but so far Darcy was undecided about her future career.

Darcy's friendship with Grady Forrester was in its early stages. When Grady had made it clear it was Darcy who attracted him and not Darcy's friend, Chrissie, she was flattered. At first Chrissie was peeved, but she soon found another young man to admire, so the girls' friendship was unaffected. Cycling Club outings were the common meeting point until the day Grady accompanied Darcy to Trespershields. That day they talked in depth on a variety of subjects and Darcy was comfortable in his company. The Dinner Dance invitation marked a point of progress in their friendship.

"Prepare yourself for your first kiss," Chrissie chided.

"I'm not sure the opportunity will arise," Darcy reacted, secretly hoping, however... that it would!

CHAPTER 5

Grady was an attentive companion, introducing Darcy to his parents, siblings and their partners. He kept her supplied with soft drinks. They sat at a round table with Grady's family. Darcy felt at ease with the conversation around the table, joining in with various discussions.

In the centre of the room was a dance floor. After dinner, when the small band began to play, Grady led his beautiful companion to the centre of the room – he was surprised how well Darcy could dance.

"Where did you learn your ballroom dancing skills?" he enquired.

"At home," Darcy responded. "Before the war dancing was a regular event at our house, when it was a hotel. During the war, when it was used as a convalescent home, Mother and Dad encouraged the patients, who were able, to dance, accompanied by gramophone music. The staff loved it and sometimes friends of my parents would attend – anything to dispel the gloom and doom of the war days," she explained.

Grady seemed impressed. As the evening progressed, Darcy danced with Grady's father and his two brothers Solomon and Winston. Returning to the table she noticed Grady was missing. She excused herself to visit the Ladies' Powder Room, stepping out into the spacious hallway. There were two corridors separated by a staircase, but there was no indication of the room Darcy was seeking. She took a guess and walked down one of the corridors.

73

As she walked, she heard muffled voices. Some instinct prompted her to be cautious. She slowed her pace and tiptoed towards the voices. Her jaw dropped as she recognised Grady's distinctive accent. She halted behind a pillar and watched. Grady and his friend were loitering under the staircase archway, beside some coat stands. What she observed next… perplexed her. The young man with Grady was a boy from school – Philip Trent, she thought, recalling his name.

She looked on as Grady slid his hand into the pocket of an overcoat. He retrieved an item from the inside pocket. It was thin, rectangular and silver coloured – a cigarette case, she guessed. Then he handed it to his companion who proceeded to place it in a different coat pocket.

Darcy placed her hand over her mouth. Something about their furtive actions caused her to retreat. She wasn't sure what she'd observed, but she knew Grady wasn't wearing an overcoat that evening. She quietly walked backwards for a few steps, then reaching the staircase quickly climbed the first few stairs.

She heard Grady and Philip laughing as they approached the staircase, so she spun around, making it look as if she were descending the stairs. Grady looked up, saw her and smiled.

"I was looking for the Ladies' Room upstairs," she explained.

He shook his head. "Wrong way," he chirped. "It's that way." He pointed to the other corridor.

Darcy followed his instructions. Returning to the ballroom five minutes later she found Grady hovering outside the room waiting for her, they rejoined the event, and the evening continued pleasantly.

Just after eleven o 'clock, Grady brought his brother's car to a halt outside Meckleridge House. He turned off the engine and applied the handbrake, then leaning over towards Darcy he took her hand.

"Thank you for being such a delightful companion this evening, Darcy," he cooed in his gravelly voice. He lifted her gloved hand to his lips. Darcy shivered with excitement. Grady slid his arm around the back of Darcy's shoulders. "You are a very attractive girl, Darcy Smallwood...may I kiss you?" he purred. Darcy nodded, not trusting herself to speak. His kiss was soft and gentle.

Pulling away, he murmured, "I think I'd like to take you on a date, Darcy ...would that be possible?"

Finding her voice, Darcy whispered, "Yes, Grady...I'd like that – what do you have in mind?" She could see his pleasing smile in the moonlight.

"Pictures?" he suggested. "I'm not sure what's on at the Rex in Malsett, but how does next Saturday work for you?"

Darcy swallowed, still reeling from her first romantic kiss. "I think I'm free," she replied.

Grady sat back. "Good, I'll telephone during the week. Maybe we could go to a picture house in Newcastle, if I can borrow this car," he remarked, tapping the steering wheel.

"Give me a call," replied Darcy.

Grady leaned forward and pressed his lips to hers again, briefly, then jumped out of the car, opened her door and escorted her to the doorstep. Placing a featherlight kiss on her lips, he bid her 'goodnight'.

As Darcy lay down to sleep later, having relayed the evening's events to her parents, she felt happy but confused. The evening was splendid. She had enjoyed meeting Grady's family; she loved partaking of the sumptuous food – delighting in the various courses; she was thrilled being whisked around the dance floor by various partners. But the highlight of the evening was Grady's kisses...three in total. His lips were so tender. She touched her own lips, recalling the sensation of their connection.

But one aspect of the evening marred her joy. What were Grady and Philip doing under the stair arch with those overcoats? They didn't appear to be stealing the item...but then what were they doing placing it in a different coat pocket? The incident troubled her.

* * *

FRANCE,
NOVEMBER 1946

Cycling during the night with only her tiny bike light to guide the way on the winding lanes stirred unpleasant memories for Chantal. Memories from a different lifetime, or so it felt. Yet…it was only a few years ago. Her courage during those dark days of the Occupation was something she didn't question. There was a job to be done; a need to be fulfilled; and she made the perfect participant in her role as *a sage femme.*

Like many French citizens during the German Occupation of France, Chantal hated the situation her country was enduring. But she had admired the daring acts of bravery carried out by The French Resistance, from afar, until one night in the summer of 1941.

Visiting Madame Bernard, after an urgent phone call, she hastened to assist the mother who was in the latter trimester of pregnancy with her second child. It was eerie cycling through the darkness, but her bike was her only mode of transport. It was also dangerous. She could be attacked so easily. Bikes were a valuable commodity, and it was a constant threat – someone who wanted her bike, could take it, by fair means or foul.

She was required to pass through one checkpoint on her way to the farmhouse on the edge of the city of Bordeaux, which lay in the occupied zone. Her first experience of the scrutiny was scary, but after showing her all important papers, including an explanation of her need to travel at such a late hour, she was allowed to pass through. It wasn't a frequent occurrence, it usually happened during daytime hours when it seemed less frightening. Over the months she recognised some of the soldiers, making the transit less of an ordeal.

But during that summer, her visits to Madame Bernard took on a new role of importance. As a regular visitor to the farmhouse Chantal would park her bike against the wall, knock on the door and step straight into the kitchen. This night her arrival was quiet, as usual, but the sight she beheld in the kitchen was far from usual. Two men stared at her, shocked and fearful, as she entered.

"Pardon, pardon," she exclaimed – all too aware the men were hastily trying to conceal the contents of a crate with a lid…Chantal's eyes were transfixed by the contents. Monsieur Bernard, her patient's husband, stepped in front of the table, obscuring Chantal's view – but she knew what she had observed…and she knew it was a mistake.

She was quickly ushered into the sitting room, where Cécile was lying on a chaise in obvious discomfort. Chantal 'flicked' into her midwifery role, attending to her patient. After a careful examination, Chantal reassured the mother.

"Cécile, you are not in labour. It could be sometime before your little one is born. You are experiencing Braxton Hicks contractions – they are a practice for the real event."

The young mother looked relieved. "Why did I not feel like this when Michel was born? I telephoned you because I thought this baby was on its way," she asked, puzzled.

"Not all births are the same, Cécile, now you must rest. You should be in bed at this late hour. You may experience them again but don't worry, I will always be willing to attend, to check you over. Now, your husband needs to make you 'une tasse de thé'.

As Chantal was packing her bag, Monsieur Bernard entered the room, looking rather threatening.

"Mademoiselle," he said sternly. "You will take a seat please. I need to speak with you." The French farmer was a burly, unkempt man, with a head of unruly red hair and a matching bushy beard. He was tall and broad, and Chantal felt threatened by his stance. In all her previous visits to the farmhouse she had scarcely spoken to the man, and now he wanted to talk to her. Somehow, refusing to obey his request seemed non-negotiable, so she complied.

Chantal noticed the look of panic on Cécile's face as her husband began to speak.

"Mademoiselle, when you arrived this evening... you saw something," he stopped abruptly, and an awkward silence ensued.

Chantal felt ill at ease and sat forward on her seat. Monsieur Bernard pulled himself up straight and stared intently into Chantal's eyes, then wiped his brow.

"Can I count on your silence, Mademoiselle?" The way he spoke and the glare he used unsettled her.

Chantal glanced warily between the French farmer and his pregnant wife. She coughed and replied. "I was called here tonight to attend to Madame Bernard. She was distressed and feared she was beginning her labour. I examined her and confirmed she is not in labour. I spoke to you and your friend as I entered the kitchen but quickly made my way into the lounge to attend to my patient."

The bulky farmer continued to stare at Chantal, unsettling her, then slowly a smile spread across his rugged face.

"Bien, bien, mademoiselle…I think we understand each other," he remarked.

Chantal relaxed and smiled. The words were unspoken but the message was clear. Chantal had witnessed something which could be beneficial to her country and she, like many of her fellow Frenchmen, would keep her counsel if she were to be questioned.

That night, more than five years ago, was to mark the beginning of an involvement for Chantal. But at that juncture, she was blissfully unaware of the events yet to take place. Arriving home, Chantal attended to her routines following a visit. Her memories were disturbing… and she doubted she would sleep. Her memories of Sam and her memories of the war days made a perfect cocktail for insomnia.

Chapter 6

CHRISTMAS 1946, FRANCE

Chantal wiped the sleepy sludge from her eyes, blinked and sat up. It was still dark. She reached out, switched on the lamp, and noted the time – six o'clock. She shivered and snuggled down under the blankets again. Five more minutes, she thought, but already her mind was racing. Today she was travelling to Lyon for the family Noël celebrations.

To Chantal the word 'family' felt fluid. For the first thirteen years of her life, she'd been an only child – an *enfant unique,* living with her loving parents. There were no other relatives in her family to her knowledge.

When her father died suddenly, she clung to her mother. About a year later her world exploded again when she was introduced to her English sister, Rachel. It was a shock, but it was welcomed. Overnight she'd acquired a family – a sister and brother-in-law and, in addition,

Tom's sister and family who lived in Lyon, became her extended family.

She was drawn to Peg Thibault, and they became good friends. She frequently travelled to Lyon to visit the Thibaults and accompanied them each August on their annual visit to Malhaven. Before she moved to England to train as a nurse, Chantal and her mother spent two Noëls with Peg and her family. But it was eight long years since she had seen any of them and only a handful of letters had been exchanged.

Chantal reluctantly left her cosy bed and braced herself to face the early morning chill. She was working for a few hours this morning, then after lunch she was taking the train to Lyon. She hurriedly dressed and placed a few extra items in her suitcase, which she'd packed the night before. She glanced at her other bag – the one containing the gifts she'd bought.

The children were no longer children – they were young adults. So, her presents were based on guesswork. How would she fit in? She mused as she brushed her blonde curls and adjusted her uniform. Really, she was a 'misfit' – she belonged to neither generation. Rachel was more of a friend than an older sister. Until she moved to England, she'd only seen Rachel twice a year – summer and a week in January when Tom and Rachel visited France.

Rachel was a good listener, and Chantal shared her secrets, such as they were, with her. She'd trusted Rachel, more than she trusted her mother. Deep down, Chantal struggled to fathom why her parents chose to abandon Rachel and withhold the information regarding her existence from Chantal. She often wondered if it hadn't been for Tom, uncovering Rachel's background, if she would have lived her life totally unaware that she had a sister! Oh, it would be so good to talk to Rachel and unburden herself.

The train rattled through the French countryside later that day. Looking out of the window the scars of war and the remnants of The Occupation were still in evidence. She lay back and allowed the rumble of the train to lull her into her remembrances. It was a luxury she rarely afforded herself, ensuring the deep recesses of her mind remained closed, in the busyness of her everyday life.

The ravages of war had also taken their toll on Chantal Martin's life. The last time she had seen Rachel she felt sure her future lay in England with Sam Carter. Who could have guessed as she waved Rachel goodbye in Durham Station in January 1939, almost eight long years would pass before they could be re-united. The war tore her country to pieces; the war tore her loving family from her and the love of her life.

Rumours of war were circulating in the months she conducted her correspondence with Sam. When her mother's illness worsened, she had reluctantly resigned her job in Newcastle. By the time Yvette Martin died, the world was a different place. She knew Sam would offer his services as a medic in the war, his letters indicated it, but as she was French by birth she remained in her homeland.

France was divided into zones around the same time she received her 'divided' letter... the letter with the missing page. She'd envisaged myriad explanations for its contents...but it was futile and torturous. So, years ago she made the decision to stop guessing. As long as the contents remained unknown – Chantal could always hope. Hope for a future with Sam, hope for a re-union with Sam.

Hope was an optimistic attitude, and she was an optimistic soul. Hope was a powerful tool, and she intended to use it to discover Sam's whereabouts. Her first attempts may have failed but the world was still in chaos in those early days when she'd first made enquiries. With the passage of time, she hoped if Tom was willing to assist her, more information would emerge.

She truly believed the love she shared with Sam Carter was meant to be and unless he was dead...where there was life... there was hope. She concluded if there was no evidence of his death – then he must be alive. Hope was an active ingredient and the more she fed it...the more real it became. I'm an optimist, she told herself, and my hope in finding Sam is my reason to live.

She must have dozed because the next time she consulted her watch she was amazed at the closeness of her destination.

* * *

"Wait there on the platform, I'll be back in a jiffy," shouted Darcy. She leapt from her seat and pushed past other passengers trying to retrieve their luggage.

"Wait, wait, Darcy," called Tom, to no avail.

"*Pardon, pardon,*" Darcy muttered multiple times, as she dodged between the exiting occupants of the train carriage. Tom's voice could be heard in the background urging her to wait, but he could have saved his agitated breath, as his impetuous daughter was soon out of earshot.

Rachel was frantic. "She'll get lost," she exclaimed, scrambling to pick up bags and follow her husband.

"Well, at least she speaks the lingo," chuckled Josh, helping his father collect their luggage.

"As usual, the little monkey's given no thought as to who would carry her belongings," sighed Tom, juggling his own and Darcy's suitcases.

"*Ou sont les toilettes?*" Darcy demanded, seeking directions from the uniformed porter.

He paused and stared at the young girl, literally dancing on the platform in front of him. He pointed to a door and Darcy took off at speed, only to come to an abrupt standstill, as she collided with a solid human object, dislodging packages from his arms and scattering them to the ground.

"Get out of my way, you idiot," she shrieked, in English.

"*Mademoiselle, pardon. Regardez ce que vous avez fait,*" came the gentle response from the lips of a bewildered young man, asking her to look at what she had done.

"*Je suis désolée*," yelled Darcy, leaving him to pick up his packages, as she dived into the ladies' toilets. Minutes later after much relief, Darcy returned to the platform, catching sight of her bewildered family. Her father eyed her sternly. She held her breath anticipating a severe reprimand.

"Never, ever, do that again, Darcy Smallwood. You could easily have become lost and ended up on a different platform," Tom rebuked her, sternly.

"Yes, Dad…but I was desperate." She smiled sweetly, pleading her defence.

"Here, get this lot," remarked her brother, pushing a bag and two parcels into her arms.

Without further conversation the Smallwood family exited the station platform in Lyon.

"*Bonjour, bonjour*," called a familiar voice. Pierre Thibault embraced his English brother and sister-in-law and led the family to his waiting car. The air was cold and crisp, and darkness surrounded them as they made the short journey from the station to the apartment where the Thibaults resided. Their arrival was frenetic, as Peg hugged, kissed and embraced her English family, showing them their accommodation.

"I've put you and Rachel in Jonty's room," she announced to her brother. "Josh…you will be sleeping in my neighbour's apartment upstairs, sharing with Jonty and his cousin, Henri. The rooms are spacious, just leave your luggage in the hallway – Jonty will be back soon, he's gone to the station to meet Henri." Peg was a born organiser. "Darcy...can you share with Sylvie?" she asked, as the young girl emerged from her bedroom to welcome her English cousin.

An hour later, unpacked and refreshed, a melee descended upon the salon. The chatter was loud with several conversations taking place simultaneously. Suddenly, the door opened. Darcy turned, eager to greet her handsome cousin Jonty, who if it were possible looked even more stunning than he'd appeared in the summer... then her heart skipped a beat. Following Jonty into the room... was the solid 'idiot' from the station! Darcy swallowed...oh dear, what was he doing here?

Peg was making introductions. "Tom, Rachel – this is Pierre's nephew Henri. He lives near Paris and is spending Noël with us." The young man, who Darcy surmised was about Jonty's age, followed his cousin as he shook hands with her parents. Jonty welcomed them with hugs and kisses. The two young men approached Josh and Darcy, standing beside the window.

"These are my English cousins," announced Jonty in French.

Darcy was on tenterhooks – why had she called this extremely handsome young Frenchman an *idiot* two hours ago? Will he recognise me – she wondered, watching him shake hands with her brother. She reasoned he probably wouldn't remember her as she was now relieved of her outdoor clothing – but he did! A glimmer of recognition caused a smile to tickle the edges of his mouth, causing a broad grin to radiate across his 'Adonis-like' face.

"*Enchanté de vous...revoir,*" he crooned, pausing before speaking the word '*revoir*'... again. His eyes laughed and sparkled...he was mesmerising!

Darcy repeated the greeting. "*Enchanté de vous... revoir,*" she whispered. "*Pardonne moi, monseuir. J'étais pressé,*" she replied, explaining she was in a hurry. As she was apologising, he continued to hold her hand and stare into her pale blue eyes.

"*Je'accepte vos excuses, mademoiselle,*" he replied.

Jonty was observing the exchange with amusement. "Have you two met before?" he asked in English.

Darcy dropped her eyes as she felt heat rising in her cheeks.

"*Oui,*" responded Henri. Then the gallant Frenchman bent forward and whispered into Darcy's ear. "*Je ne suis pas un idiot.*" His closeness caused delightful shivers to run down Darcy's spine and her bright pink visage to radiate. The moment passed, and the young men departed to explore their accommodation with Peg's elderly neighbour. Darcy was encased in a warm glow of something surreal.

"Only one more guest to arrive," remarked Peg excitedly, "then are ready for '*Le Réveillon*' tomorrow evening."

Seeing the perplexed look on Darcy's face, Sylvie, her cousin explained. *"Le Réveillon'* is the name we give for our special Christmas Eve meal. Be prepared to sit at the table for hours, Darcy – but I can promise you a feast *'par excellence'*. Ma mère has been organising the food for days."

Rachel was listening to her niece describing the event. "Do you exchange Christmas presents at this meal?"

Sylvie shook her head. "We don't – in our household, present giving is left until Christmas morning. Most French families, however, do exchange gifts at *'Le Réveillon'*, but we are an Anglo-French family, so we adopt traditions from both countries, and we attend mass after *'Le Réveillon'.*"

Darcy nodded. "Yes, we usually go to church for a midnight service on Christmas Eve."

A rattle sounded on the door. "I guess that will be Chantal," announced Peg gleefully, jumping up.

Darcy glanced around the room. She'd visited her aunt and uncle's home as a child, but her remembrances were vague. She noted how spacious and tastefully decorated the salon appeared, with neatly upholstered chairs and a chaise. In the corner stood *un sapin de Noël* adorned with ornaments and sweet delights. The fireplace was dressed in festive tree boughs, laced with red ribbons and bearing candles. Aunt Peg has a lovely home, thought Darcy. A commotion in the doorway halted her observations.

"Bonjour, bonjour, everyone," declared Chantal excitedly.

Rachel and Darcy stepped forward to embrace the new arrival. The three women hugged and kissed; tears of joy flowed, and greetings resonated throughout the room. Eventually, as Chantal was released, she acknowledged the remainder of the guests in the crowded salon. "Where are we all sleeping?" asked Chantal, looking around.

"The boys are staying upstairs in Madame Levigne's apartment. You also, Chantal," announced Peg.

Chantal smiled. Peg's elderly neighbour was no stranger to Chantal – she was her mother's friend, and she'd stayed in her apartment in past years.

"I'm looking forward to seeing her again, we have corresponded over the years," she commented. Loud laughter caused Chantal to glance towards its source. Three young men were obviously sharing something amusing. Chantal approached them. "My, my...how you have grown," she declared, embracing Jonty and Josh as they stood up. She took the outstretched hand of the third young man. "I don't think we have met before," she remarked, as Jonty made the introduction.

"This my cousin, Henri Dukas, from Paris," he explained, smirking. "Sorry, Chantal, I'm just getting over some pert comment my dear cousin passed earlier... nothing to do with you!"

The young Frenchman shook hands with Chantal, his eyes were sparkling. "Delighted to meet you," he remarked.

"I was sorry to hear of your loss," she added, as Henri nodded.

Sylvie bent over and whispered to Darcy. "Henri's father died a couple of months ago – his mother has been dead for years. He is an *enfant unique* so has been visiting us regularly as mon père is his guardian now."

Darcy regarded Henri with compassion. What a sadness for him to have lost both his parents and have no siblings. As if he realised he was the object of their conversation, Henri looked up and his eyes locked with Darcy's. Once again, Darcy experienced a strange sensation but was unsure if it was born out of sympathy for this young man's circumstances...or otherwise.

* * *

"Joyeux Noël, Joyeux Noël," the greeting resonated as the occupants of the spacious apartment in Lyon sat down at the extended dining table to celebrate *'Le Réveillon'* on Christmas Eve. The preparations prior to the event were busy, but Peg was well organised, and each person was given a task to perform. The atmosphere was buoyant and rewarding. The young men had been dispatched to the market – *'Le Marche de Noël'* to source *croustellons* – small sugar-coated doughnuts and *batons de sucre*. "We call these candy canes," remarked Josh, as Jonty pointed to them on the market stall.

Tom and Pierre were commissioned to purchase bottles of wine and the ingredients to make '*vin chaud*' – mulled wine and hot apple cider. Chantal, Sylvie and Darcy were sent to procure the fish order – scallops and oysters. Meanwhile back at the apartment Peg and Rachel began the task of assembling '*le repas de Noël*', the traditional thirteen desserts.

"So much food, Peg! How have you managed with all the rationing?" Rachel enquired.

"Weeks of careful planning, Rachel. Fortunately, many of the required ingredients are dried fruits and nuts, so I have acquired them over many weeks and Madame Levigne has helped with her rations."

When the younger ladies returned with the fish order, Peg instructed them to lay the table for the evening meal and decide where to hang the mistletoe.

At seven o'clock everyone sat down, dressed appropriately, and the feast began. Three hours later, having partaken of hors d'oeuvres; appetisers; fish and meat dishes; vegetables; the special desserts and cheese, Darcy felt she was ready to explode.

"We keep our speciality dessert until tomorrow," Peg declared. "On Christmas Day we eat our '*Bûche de Noël*' or Yule Log as you call it in England."

Tom exclaimed, "Peg, you are a genius," then standing, glass in hand, added, "I'm going to raise a toast to my dear sister for all her hard work and organisation."

The assembled group raised their glasses and drank a toast to an embarrassed Peg Thibault. When the dishes were tidied away, everyone donned their outdoor clothing and walked the short distance to the *L'eglise* for *Le mass de minuit*. Christmas Eve 1946 had been celebrated in style – a welcome treat after the restrained celebrations of the war years.

On Christmas Day morning, gifts were exchanged and after a lunch comprising leftovers and the *Bûche de Noël* – the sumptuous rolled sponge, filled with chocolate buttercream and decorated with meringue and marzipan – Peg conducted an afternoon and evening of parlour games. "What a joy to have a captive audience for my games," she declared, clapping her hands. Everyone partook of the fun and frolics – but one person dared to engage in an extra Christmas custom.

Since arriving in Lyon, Henri Dukas had found himself admiring Darcy Smallwood from afar. Their initial collision in the station and introductory comments in the apartment, when he revelled in watching the pretty English girl blush profusely, caused some stirrings. He observed her closely and the more he watched...the more he liked what he saw. Her looks appealed to him – slim, petite in stature, but feminine in all the correct places. Her blonde, bouncy curls, pale blue eyes, chubby nose and slender neck drew his attention. But it wasn't just Darcy's outward looks which appealed. Henri was intrigued by her bubbly personality, her 'have a go' attitude and competitive spirit when playing Aunt Peg's parlour games. She possessed a vitality he admired, and he knew he wanted a further connection with this *'belle fille Anglaise'*.

Opportunities to converse were limited, but he'd noticed her stealing a glance in his direction several times. So, he decided to be a 'daredevil'. Henri waited until Darcy left the salon, then quietly slipped out of the room into the hallway, while the others were preoccupied. He reached up and unhooked a sprig of mistletoe then loitered beside an alcove, awaiting Darcy's return. He figured she was in her bedroom. Minutes later he heard the door to her room close and, hoping no one else would appear in the hallway, he stepped out into her path.

Signalling for her to remain silent, he took hold of her arm and guided her towards the wall. Darcy emitted a tiny squeal of delight. *"Ssh, ma belle fille,"* Henri spoke softly, then producing the sprig of mistletoe he held it above her head. She smiled…he raised his eyebrows questioningly… and she nodded. Gently he brought his lips to meet hers. It was a brief, tantalising kiss, but to Darcy it was exciting. *"Trop belle,"* he exclaimed, releasing her, delighted to note she was once again flushed.

"Henri, *quelle audace*," Darcy declared, and stepping away made her return to the salon. Henri watched her and grinned. Before opening the door, she turned back and smiled, coyly.

"Mmmmm," muttered Henri to himself. *"Bon, très bon."* Then he walked over to re-hang the festive bough.

Chapter 7

"So, why don't you celebrate Boxing Day?" Darcy asked her cousin Sylvie, after breakfast.

"Boxing Day?" enquired the young French girl who was obviously unfamiliar with the phrase.

"The day following Christmas Day…we call it Boxing Day. It's a holiday for most people in our country," she explained.

Sylvie shook her head. "Most people in France return to work the day after Noël. However, ma mère treats it as a special day, but often mon père is needed at his work, but not today, he has managed to organise some holiday."

Peg Thibault relished in combining French and English traditions, so the guests were instructed to dress for a festive hike.

The party of ten assembled after 'petit dejeuner', suitably kitted and booted to face the chilly December morning. "Bon," declared Peg. "I wish to show you my adopted home, the city of Lyon, post-war. It is the third largest city in France."

Rachel and Tom had visited Lyon before, but it was a new experience for their offspring.

They left the quiet residential area where Peg and Pierre had lived since their marriage, twenty years previously. On their route Peg stopped and pointed out various styles of architecture and gave a general background to the city being at the confluence of two rivers – the Rhone and the Saone. "We enjoy an alpine climate here in Lyon," Peg added. "Now, you will soon notice Lyon is a city of steep climbs. In our neighbourhood we were fortunate to escape structural damage during the war, but that was not the case elsewhere."

Rachel linked arms with Tom.

"My sister has missed her vocation – she would have made an excellent tour guide," Tom quipped quietly to his wife, as Peg continued.

"The city stands on the site of a Roman colony and while we are feeling fresh, we will visit Croix Rousse. It's set on a hillside with a steep gradient, winding streets and passageways."

The group followed their guide, carefully navigating the challenging terrain.

Inevitably the subject of the German Occupation was mentioned. Chantal walked alongside Sylvie and Darcy. "What was it like living in an occupied country?" Darcy asked her cousin.

"Not good," replied Sylvie, "very restrictive. No freedom to go where you wanted to go. We kept our heads down; obeyed the rules and adapted to the food shortages. Mostly, we stayed out of the way. But I was a child, I did what I was told. Ma mère and mon père – they sheltered us."

Darcy pondered her young cousin's response, then looked at Chantal. "How about you, Tallie? What was it like for you in Bordeaux?"

Darcy felt her aunt stiffen and detected a tremble in her voice.

"It was awful – I lived alone. My mother had recently died and like Sylvie I tried to stay out of the way. But in my work as a *sage femme*, I often needed to venture out at night – I held a special pass to explain my need to be travelling."

Darcy looked shocked. "That sounds scary!"

Chantal nodded.

After wandering through streets and courtyards, Peg stopped and beckoned the group to come closer. "Lyon has a proud heritage. We were known as the 'Capital of the Resistance' during the war. There are many accounts of the brave actions of members of the Resistance – brave but also sad. So many paid with their lives to free our country from the invading forces. The citizens of Lyon were resilient, and the city was eventually liberated in September 1944, just over two years ago." Peg spoke softly – the mood of the group became sombre.

Eventually, Peg brought them to a French tearoom. Everyone needed a hot beverage and enjoyed warming themselves and partaking of the delicious pastries on offer. As the group chatted, the restrictions caused by the Occupation weighed heavily on Darcy's mind.

"How did it feel for your city to be liberated, Aunt Peg?" she asked with curiosity.

Peg smiled as they ate their snack. "It was such a relief! People crowded onto the streets, waving flags, as tanks rumbled through the city."

"People were hanging over the balconies of their apartments, clapping and cheering and waving flags," added Pierre, chuckling.

"Everybody went wild, but it was sad when we saw, at first hand, the devastation of the collapsed bridges and blocked roads," commented Jonty, recalling the scenes he'd viewed.

"But we are free people again," declared Peg, "and our city is bouncing back. We are so grateful to be alive and free. We must press forward. Now, drink up everyone… our tour continues."

The group continued their city tour. Darcy walked with her aunt who seemed tense and lost in her thoughts.

* * *

Chantal was enjoying the reunion with her family. She was enamoured with the attractive young woman who was snuggling beside her on the chaise, after returning from the walk.

"You are so pretty, Darcy," she remarked. "Tell me about yourself. I feel we have lost so much time. You were only nine years old when I last saw you."

Never one to be shy, especially when talking about herself, Darcy began to speak. She told her aunt about her schooling and how she was excelling in her French language studies.

"I also enjoy art – still life in particular, portraits are my preference. My favourite hobby is cycling – remember when you taught me to ride a bike?" Chantal smiled. "Well, I joined the local Cycling Club, last year. We have about twenty-five members and most Saturdays we take off into the hills and dales in northwest Durham."

Chantal was interested to hear these details. "*Bon*, cycling is important to me also – it is vital in my role as a *sage femme* to visit my patients."

Darcy looked perplexed. "But I thought you worked in a hospital – you did when you lived in England," she commented.

Chantal smiled. "No, my work in France is different. My mother was a *sage femme* in the community until she retired. I was asked to help when I was looking after my mother. At that time, I fully expected to return to England. However, there was a shortage of staff and after my mother became ill, I was unable to return."

Darcy noted the sad countenance on her aunt's face.

"Tell me about your friends, Darcy."

The young girl chuckled. "Male or female?"

"Both," replied Chantal, grinning. "I'm good at keeping secrets," she added with a twinkle in her eye.

"Well, I've got a best friend – she's called Chrissie, and we have been friends forever…until–" Darcy broke off.

Chantal reached out and squeezed her niece's hand. "Until what?" she whispered.

"Err…I…sought of gained the admiration of the boy she had a crush on," Chantal gasped.

"Oh, gosh – that's tricky. Has it spoilt your friendship?" she asked.

Darcy shook her head. "It was awkward in the beginning, but once Grady made it obvious it was me he fancied and not Chrissie, she soon found someone else to swoon over. We are good friends again."

"So, this Grady – tell me about him." Chantal noticed how animated Darcy became at the mention of this boy's name.

"Grady's mother is American. He's a year above me at school and…he's rather special. He's tall and very good looking. He makes me feel all gooey inside when he talks to me. We've been friendly for months – he's also in the Cycling Club," she paused, looking dreamy. "He asked me to go to a posh dinner dance in November – oh, Tallie, it was great. A proper 'grown up' affair. I wore a long evening gown, and he picked me up in his brother's car. I felt like a princess."

Chantal smiled, enjoying the descriptions. "Have you seen him since?"

"Oh, yes, I see him at school – he's a prefect and I try to loiter where I shouldn't, so he can be all manly and tell me off. He turns my insides to jelly when he orders me to go elsewhere, but he winks at me, so I know it's all an act. Anyway, we went to the pictures in Newcastle, the week after the dinner dance – he took his brother's car. Then last week we went to the Youth Club Christmas party in the church hall. That wasn't a proper 'date', but we sat together and danced together all evening and he walked me home." Darcy was breathless by the time she had finished.

Chantal was so taken with this bright, bubbly girl. She bent over and whispered. "Has he kissed you yet?"

Darcy gasped and put her hand over her mouth to hide her response. "Mmmm, yes, he has, but don't let on to my parents...my dad is so old fashioned he would 'freak out' if he knew."

Chantal sniggered. "Oh, I think you underestimate your dad, Darcy – he was young himself...once upon a time."

Peg entered the room. "Attention everyone, we are going to continue our Monopoly Tournament," she announced.

Groans resonated from the young men who were playing cards beside the window. But Peg was not to be deterred, and Round Three of the games tournament was soon underway.

* * *

Wiping the dishes in the kitchen later, Chantal watched Tom with his sleeves rolled up and his hands in the sink. "Tom," she paused, looking to see if anyone else was around, "I was wondering if you might be able to help me."

He looked up. "I'll try, what's your problem?"

Chantal had rehearsed her little speech but felt awkward. She knew what she wanted to say, but phrasing it wasn't easy.

"It involves finding a missing person," she began, "he may not be 'missing' as such, but I want to trace him." She stopped and leaned back against the draining board. "Do you remember Sam Carter, the doctor I befriended before the war?"

Tom dried his hands on the cloth Chantal was holding. "Yes, I remember him – he was a doctor at the Infirmary in Newcastle – wasn't he?"

Chantal nodded. "Well, he joined up, as a medic, and the last I heard of him, he was going away, but he couldn't say where. His last communication was sent in June 1940. I don't even know which branch of the forces he served in."

Chantal was silent and Tom sensed her pain. She continued wiping the glasses.

"You were in love with him – weren't you?" he asked gently.

Chantal's bottom lip quivered, and she grabbed it with her teeth. Tears filled her eyes. It was the first time she'd spoken audibly about Sam for years and it hurt... just saying his name aloud felt painful.

Tom placed his hand on Chantal's shoulder. "There are channels of enquiry available, Chantal, but what about his workplace – have you checked to see if he has returned?"

Chantal looked up and stared into Tom's face. "I contacted the hospital eighteen months ago – it took ages for them to reply. But all they said was he had joined up and left their employment."

Tom was quiet for a few minutes.

"What about his family? He used to visit them – didn't he?"

Chantal dried the last of the glasses. "I have no address for him, Tom, only a city – Edinburgh...and I live and work in France. I feel helpless." She made a fist with her hand and struck her chest. "I have this strong sense of hope, Tom...it's in here. I'm sure he's still alive... but how can I find out?"

Tom looked thoughtful. "Many people who were displaced during the war, are only just being found you know – so you may well be right. Listen, Chantal...I'm not exactly sure how to tackle this, but I'll give it a good shot. I'll chat to Pierre...he may have some suggestions. Take heart, Chantal – where there's a will, there's a way. I've had a little experience in finding missing people before." He grinned, recalling the inquiries he had made concerning his wife's family. "Before we leave, Chantal, write down everything you can remember about Sam. Any little detail about his background, and if possible – a decent photograph of him."

Chantal nodded. "I've already done that, Tom. I'll give it to you," she added and smiled. "Thank you."

"Stay positive," Tom remarked, thinking how alike Chantal and Rachel looked, when they smiled.

* * *

So much food to eat called for plenty of exercise, so Peg suggested another walk the following day. Pierre was needed at work. Darcy and Sylvie walked with the boys. After walking a short distance, Darcy found herself chatting to the handsome Henri.

"What are you doing?" she enquired in her forthright manner, referring to his career.

Henri misunderstood and turned to look at her. "Trying to befriend a very attractive young English girl," he remarked with a distinct accent, which caused Darcy's heart to race.

"Monsieur...do you usually kiss a girl, before you befriend her?"

Henri grabbed her arm and pulled her to one side. "I hope my behaviour did not offend you, mademoiselle?" he queried with a fixed gaze. "I confess I was determined to kiss you from the moment we collided in the station. Meeting you again seemed like it was meant to be."

Darcy looked up and realised they were falling behind the rest of the group.

"We must catch up, Henri, and in answer to your question, I was not offended. But you have not answered my question about what you are doing in your studies?"

Darcy and Henri walked on together to rejoin the group.

"Ahh, that is a good question…I am at, what do the English say…at a road join?"

Darcy sniggered. "You mean at a crossroads? You are unsure which way to take?"

"Exactly," he replied. "I have no idea what I am going to do with my life."

Darcy felt embarrassed, having momentarily forgotten he was recently orphaned.

"Oh, Henri, forgive me please – my question was insensitive."

The young Frenchman looked serious. "Pierre is my guardian – he was my mother's only brother. Since mon père became ill, I have worked in his clock repair shop – but now he has died, the shop is for sale. My home is an apartment above the shop, so when the business sells, I will have no home."

Darcy was moved by his openness. "But who has been looking after you, since your father's death?" she probed.

"I look after myself, Darcy. I am quite capable. I was looking after my father for months before he died. I am… how do you say…the domestic – is that correct?"

Darcy was overcome. She reached out and touched Henri's arm. "We say domesticated, Henri. But I admire your tenacity – it can't have been easy for you." Darcy removed her gloved hand from Henri's arm.

"It is life, my English girl. I was more fortunate than others. At least I was protected during the war years. The occupying forces needed clock and watch repairs. My father disliked helping them, but he was only doing his job. It was a natural choice for me to join his business when my school studies finished. But now, I am ready for something different. When the business sells, I will move here to Lyon, to live with my uncle and his family."

They rejoined the group who were waiting in the square.

The Joyeux Noël celebrations were nearing an end. Chantal was due to return to Bordeaux, the Smallwoods to northeast England, and Henri to the outskirts of Paris. Rachel, having enjoyed catching up with her sister, wanted to ensure there was a date planned.

"When are you going to visit us in England, Chantal?"

"Soon, Rachel – I am looking forward to visiting England again."

Rachel took hold of her sister's hand. "Tom has told me you have asked him to help you trace Sam. I'm sure he will leave no stone unturned. I know how much Sam means to you... but...I mean this kindly, Chantal... you must be realistic. Many servicemen, even medical personnel, did not survive the war."

Chantal stared at her sister. "I am sure he is still alive, Rachel. I will not give up hope."

The sisters hugged. Rachel felt saddened – her sister could be setting herself up for disappointment.

* * *

As Chantal was packing her suitcase in Madame Levigne's apartment, she was humming to herself. This Christmas celebration had been a tonic – an opportunity to meet and mix with her family and extended family. A gentle tap sounded on the door.

"*Entre*," she instructed.

Darcy popped her head around the door.

"Aunt Peg asked me to deliver some soup and bread for Madame Levigne," she said. "I heard you humming." Chantal stopped her folding task and enveloped her young niece in a tight embrace.

"Oh, Darcy, it's been such a pleasure to see you again, all grown up – a young woman now! I think you are going to break many hearts over the next few years. So many young men will fall for your charms," she remarked. "But a word of advice, Darcy...guard your heart, there will be lots of admirers, but somewhere out there will be a special person – he will make your heart thump, your eyes sparkle and your voice sing."

Darcy looked at her aunt and asked the question she'd been wanting to ask for days. "Tante Tallie...is there someone special in your life?"

Chantal took her niece's hand and led her to the other side of the bed to sit down. "Yes, Darcy…there was…there is…but I don't know his whereabouts."

Darcy's jaw dropped. "Is it because of the war?"

Chantal nodded. "He was a doctor at the same hospital, where I worked as a nurse, in Newcastle. We became friendly. I was sure we had a future together. But then I was needed in France to care for your grandmother and when she died, the world was a different place. The war had started, and I could not return to England. At first, we corresponded frequently, then he told me he was going away – I assumed he meant on military service. That was over six years ago, and I have not heard from him since."

Darcy reached out and hugged her tightly. "Oh, Tallie, that is so sad. There must be some way he can be traced?"

Chantal gazed into the innocent face of her niece – young and invincible. "I'm hoping your father can help me. I have given him all the information I know. I've never given up hope that one day we will be reunited."

The young girl looked so concerned. "Tallie, if I can help in any way, I will," she added, squeezing her aunt's hand.

* * *

A long journey lay ahead, one which Darcy was not relishing. Trains to Paris, then to the channel port; a sea crossing; another train to London, then after an overnight stay at a hotel – another train north, to Durham. She looked dreamily out of the window as the train rattled towards Paris.

"Your mother and I have some news," announced her dad, pulling her from her reverie.

Darcy was wide-eyed, staring across at her parents.

"Not that sort of news…please not – it would be so embarrassing!" she spluttered, glancing at her brother, sitting beside her.

Tom appeared puzzled, as Rachel started to laugh.

"No worries there," Rachel remarked, as Tom caught on to Darcy's line of thinking. He grinned at his wife.

"We *are* going to have an addition to the family," he remarked. "But not in the way you are thinking, young lady!" Darcy looked aghast and Josh chuckled, having already heard about the plan.

"Henri Dukas is coming to stay with us for a few months, over the summer," Rachel announced, excitedly. "He is going to help your father set up his horticultural business."

Darcy shook her head in bewilderment. "He's going to do *what*?" she exclaimed.

Chapter 8

The train chugged northwards – had they done the right thing? Tom wondered as he surveyed the bland winter landscape. Was he caught up in the young man's plight, jumping in with the offer, before consulting their own children? He looked across the carriage at his beloved offspring. They were so blessed to have two healthy, well adjusted, and outgoing children, who thankfully were sheltered from the brutal effects of war. So, why not share their blessings with others? Finding themselves in Henri's situation – surely Darcy and Josh would have welcomed the opportunity to spend six months in the care of a loving family – even if it did mean moving abroad?

"Will he be living with us…as in our house?" asked Josh, after a few minutes.

Darcy stared at her brother in disbelief. "Of course, stupid. You didn't think he'd be sleeping over in the stable block – did you?"

Josh looked bemused – the workers in their market garden, lived there. "Only asking," he replied, pulling a face at his sister.

Rachel jumped into the conversation. "Your father and I are not planning to re-open the hotel business for at least another year. So, there will be plenty of accommodation in our house. I'm not sure how much you know about Henri's circumstances. His mother was Pierre's sister – she died a few years ago. She was an invalid and used a wheelchair. Henri's father, Leon, was much older than his wife. They lived on the outskirts of Paris, where Leon worked as a clockmaker and repairer. Henri was their only child and hoped to continue his studies at university, but when his father took ill, he was needed to assist in the business. Sadly, Leon passed away a few months ago." Rachel paused and glanced at Tom, who reached out and squeezed his wife's hand, then continued the explanation.

"Your Uncle Pierre approached me not long after we arrived in Lyon. He is Henri's guardian now. The young man has been forced to grow up quickly. Pierre thought it would be wise to give Henri the opportunity to see life outside of Paris and away from the clock repair shop. So, to that end and with Henri's agreement, the business and adjoining apartment were offered for sale. Surprisingly, it was purchased quickly, and the new owners take over at the end of January. This means Henri is moving to Lyon to live with the Thibaults quite soon."

Darcy was thoughtful, absorbing the details of Henri's background. This young man had captured her attention since their impacting introduction in Lyon station.

"What is he going to do?" asked Josh.

"Well, this is what Pierre wanted to discuss with me. He hopes Henri will attend university in the future, to further his studies, but in the short-term Aunt Peg suggested he could visit England. She was sure I could offer him some work on the farm, but after talking to him, it transpires he might be interested in my new business venture. He has an eye for detail."

Darcy turned abruptly. "What's your new business 'thingy' about?"

Rachel sighed – as usual Darcy had only listened to half the story.

"Your father wants to set up a horticultural venture to run alongside the market garden."

"I don't get it – how do the two things differ – they're both about plants?"

"Horticulture is plant propagation – a process of multiplying a species and can be done in more than one way. It's a subject dear to my heart and fascinates me," Tom explained.

"When he was a young man, your father gained a degree in Botany and was all set to pursue a career in that area, until he inherited a share in the Meckleridge Estate," Rachel informed her daughter.

Darcy stared at her dad – this was news to her – she'd always thought he'd been a hotel and farm owner.

Tom wiped the condensation from the train window. "I don't suppose we'd have given up the hotel business, if it hadn't been for the war. But now we are in this position, we think it might be a good idea to change direction. The income from the farm and market garden gives us a decent living and your mother is set to advertise for more students to tutor… so, that paves the way for me to explore my passion with plants. Henri Dukas is a bright young man and is keen to help me. It's only in the discussion stage at present, but as soon as arrangements can be made, Henri will come to England for six months."

Darcy was unsure what to make of this new turn of events. "I guess it means I'll have an extra brother hanging around over the summer," she remarked, distantly.

"I don't envisage him hanging around, Darcy," commented Tom. "I see it as an extension to his education and Pierre agrees with me. He won't receive payment for this work – only his board and lodgings with us. What I ask from you two is that you welcome him…be friendly, don't alienate him, include him in your activities. He speaks English quite well… but help him to improve."

The family lapsed into their own thoughts and sometime later Darcy reached into her bag and retrieved her sketch pad and a pencil. In a short time, she'd drawn a remarkable likeness of Henri Dukas, totally from memory.

"You must have looked at him frequently, to remember all those details," remarked Josh, grinning as he peeped over her shoulder.

"I have a photographic memory," she announced pertly.

Josh bent forward and whispered, with a smirk on his face, "Or a sneaky fancy for the Frenchman."

Darcy elbowed him, began to blush, and hastily snapped shut her sketch pad before her parents could see it.

* * *

Chantal checked the letter she had just penned to Tom. It was in addition to the facts she had given him when she was in Lyon. She'd forgotten to give Sam's birthdate – 12th May 1904 – and to include a decent photograph. The twelve-year gap in their ages didn't bother her.

She perused the photograph – although Tom had met him, she gave a description anyway. He was just over six feet in height with a broad build and was usually clean shaven – but she doubted that fact would have any relevance. His hair was brown and wavy... but he could be grey by now, she thought. He spoke with a distinct Scottish accent, and she knew his family lived in Edinburgh but was unsure if that was his place of birth. In answer to Tom's embarrassing question – she was unaware of any distinguishing birthmarks or other features.

Chantal was mindful of the fact Sam was one of millions of displaced people since the end of the war. How could Tom achieve anything different? However, she was not despondent. Somehow, having asked for Tom's assistance, she felt encouraged – she was doing something positive and just the act of posting this letter was a first step on the journey to trace Sam Carter.

As she took the letter to the bureau de poste, the following morning, she was reminded of the quotation by the 18th century poet ... *'Hope springs eternal'*. That's me, she thought, smiling to herself.

* * *

On receipt of his sister-in-law's letter, Tom telephoned The Royal Victoria Infirmary in Newcastle and spoke to the staff administrator, who promised to make inquiries concerning Sam Carter.

"Gosh, Sam is only two years younger than me," commented Rachel as she re-read her sister's correspondence. "Somehow, I imagined he was just a couple of years older than Chantal. They looked a similar age," Rachel mused, reflecting on the times Sam had visited their home. "Tom, I've had an idea, why don't you contact Lesley Griffiths? I suspect an appointment with a staff administrator at the hospital will only confirm the information Chantal received last year."

Tom was thoughtful. Lesley Griffiths was the almoner at the local Malhaven hospital. She had overseen Meckleridge House when it was requisitioned as a convalescent home during the war.

Tom stood, walked over to his wife and placed a finger under her chin. "You're not just a pretty face are you, Rachel Smallwood," he quipped. "I'd never have thought of Lesley Griffiths; she may be just the person who can help." He bent forward and kissed his wife lovingly. The following day he telephoned the hospital almoner.

"Tom, how lovely to hear from you. How are things at Meckleridge? I do miss visiting the house...how are the family?"

Tom chatted for a few minutes, then explained the purpose of his call.

"I sympathise with your sister-in-law, Tom," Lesley commented. "The administration department receives many requests of this nature and naturally they are careful to whom they pass on information. Unfortunately, she is not a relative, so I doubt you will get anywhere with your enquiries. However, if you can send me some information about this missing person, the next time I am at The Infirmary, I'll look at some old records. I'm not promising anything, but there may be a former address or name of a next of kin – some tiny detail on a record card which may prove helpful."

"Lesley, you are a gem. Thank you," Tom replied.

Over the following week, Tom made many telephone calls. He was passed from one military department to another and was told he would be sent various forms to complete and return.

When the forms arrived, Rachel stared at them. "Where do we start, Tom?" she declared. "We don't even know which branch of the military he served in – Army, Navy or Air Force – he was a doctor, he could have been with any of them!"

Tom shook his head, scanning the forms. "They ask if the missing person was killed, wounded, captured, executed or did they desert…how do we know? He joined up and then…. vanished! We need to be prepared – it's likely they'll tell us he was missing in action – it's so unsatisfactory."

Once again, Tom was so thankful his occupation as a farm owner was a reserved occupation.

Rachel flicked through the forms. "It asks for his last known address – perhaps Chantal can supply that information."

* * *

WINTER 1947

Snow began falling during the third week of January that year. It wasn't unusual for heavy snowfall in northeast England, but most of the country was affected this time. The temperatures plummeted and within a couple of weeks large snowdrifts were evident as winds whipped up the relentless snowfall.

"I'm not going to attempt to walk to school in that," declared Darcy, after a few days.

"No, I agree. It's not safe. It's a while since we experienced such an accumulation of snow," remarked Tom. "Judging by the radio news it's widespread across the country. Good job we've got plenty of supplies in stock."

The following weeks saw conditions some folk described as 'worse than the war'. Electricity cuts were put in place and radio transmissions were limited. Living in the dim glow of candlelight became the norm. Gas pressure was low, and water pipes were frozen. Huge icicles hung from the guttering of the house and large snowdrifts resembled mountain peaks.

Tom and his Polish employees helped on the farm, as there was limited work in the greenhouses. Rachel, assisted by Darcy, cooked and baked for all the workers – a community spirit based on survival existed.

"It will pass," Tom encouraged his staff. But it was seven long weeks before the snow eventually stopped falling. When the thaw set in, the snow began to melt as the sub-zero temperatures rose and the land became sodden with water. "Thankfully we aren't prone to flooding," Tom observed, thinking of the low-lying areas which were suffering.

Throughout the extended winter of 1947, communication from France was non-existent. Darcy kept herself busy reading up on her school subjects and helping her mother. Slowly, daily activities returned to normal, the schools opened, and post began to arrive in batches.

Several letters arrived all together from Chantal. Each one asking if Tom was making any progress with his enquiries.

"I hope by now she will have received our letter explaining how everything ground to a halt during the Big Freeze," remarked Rachel.

Tom was reading letters from Peg. "Henri is living in Lyon now," he commented. "According to Pierre he is being very industrious, spending hours at the library reading up on horticulture." Tom opened a letter from Henri. "Oh, Henri is asking if I can provide guidance on specific subjects he can read about. Trouble is, Rachel – I'm rusty, it's years since I studied," Tom moaned.

Rachel looked up. "There are boxes of stuff belonging to you from your student days, up in the attic."

"Good thinking, Rachel. I must go up there and have a rummage. Pierre says Henri's father's will is all sorted now, so financially he has resources behind him. He has organised his passport and is eager to make the journey. They want us to suggest a suitable date for his arrival!"

* * *

The impending arrival of the young Frenchman began to excite Darcy as soon as she heard the news. Since arriving home from France she'd seen Grady a few times. At first, the snow was an adventure. They went sledging, engaged in snowball fights and built snowmen. But then when it became serious, they applied their youthful energies to delivering much needed supplies to help older, less able residents in the town. They worked well together in a team, organised by the Cycling Club leaders – swapping bicycles for wooden sledges. During these outings, Darcy enjoyed her flirtations with Grady Forrester.

One afternoon Grady trudged his way through deep snow to deliver some food supplies to Meckleridge House. Tom and Rachel were over at the farm and Josh was in his bedroom. Darcy and Grady were in high spirits, laughing and joking. They were enjoying an easy banter, sipping a hot drink at the kitchen table. Darcy decided to ask a question which had been puzzling her for weeks.

"Grady, do you remember that night of The Works Annual Dinner Dance?"

Grady became serious. "Yes, of course I do…why?"

Once started, Darcy was fearless. "Well, I saw something that night which I don't think I should have seen…" She stopped.

Her companion was staring at her in a strange way. His eyes were hard and piercing…penetrating. "Which was what?" he enquired, intensifying his gaze.

Darcy swallowed, beginning to wish she'd kept quiet.

"I saw you…and your friend Phil…messing about with some overcoats," she blurted out. "I was searching for the ladies' room, and I heard voices and…" Suddenly, the atmosphere became tense, and Darcy felt nervous – why did she ask this question?

"What do you mean by 'messing about'?" Grady asked, his voice flat and contentious.

Putting aside her fears, Darcy spoke with bravado. "I saw you remove something from a pocket… hand it to Phil…then he placed it in another coat pocket. I'm curious to know what you were doing."

Darcy stiffened, as she watched Grady place his mug on the table, scrape back his chair, stand and walk around behind her. He stood over her for a few seconds, then put his hands on her shoulders. Was he angry? Was he being playful? She shook involuntarily, fear rising.

He bent forward and whispered in her ear. His breath felt warm against her skin, which was prickling. Grady's tone of voice was menacing. "I think, Darcy Smallwood... you should learn to keep your mouth shut...and to mind your own business." Darcy felt his fingers penetrating the flesh on her shoulders through her thick jumper. "Do you understand me?" he added, continuing to grip her shoulders.

It was only momentary...but sufficient to alarm Darcy. At that point, a voice called from the hallway. Grady released his hold and quickly stepped back to retrieve his drink, as Josh entered the kitchen. The episode passed. Josh chatted to Grady as he donned his outdoor wear, then he left to walk back home. The incident was not referred to again.

That encounter with Grady mystified Darcy. What was he hiding? What was he doing? And more importantly... why did she feel he was threatening her? Darcy decided to write to Chantal. She found writing gave her a channel through which to express herself more clearly. She told Chantal about the Big Freeze; about school being closed and studying at home; about helping with the Cycling Club sledge missions. Then she confided the incident with Grady in the kitchen.

'Do you think I should end my friendship with Grady? I would appreciate your advice, Tallie. I can't talk about this to Mother, Dad, Josh or Chrissie. Please reply soon.'

The next day she posted the letter.

* * *

"Nature has an amazing way of recovering," Tom remarked, one morning in early April. The Big Freeze and the difficulties which had ensued seemed like a distant memory. "I wonder how The Bungalow fared during the storms?" he commented to Rachel.

"Perhaps we should visit and see if there's been any damage?"

A rattle at the front door distracted Tom. It was the postie.

"Morning, Tom – here's your letters," announced the postman in his usual jovial manner. "It's good to be getting back to normal. I think we've cleared the backlog of post."

Tom and the postie continued to chat as Jess, the dog, received her regular welcome.

Tom ambled through to the rear lounge, flicking through the pile of post – bills, private letters and two official brown envelopes. Tom took the latter and sat down. The first envelope was a reply from the Royal Victoria Infirmary – it was courteous, but brief.

'We can confirm Doctor Samuel Carter was employed on the staff of this hospital until he joined the military service as a medic in early 1940. We have no knowledge of his present whereabouts.'

Rachel walked into the room and Tom passed the letter to her. "As we expected, why would they know? It was his place of work, and he left…end of story. It's a dead end, Tom. Our only hope is the military services, unless Lesley Griffiths remembers and gets back to us with some information."

When Darcy returned from school, she opened a letter addressed to her from Chantal. After commenting on her daily routines and the activities Darcy relayed about the Big Freeze, she mentioned Darcy's advice request.

'Be careful, Darcy. I think this young man, Grady, may not be what he seems. My advice is to avoid ending your friendship abruptly, as it could cause a potential problem for you. Better to keep him as a friend than turn him into an enemy. Remain friends but be on your guard. Be cautious and watch out for any signs of strange behaviour.'

Darcy pondered her aunt's advice. She liked Grady Forrester and apart from the isolated incident in the kitchen she was happy to remain friendly. It was as if the episode had not taken place. The next time they met he was attentive, funny and witty. She enjoyed being with him, he was so handsome. She relished seeing other girls looking at her enviously when they were together. But her dad always impressed upon her and Josh how important it was to be truthful and somehow, she felt Grady was being evasive, hiding the truth. Maybe she should have held her counsel? She mentally chastised herself for seeking an explanation, but the episode had left her with an uneasy feeling.

As she went downstairs the telephone rang. "Hello, can I speak to Tom Smallwood please, it's Lesley Griffiths speaking." Darcy remembered the friendly hospital almoner.

"Hello, Miss Griffiths, it's Darcy speaking, I'll go and fetch my dad."

Tom appeared and took the receiver. After exchanging pleasantries, he picked up a pencil and began to jot down some notes. Ending the call he walked into the rear lounge.

"That was Lesley Griffiths," he said to Rachel. "She apologised for the delay in responding, but she was stranded at her parents' home near Durham for most of the inclement weather. Anyway, things are back to normal, and she has some information for us concerning Dr Carter."

Darcy looked up, sitting on the rug stroking the dog. "Who is Dr Carter?" she asked.

Rachel frowned; this information was not for Darcy's ears…but it was too late, she had heard.

"Dr Carter was a friend of Chantal's who went missing in the war," Rachel explained. Vague memories of the man her aunt had brought to their home tugged at the back of her mind, and she also remembered her brief conversation with Tallie in Lyon.

"Oh, I remember... Tante Tallie was in love with him, wasn't she?"

Rachel stared at her teenage daughter. Not much escaped this young girl. She possessed a knack for remembering faces and obviously she could remember the handsome Dr Carter.

Chapter 9

There was no point in withholding Lesley Griffiths' findings from Darcy. If Darcy wanted to know something she would delve and delve until it became apparent.

"What did she say?" asked Rachel.

Tom consulted his scribbled notes. "Not much – but it may prove helpful. He left his employment in Newcastle in February 1940. He joined the naval branch of the services as a medic."

Rachel's eyes lit up. "Good old Lesley – at least we've got something to work on – a branch of the services and the date he joined up...anything else?"

Tom looked back at his notes.

"Yes, his full name is Conrad Samuel Matthison Carter, born 12th May 1904."

Darcy chuckled. "And I thought Darcy Rose Smallwood was bad enough. Good grief, poor man...what a handle!"

Rachel glowered at her teenage daughter. "Your names are significant, Darcy," she retorted, then looked at her husband, expecting more information.

"That's all she could glean, but with a name like that it should be easier to trace him. Sam Carter was a name likely to be repeated on lists."

Rachel looked thoughtful. "It's possible he might have used his first name, Conrad… and maybe Matthison was his mother's maiden name. These are all helpful pieces of information; if you draw a blank with the services, then you could extend your enquiries to Edinburgh, Tom – what a good job we thought about Lesley Griffiths."

Darcy was listening intently. "Why Edinburgh – I thought he lived and worked in Newcastle?" she asked.

"His family belonged in Edinburgh – he used to visit them," Rachel explained.

Darcy was sitting contemplating. "So, are you two supposed to be finding this Sam Carter?" she asked.

Tom looked up. "That's the general idea. We are helping Chantal, Darcy. Thousands of people went missing during the war, for many different reasons. Chantal has not heard from Sam for over six years. However, they were not engaged, so there was no reason why she would be informed, if anything had happened to him. She didn't visit his family and it's unlikely they knew of her existence."

"What are you going to do with this information?" Darcy asked, intrigued.

Rachel looked thoughtful.

"With this information we can complete the forms for the naval branch of the services – it's narrowed down the width of the search; until today he could have served with any area of the armed forces."

Tom listened and sighed – he felt dejected, nevertheless. Even with these extra details... this was going to be a long, drawn-out procedure.

* * *

"Come and dry the dishes, Darcy," called Rachel, after supper.

Her daughter sauntered into the kitchen as if next week would do. In her usual style Darcy jumped straight into a conversation.

"This boyfriend of Tallie's... were they...you know... lovers?" she queried.

Rachel gasped at her daughter's bluntness. "Darcy – that's a personal detail, to which only Chantal could supply the answer. And it's none of our business. Suffice it to say, they were 'serious' about each other. We liked him and he visited here regularly during the summer and autumn before Chantal returned to France. I know your aunt was in love with him, but I don't think the subject of marriage had been mentioned." Rachel paused, reflecting. "Probably the imminence of war and all the unpredictability it brought, prevented them from formalising their relationship. Chantal was needed in France to attend to our mother...maybe if that hadn't happened, they might have married before the war started." Rachel dried her hands and sat down at the kitchen table.

"When did Chantal return to France?" Darcy asked.

"In January 1939, eight months before the war started. She expected to return to Newcastle, but eventually resigned from her job, when our mother's illness worsened. Chantal is convinced Sam is still alive, Darcy. I tried when we saw her over Christmas to help her consider the possibility, he may not have survived the war – but perhaps this new information will help to trace him." Rachel was lost in her thoughts, reflecting on the sadness she had experienced in not being able to travel to France to support her sister at Yvette's funeral.

Darcy sat down opposite her mother. "Can I help? I think it's a fascinating idea to search for a missing person," she stated.

Rachel looked at her daughter – she was a caring girl.

"I'm not sure there is anything you can do to help, Darcy, other than support your aunt. Keep writing to her – I'm sure she enjoys hearing your news. This enquiry to the naval services could take weeks, even months, before we receive a reply." Rachel paused. "It's going to take courage for Chantal to face a negative outcome, Darcy, and we need to help her if, or when, it happens…but let's remain positive. Now, changing the subject, your father has replied to Pierre suggesting Henri arrives to commence his stay at the beginning of May."

CHAPTER 9

Darcy turned her thoughts from her aunt to the handsome Frenchman – she was eagerly anticipating his visit.

* * *

FRANCE

Chantal couldn't settle. Rachel's letter had arrived that morning just before she left on her midwifery rounds. It informed her of the almoner's information...Conrad Samuel Matthison Carter...she ran the name along to the rhythm of her cycling – somehow it fitted.

She'd been totally unaware of Sam's other names. Was there a reason he'd omitted sharing his other names? They suited him – surely this would make it easier to trace him. It was certainly a unique name. There was something pricking at the back of her mind though, and it was annoying her.

She set about her daily duties methodically, caring for the mothers at their various stages of pregnancy. Often mothers talked about name choices. Had she ever delivered a 'Conrad'? She didn't think so, but she had assisted in the births of several Samuels in her years as a *sage femme*. She smiled. It was a tiny piece of information, but it brought such hope. Chantal was 'charged'. It was only a detail, but what a difference it could make. There was a fine line...a thin line between holding on... or giving up and the difference was called – *hope*.

That evening Chantal's hope in her belief that the love of her life, Sam Carter, was still alive, was strengthened. She was relaxing in her own lounge in Margot's home. She'd established a routine of retiring to her own rooms after their shared meal. She reread her sister's letter. The Navy – now that was a surprise. Sam had joined The Navy in his role as a medic. She lay back and tried to imagine him in a naval uniform – her heart pounded with her visualisation – he would look so handsome. He would have been part of a medical team serving on a ship – was that safer than being deployed to a field hospital near a battlefield? It was all conjecture. Vague memories of films she'd seen at the cinema set in war zones came to mind. Hospitals in fields; hospitals on ships as well as regular hospitals. Sometimes hotels and grand houses were turned into military hospitals.

Now she knew he'd joined The Navy, she could picture him down on the lower decks caring for the wounded servicemen, carrying out procedures to the sway and creaks of an ocean-going vessel. They were only snippets of information, but these thoughts brought her comfort, just being able to visualise him at work.

The telephone rang, jolting her from her reverie. She jumped up and met Margot in the hallway. "For you, Chantal," the older lady remarked, handing the receiver to the young midwife.

Chantal's mind was racing through her patients who were close to their due date, but was surprised to hear Peg Thibault's voice answer.

"Peg, how delightful to hear from you," she exclaimed. It was rare for Peg to telephone, but she had given her the number of her new residence in case of emergencies.

"Don't panic, Chantal. Everyone is fine. I have a proposition to put to you."

"Yes?" responded Chantal expectantly.

"Our nephew Henri who you met at Noël, is going to stay at Malhaven for the summer and he is hoping to travel at the end of this month. Pierre and I have been chatting. It's a long journey for him and although he is more than capable, we wondered if you had any plans to visit England now travel is easier."

"Well, yes, Peg – I was hoping to visit in August, like we used to do, but how would that help Henri?"

"Chantal, if you were able to take leave from your work, we would pay your travel cost, if you could travel with Henri at the end of the month."

Chantal gasped. The thought excited her. "Oh, Peg…I would love to do that and it's kind of you to offer to pay my fare. I have accumulated holiday time. Can I let you know tomorrow?"

A visit to England…just what she needed. Walking back into her lounge her eyes landed on the ornament 'the boy with the fish'. She walked over to the sideboard, picked it up and turned it over. There inscribed into the ceramic base was the name given to his work by the potter…it read *Conrad*. Her heart quickened…that was it…the elusive thought she'd been trying to pinpoint all day since receiving Rachel's letter giving Sam's full name. It explained why he had given her the ornament – because it bore his name! Oh, Sam, why were you so secretive?

* * *

ENGLAND

News of the two French arrivals sent Rachel into overdrive. She fretted and fussed, moving furniture and hanging new drapes.

"Rachel, slow down," Tom exclaimed, after assisting in the transportation of a bookcase up to Henri's designated bedroom.

"I want him to feel comfortable, Tom, it's going to be his home for six months – he's not a hotel guest. He will need places to store things. You could help by retrieving those boxes from the attic – the ones from your student days. I suggested it weeks ago, but they haven't made an appearance."

Suitably chastised, Tom kissed his wife. "Your wish is my command, my darling," he quipped and set off for the attics.

Meckleridge House boasted ten bedrooms and several large attic rooms. During the hotel days, the family frequently utilised this space as extra accommodation, when the hotel was at capacity. Over the years the attics were upgraded, but during the war they were just used for storage.

Darcy spied her dad taking the back stairs to the attic floor. "Do you need any help?" she called.

"Yes, please," Tom replied.

"I'll help you...if you'll help me," declared Darcy, grinning.

"Oh, in what way?"

"Well, I've got this cycling event on Whit Monday and with that harsh winter I've hardly used my bike, so it needs a good overhaul. You know how useless I am at that sort of thing and Mother goes on and on about safety." Darcy was carrying boxes down the narrow wooden steps, leading from the attic floor.

"You are not 'useless' at cycle maintenance, Darcy. I taught you the basics years ago. The truth is you don't like spending the time checking the mechanical stuff and getting your hands dirty – do you?"

Darcy placed the boxes against a wall at the base of the steps and grinned. Her dad was dusting debris off his jacket, as she reached up and gave him a hug.

"Dad, you're a gem. I've got far more important things to sort like choosing my outfit. You won't forget, will you? The event is the day after tomorrow, so you've only got today to sort it."

Tom squeezed his boisterous daughter. "Aye, aye, captain," he joked, releasing her. "Between you and your mother, I never have a spare minute," he chuckled, watching the receding figure of his attractive daughter sauntering back to her bedroom. She'll break a few hearts he thought, admiring her from afar.

* * *

The green in front of the Town Hall was the starting point for the cycling event. It was an architecturally pleasing, stone building, dating back to the late 1800s. These days it was used as a Bank on the lower floor and apartments on the upper floors. Grady was waiting as Darcy arrived.

"Hello, beautiful," he crooned, casting his eyes appreciatively down her slender figure, as she brought her cycle to a halt beside him. She loved being the recipient of his admiring glances. She'd spent ages perfecting her outfit and styling her hair.

"Waste of time," her mother chided, passing her room earlier. "All this time spent doing your hair – it's going to be windswept in no time."

But Darcy ignored her mother's comments and continued to add the finishing touches to her cycling outfit – shorts, blouse and canvas shoes.

"How's the bike?" asked Grady, as she straddled her cycle.

"Okay, thanks to dad. He checked it over, oiled it and put air in the tyres – all good to go!" Darcy felt good under Grady's scrutiny. There was no doubt in her mind she had captured the attention of the most handsome young man in their school. She enjoyed holding the position of 'Grady Forrester's girlfriend'.

"And how is the rider of this excellent machine?" he asked, raising his eyebrows.

"Never felt better," she responded, flicking back her blonde ponytail and touching some stray locks on her forehead. Grady bent over and smoothed another stray lock behind her ear. His touch sent shivers down her spine, causing a pleasing sensation in her stomach.

"Later, beautiful – we'll catch up later," he added, winking at her.

Cycling was becoming acceptable as a sport for female riders. The leaders of the Malhaven Cycling Club were a married couple, who embraced equality for women as far as cycling was concerned. The cycling event involved mixed pairs. They were to be marked according to time in between various points. Grady and Darcy made up a pair and were confident as the event commenced, anticipating a good time score. The prize was the accolade of achievement and a small metal cup. The course was divided into four sections all starting and ending at the Town Hall. In between the sections each pair could rest and take refreshment.

When the event was first mooted, the previous autumn, Grady and Darcy's acquaintance was new, but in the intervening months their friendship had developed. Lack of practice during the long wintry months raised concerns, but everyone faced the same situation. Darcy hoped the unpleasantness from their confrontational discourse in the kitchen a few weeks ago, would be forgotten. At the halfway point, around midday, Rachel and Josh arrived to cheer them on.

"Where's Dad?" enquired Darcy.

"He's gone to the station to collect our French visitors," her mother replied. With all the excitement of the cycling event, the arrival of Chantal and Henri had slipped her mind. "If the train is on time, he'll bring them here before going home," Rachel added.

Coming in at the end of the third leg of the race, Darcy and Grady were greeted with the news they were one of three couples in the lead. Darcy was jumping up and down at the news.

"Save your energies, beautiful," Grady urged. "The last lap can prove tricky; remember there are a couple of hills involved."

Darcy knew how challenging the terrain could be. Couples leading at this stage could easily lose valuable minutes on the final leg. But Darcy and Grady made a good team. They felt like equals and it heartened Darcy to think she could be equal to a man in this sport. She was fortunate to be partnered with Grady. He could easily have taken his choice from other athletic women in the Cycling Club, who oozed confidence, capability and stamina. But he had chosen her, Darcy Smallwood... petite, slight, and with a featherlight build.

Arriving back at base, they dismounted. It would be thirty minutes before the winners would be declared, after all the participating pairs' times were totalled. Rachel was plying Darcy and Grady with food. Grady's parents were not in attendance, but his brother and his fiancée were there to support him. The minutes were ticking by. Darcy was disappointed her dad, and the French visitors, had not arrived in time to hear the results. But just as the judges were walking to the steps of the Town Hall to announce the winners, Darcy spotted three figures hurrying across the grass.

Chantal opened her arms and embraced her niece. "Hello, hello, Darcy – still cycling I see!"

Darcy whooped with joy and hugged her aunt. Behind her dad stood a tall young man with dark hair and a neat beard, grinning broadly. He stepped forward and opened his arms. Darcy did not hesitate, she jumped into his outstretched arms. He lifted her off the ground and swung her around – her ponytail flying.

"*Ma petite fille Anglaise*," Henri declared.

Grady, standing by, observed the scene, calling out in agitation. "Darcy, over here now…the results are about to be announced." He grabbed her hand and pushed forward to stand at the base of the steps.

A man with a megaphone spoke. "The winners of the Malhaven Cycling Club Time Challenge, by a small margin of seventy seconds are…" the megaphone squealed; the audience gasped; the judge fiddled with the switches and coughed.

"The winners are – Mr Grady Forrester and Miss Darcy Smallwood."

Grady bent forward, clasped his partner tightly and kissed her firmly on the lips. Cheering resounded from the assembled crowd. Grady continued to hug Darcy tightly and whispered in her ear, "Well done, partner."

Darcy pulled back and repeated the phrase to Grady. They received plaudits from their families and Cycle Club members. As the euphoria of the moment ebbed, Grady slid his arm around Darcy's shoulders. Then he nodded towards the Smallwood family group.

"And who, may I ask, is *he*?" Grady queried.

"Oh, that's Henri...he's a sort of cousin," replied Darcy, feeling flustered. She wriggled free from Grady's arm, but he reached out and pulled her back, as she attempted to move towards her family.

"Well, make sure he knows who you belong to, Darcy Smallwood," he added.

Darcy turned and retaliated, "I don't belong to anybody, Grady Forrester," then she walked over to join her family.

Chapter 10

MAY 1947

The warmth of the delightful Whitsuntide Monday was still in evidence, as the two Smallwood siblings and their French guest walked along the road into Malhaven. Their destination was the church hall and that evening they were attending a Barn Dance.

"What is ze Barn Dance?" asked Henri.

Darcy giggled – she loved Henri's accent.

"Please explain, my friends."

"It's just a get together with dancing, Henri," she replied. "Lots of traditional dances with a folk band playing. It's great fun, everyone makes mistakes. There will be a caller, giving instructions."

Henri's face was a picture, as he tried to understand the scenario Darcy was describing. "I cannot dance," he declared, looking despondent.

"Fiddlesticks…you've got two arms and two legs… you'll cope," she laughed.

Henri was struggling to follow the young English girl's explanation and Josh noticed his bewilderment.

"Stay with me, Henri and copy what I do. It's a laugh...nothing serious. There's some good grub and lemonade to drink."

Henri nodded, his English was good, but some words escaped him. "Grub?" he questioned, thoughts of little insects filling his mind.

"Food," clarified Josh. "You'll soon learn the local lingo, Henri."

They arrived at the venue.

The Cycling Club Barn Dance was a much-anticipated occasion. The local Youth Club frequently held such events. Since the end of the war, they'd proved a popular jaunt for the youngsters in the town. But tonight, it was a private function for Cycling Club members and their guests. It was an opportunity to celebrate the efforts of the teams who had participated in the Time Trial Contest and the opposing team, The Malsett Cycling Club, were also invited. Fortunately, the church hall was a sizeable venue with a stage, where the folk band was already tuning up. Within minutes of their arrival, Grady was at Darcy's side.

"Are you going to introduce your new friend?" he asked, indicating the handsome Frenchman.

Darcy smiled. "Ahh, yes. Grady this is Henri Dukas. He lives in Lyon, France, with my aunt, uncle and cousins. He is spending the summer with us, helping my dad with his new project." She turned to their guest. "Henri, this is my friend, Grady Forrester, we attend the same school."

Grady eyed the tall well-built Frenchman with interest as they shook hands. "Welcome to England, Henri. I hope you enjoy your stay," Grady added in greeting.

"*Merci*, thank you for your kind welcome, monsieur, I am delighted to be here. It is my first visit to England," replied Henri.

Darcy looked between the two young men. They matched each other in height and build, but Grady was fair haired and clean shaven, whereas Henri's hair was dark, and he wore a neatly trimmed beard.

Standing between them, Darcy sensed something – a hint of antagonism perhaps...why? Josh guided Henri over to meet some of his friends.

Grady draped his arm casually around Darcy's shoulders. "A sort of cousin...you said," he commented, watching Josh and Henri cross the floor.

"He's not related to me," explained Darcy. "He's my cousin's cousin on their father's side of the family. His parents are dead, and my uncle is his guardian until he reaches twenty-one."

Grady was caressing Darcy's shoulder, as he continued to observe Henri. "Why isn't he at university?" he enquired, in a demeaning manner.

Darcy looked up at Grady. "Grady, I have no idea – he's recently lost both his parents, and he has no brothers or sisters. His only relatives are my uncle, aunt and cousins. He's had a great deal to cope with recently. Not everyone comes from the privileged background you enjoy," she rebutted.

Grady swung her around to face him. "Oooo, tetchy, aren't you? Coming to his defence, I see." He flicked Darcy's chin and grinned. "I think he looks big enough to take care of himself...he is *un grand garçon*, if my French is correct! Come on, time to dance, beautiful." Grady took Darcy's hand, and they walked over to make up the numbers in a group on the dance floor.

Within minutes they were performing the circles, turns and reels of 'The Dashing White Sergeant' dance. The pair frequently partnered each other at the local dances and were quite adept at the routines. One dance led to another, and Grady was not about to leave his attractive girlfriend to be swept away by any other admirers. But after completing the strenuous demands of the traditional dance known as 'Strip the Willow', they were both exhausted and found a seat.

Regaining her breath, Darcy scanned the room trying to locate her brother and Henri. "I wonder where Josh and Henri are?" she enquired.

"Over there," indicated Grady, beckoning to an alcove where a crowd of youngsters were gathered, near to the table currently being set up with food. Darcy followed his direction and noted Henri talking animatedly with a young girl, one of Josh's friends.

"He seems to be finding his feet, so you don't need to worry about him," groused Grady, pulling Darcy onto his lap and jiggling her up and down to the beat of the music.

"Grady, I must go and talk to Henri – we promised Dad we'd look after him," she objected, jumping off his lap.

He grabbed her arm and instantly protested. "And what about me...what will I do while you are playing 'mother hen' to your French guest?"

Darcy pulled free from his grasp and placed her hands on her hips. Grady eyed her with a glint in his eyes. She looked so cute when she was riled.

"You, Grady Forrester, can make yourself useful. Go and get me a glass of lemonade – I'm parched with all that physical exertion. I'll meet you by the food table," she quipped, flouncing off.

Grady twisted his face – he was not enamoured by the arrival of this young Frenchman.

* * *

Darcy placed the small trophy – a metal cup displaying a gold ribbon – on the mantel shelf in the conservatory. She stood back to admire it.

"Ah, there you are," said a voice behind her. It was Chantal. "Congratulations on winning the cycling event yesterday. Sorry I wasn't up when you arrived home. It had been a long day, and I was ready for sleep."

"Oh, thanks, Tallie," replied Darcy, flinging her arms around her aunt's neck and hugging her tightly. "I thought you'd be having a 'lie in' this morning?"

"Not me, Darcy. I'm an early riser – it's a habit. I often leave for work before seven o'clock. Come and sit down and tell me all about the Barn Dance."

Chantal and Darcy sat down on the settee. The early morning sunshine was casting its sparkling beams into the corner of the room.

"Oh, it was great fun. I love barn dances, and I think Henri enjoyed himself. It fell to Josh to look after him though, and I felt a bit awkward about that, but Grady kept pulling me up for dances, so I was kept busy for most of the night."

Chantal placed her hand on Darcy's leg. "How is your friendship with Grady progressing?" she enquired.

Darcy was thoughtful for a few minutes – Tallie was the only person who knew about the episode in the kitchen with Grady.

"I like him. We've been dating since last autumn, although it's very casual. He's off to university in September, if he gets the results he wants in his Highers."

Chantal bent forward and looked at Darcy. "Have there been any more incidents like the one you wrote and told me about?"

Darcy shook her head. "No, it's as if it never happened and honestly, I struggle to remember it now, because he's been so caring since then."

"Describe 'caring', Darcy."

The young girl sighed, then her face lit up. "Well, he's given me gifts – a box of chocolates, a decorated hairpin, a silk scarf and a new notebook. He's taken me out to a restaurant for two meals. He makes me feel special... and wanted. And in case your next question is...you know...has he? Well, my answer would be – he's a perfect gentleman...and yet...oh, Tallie, I don't know. I'm so inexperienced... but sometimes I feel like I'm his 'property' – does that make sense?" Chantal raised her eyebrows as Darcy relayed Grady's words after Henri's arrival. "I told him in no uncertain terms I don't 'belong' to anybody. Then last night at the barn dance he never left my side and insisted on walking me home, even though Josh and Henri were there."

Chantal was quietly reflecting on her niece's comments.

"Well, just remember my advice, Darcy – be cautious and watchful of his behaviour. There's a narrow line between affection and possessiveness."

Darcy nodded and Chantal squeezed her hand.

"Changing the subject, Tallie. Will you tell me some more about your missing doctor friend. Mother and Dad are very careful what they say in front of me. I was present when the hospital almoner telephoned, so I know a little bit."

Chantal clasped her hands to her face – perhaps this young girl was just the one with whom to share her feelings. Rachel was caring and a good listener but not quite a confidante. When she had returned to France to care for her mother, her former school friends were married and the passage of time made it difficult to resume friendships – consequently she'd become 'a loner'. She felt a close bond with Darcy.

"Oh Darcy, where to begin. We met at the hospital in Newcastle where I did my training. I fell for him immediately, but I was a student nurse, and he was a doctor. I watched him attending to his daily rounds. He was so caring, made his patients feel at ease. His Scottish accent added to his charm. It was weeks later before we met formally at a drinks 'do' for a retiring ward sister. We stood and chatted most of the evening and he asked to walk me back to the nurse's home. He invited me out the following week and from then on, we met regularly, or as regularly as you can, when you both work shifts. He's very handsome."

Darcy nudged her aunt and grinned. "I've seen his photograph – he looked 'dishy'!"

Chantal smiled at Darcy's response. "He's more than 'dishy', Darcy. He's so loving, kind and thoughtful and makes me melt inside when I think about him. Even now after eight long years, I can feel his presence. The way I floated when he kissed me, tingled at his touch," Tears were impossible to hold back. Chantal rummaged for her handkerchief, dabbing her eyes. "He's alive, Darcy... I know he's alive." She sobbed quietly. Darcy sensed the depth of her aunt's devotion. "We experienced such a connection in our short time together – a blending of heart and soul, mind and body...we were one...we were complete. It's impossible for me to believe he has left this world. I just know he's out there...somewhere. Whatever has happened, whatever is preventing him from contacting me...it will be overcome...and one day, I hope ...to feel those arms around me... feel those tender lips touching mine and we will be together again...forever."

Darcy swallowed, tears filling her eyes in response to this profound declaration of love, devotion and hope. She embraced her aunt tightly. "Oh, Tallie, I'm so sorry. It must be heartbreaking not knowing."

They sat together in silence for a few minutes, then pulling back, Chantal's brow puckered with intensity. "If we possess a hope that something is going to happen, then we can cope with the 'not knowing', Darcy." Chantal formed a fist and tapped it against her chest. "Hope helps me to move forward, shows me the path to take. I have this urgency within me to plod on. I need to face each new day positively – I won't allow negative thoughts – like length of time; no communication; no information to cloud my determination. I go forward, Darcy...and one day, I'm sure Sam and I will meet again."

Darcy was choked, so moved by her aunt's tenacious belief. "Tallie...I want to help you...help you find Sam. I'll do anything I can to assist you."

The pair hugged.

"Thank you for listening to me, Darcy. Thank you for your understanding and concern…it's been such a release to be able to vocalise my feelings. Until now, I had no one to share this with…but now… I have you – you are so precious to me."

The door opened and Rachel walked into the room, surprised at the sight of the occupants.

"Oh, good morning, you two – I didn't realise anyone was up yet…how long have you been down here?"

Chantal stood and stretched. "Quite a while, Rachel. I rise early and I've just been having a lovely chat with my niece. Now can I help to prepare breakfast?"

Fourteen years may separate us, thought Chantal as she walked through to the kitchen, but a link has been forged this morning with Darcy…a link which bridges the generation gap.

* * *

"Tell me what I will be doing please?" Henri was sat across from Tom Smallwood in his office.

The meeting was to outline the plan for the young Frenchman's extended visit to Malhaven. Tom smiled, he liked Henri and was optimistic about the arrangement.

"Well, Henri, it's an open book at present. I hold a degree in botanical science – the study of plants has always intrigued me. However, I have spent the last twenty-five years managing a hotel and overseeing a farm. During the war I developed a market garden. We possessed the land, so to help the war effort, we extended the fruit and vegetable growing, to cover our own needs, the needs of the convalescent home, housed in the former hotel, and we also supplied local shops. The supply side of things has expanded to the neighbouring town, since the home is no longer required. Meckleridge Estate is a thriving business. I employ excellent staff to attend to the day-to-day running of the estate, so I am only needed in a managerial capacity." He paused.

"For years I've wanted to indulge my passion for horticulture – to cultivate new plants, in particular roses... I possess a dream to develop a new species of rose one day! My wife understands my passion for this and has encouraged me to change direction – in the short term 'give it a go'. It will be helpful to have someone working alongside me, so this will be your role. I will welcome your assistance and input, and I trust it will be beneficial to us both, if I can pass on the knowledge I have in this area."

The young man listened attentively. "I'm looking forward to learning, sir. I followed your suggested reading and have enjoyed it. Working with my father in his clock repair business I developed an interest in detail which I hope I can carry over into horticulture. I see you have placed many study books, concerning the subject, on the bookshelves in my room which I will read. But now I am ready...how do you say it in English...to get my hands dirty?"

Tom laughed at Henri's expression. "That's good, Henri, but let's begin the way we mean to go on. Call me Tom, I'm not one of your tutors at school and please call my wife Rachel." Tom stood.

"Now today we will commence with a tour of the estate – the gardens, greenhouses and over to the farm. I hope you have working clothes," Tom added, looking at the smartly dressed Frenchman. "I can supply wellington boots, but I suggest you purchase sturdy work boots soon."

The two men left the office.

* * *

"Where did you learn to speak English so well?" Tom enquired curiously, as they set off into the grounds of Meckleridge.

"As a youngster, I became friendly with a boy in my street. His name was George, and his family were from England. I taught him to speak French, and he taught me English. Of course we took English classes at school, but chatting with a friend is an excellent way to learn a language."

Tom whistled for Jess, and they walked over to the greenhouses. Once inside, Tom explained the processes. He introduced Henri to the Polish gardener Ivor, who oversaw the market garden for Tom.

"Welcome to England. I think you will be happy working here – Tom is an excellent boss," commented Ivor.

After touring the greenhouses, Tom led Henri into a walled garden. The young man gasped as they stepped inside. The perfume from the roses was intoxicating. Neat beds of roses were interlaced with gravel paths. On the walls, climbing roses were trailing up the trellis work.

"Tom, this is magnificent," exclaimed Henri.

"It's my passion, Henri. I was involved in the creation of this beautiful garden as a young teenager and it holds a special place in my heart," he added wistfully, touching the delicate petals of a yellow rose. "We must press on and go over to the farm."

Making their way along the winding track leading to the farm buildings, Henri heard a car approaching from behind; the horn tooted.

"Look out, Henri, danger approaches!" laughed Tom.

Henri stepped onto the verge as Tom's Austin car pulled to a halt. He was surprised when he noticed the driver… it was Darcy behind the wheel, accompanied by Chantal.

"Darcy!" exclaimed a startled Henri.

"*Bonjour*, Henri," she responded. "Don't look so scared, I'm quite proficient. My driving test is due next month, then I'll be able to drive on the roads," she announced, preening.

"Oh, the poor residents of Malhaven, they don't know what's about to hit them," chuckled Tom, as Darcy revved the engine.

"Must scoot," she added, "food to deliver. Oh, I almost forgot, Mother asked me to give you this, it came in the post," she commented, handing her dad an official looking brown envelope. Tom took it and placed it in his pocket. "I see my wife has roped you in already," he remarked to Chantal, who was balancing a covered tray on her lap, "No one has a holiday around here," he chuckled.

Darcy drove off.

"She'll pass her driving test – easily. She's been driving around the estate since her feet could reach the pedals. As you know she's a cyclist and she can also drive a tractor."

Henri could sense Tom's admiration for his daughter.

"Do you drive, Henri?"

"I do, but only recently. Uncle Pierre taught me as soon as I moved to Lyon. Living in Paris we didn't own a car – I cycled everywhere."

"Driving will be useful around the estate," Tom added, as they arrived at the farmhouse. Distinct farmyard smells filled their nostrils. They waved to Darcy, starting up the car – her delivery completed.

Bennie, the farm manager, was standing in the farmyard – he was a brusque weatherbeaten chap, around Tom's age. Tom introduced him to Henri.

"Great to meet you. Come on in, the wife will have a brew ready," he remarked.

Tom indicated for Henri to follow Bennie.

"I'll be with you shortly, I just need to check something," commented Tom. He walked over to a corner of the farmyard and retrieved the brown envelope Darcy had given him earlier. It looked official...it felt ominous. Placing his finger under the seal, he tore it open. Carefully unfolding the contents, his eyes scanned the words, and his body tensed.

Chapter 11

"Make a cup of tea, Rachel, and ask Chantal to join us in the conservatory in fifteen minutes," Tom called as he strode briskly through the back door.

Rachel was polishing some silverware at the table in the back lounge. "Why?" she asked, puzzled.

"Just do it, Rachel," he shouted, disappearing towards the hallway.

Rachel was alarmed. Tom rarely, if ever, raised his voice to her.

Obeying the summons, Rachel and her sister were seated in the conservatory fifteen minutes later. Tom, having left Henri with Bennie for a tour of the farm, walked into the room, closed the door and picked up his cup of tea. His wife and sister-in-law watched him with concern etched on their faces.

"Thank you, Rachel. I'm sorry my manner was brusque earlier, but I was concerned regarding a communication I received."

"Oh, no…that brown envelope – I have a bad feeling about it," Rachel gasped, clutching her head in her hands.

The door sprang open, and Darcy bounded into the room. "What are we going to do about..." her voice trailed away at the sight of her parents and aunt.

"You may as well join us, Darcy," said Chantal. Then looking at her sister who was about to object she added, "She's part of the family, Rachel, I want her to be here," commented Chantal.

Darcy looked from one person to another. "Why? What's going on?" asked the bewildered girl.

Rachel was becoming impatient with her daughter. "Sit down, Darcy, and shut up!" she declared.

Darcy sat down, knowing better than to argue with her mother when she used that tone. Three pairs of eyes were fixed on Tom as he pulled the brown envelope from his pocket.

"This arrived today – I read it earlier." He paused, looking solemn. "Chantal, you are already aware Rachel and I completed forms, on your behalf, after we learned Sam's full name and the branch of the forces he served in. I thought it would be months before we received a reply, but it's only been a few weeks." He paused, as Rachel shuffled in her chair.

"Please read it, Tom," Chantal urged.

Tom took a deep breath and began.

'Dear Mr and Mrs Smallwood,

Thank you for completing the form giving the last known particulars of Conrad Samuel Matthison Carter. We can confirm he served with the medical corps of His Majesty's Royal Navy. He enlisted in February 1940 and after initial training was completed, he was deployed to serve on HMS Precious.

I regret to inform you that because of enemy combat, this vessel was sunk on 9th June 1940 in the North Sea. The aforementioned Conrad Samuel Matthison Carter was listed as missing.

I trust this information will help to answer your query. I will arrange for a newspaper report of the incident, to be forwarded to you, in due course.

Yours sincerely,

Frederick Grainger.'

Rachel took a sharp intake of breath; Darcy's jaw dropped…but Chantal remained motionless. Tom folded the letter and handed it to Chantal.

"I'm so sorry, Chantal, this is an official letter. After an absence of such length, it was an inevitable outcome."

Rachel and Darcy enveloped Chantal in a tight embrace.

* * *

Tom and Rachel were preparing for bed later.

"Thankfully, Chantal was here with us when that devastating news arrived... can you imagine trying to pen those words? Worse still...the prospect of Chantal receiving the news with no one there to comfort her. It doesn't bear thinking about."

Tom nodded, lying down in bed. "Yes, but she's amazing, Rachel – no tears; no outburst; just that one statement...Sam isn't dead."

Rachel was placing her dress on a coat hanger. The day had passed uneventfully, Chantal was subdued but showed no signs of distress.

"Perhaps it's her way of handling the news – a kind of 'coping mechanism'. She holds on to this unwavering belief that she would know if Sam was dead. I think it will take a long time before the news sinks in and she can finally accept the facts. We need to help her, Tom...but I don't know how. She's returning to France next week and we won't see her until August." Rachel climbed into bed beside Tom.

"She's tough, Rachel. She's made of strong stuff. I think she'll cope. She's got her job and by the sound of it, her lodgings are working well for her – at least she sees someone when she returns home these days – not like before when she lived on her own. Do you think she has any friends?"

Rachel shook her head. "None that I am aware of anyway. She told me at Christmas, when she returned to France before the war, all her friends were married, and I don't think she's made any new ones. I think she's a loner – her job keeps her busy, and she reads. It was always her intention to return to England – she's been living in a kind of 'limbo'."

"She needs to draw a line under it, Rachel. Maybe she should move back to England and get work over here – that way, we could look out for her," suggested Tom.

Rachel was thoughtful, considering Tom's idea. "I'll leave things until August, Tom – give her time to grieve. As you say, she's tough and fiercely independent. I doubt if any suggestion I make will help her."

* * *

The new routines kept Henri engrossed and by the time Chantal returned to France he was feeling quite at home. Propagating and nurturing new plants was absorbing work and Darcy was surprised how little she saw of him. If he wasn't working in the greenhouses, he was in his room studying the various books Tom provided for him. A week after Chantal departed, Grady cycled over to visit Darcy.

"How's Henri?" he enquired.

"Okay, I think. I hardly see him. He spends most of his days in the greenhouses. Let's pop over there," she suggested, striding out of the house before Grady could respond.

He followed, admiring her figure. "What is he doing exactly?" Grady asked.

Darcy shrugged her shoulders. "No idea, you'll have to ask him."

They walked around the side of the house, across a lawn towards the greenhouses. It was the first time Grady had seen this area of Meckleridge House.

"Goodness!" declared Grady. "I didn't realise your grounds were so extensive."

Darcy stopped. "We have more greenhouses than before the war," she explained. "And you see those vegetable plots over there–" she pointed– "all that used to be lawns, garden beds and bushes. Dad put the land to good use to help the war effort."

They continued walking and arrived at the greenhouses. Darcy peeped inside two of the glass structures, before spotting Henri's tall figure stooped over a wooden workbench.

"There he is," she remarked, opening the door which scraped across the cement floor.

The humidity in the greenhouse hit them as they stepped inside.

"Wow, it's stifling hot in here!" exclaimed Grady, as they walked the length of the narrow pathway between the benches, towards the solitary figure.

"Hello, Henri," Darcy greeted the Frenchman, "I've brought someone to see you."

Henri looked up and smiled at Darcy as Grady spoke.

"*Bonjour,* Henri – how are your settling? I see you have green fingers."

Henri looked down at his soil-covered hands, quite puzzled. "Green fingers?" he queried.

Grady started to laugh. "Not literally, Henri – it's an expression we use to describe someone who is good working with plants."

Henri smiled. "It will take a while for me to learn these phrases."

Grady pointed to the pots in front of Henri. "So, Henri, tell me what you are doing in here?"

Henri was busy re-potting some young geranium plants and explained the process as Darcy watched and listened with fascination. He reached over to another bench and picked up an established plant.

"See, this is what it will look like in a few weeks," he commented, placing the terracotta pot in Grady's hands.

'Achoo! Achoo!' Grady sneezed, and after sneezing several times, he thrust the pot at Henri and headed back towards the door.

"Oh, dear...Grady... does he have the allergy?"

Darcy pulled a face. "Seems like it. I'd better follow him," she added, walking outside to join Grady. Darcy stood for five minutes listening to her boyfriend sneezing loudly.

"That wasn't good," he spluttered, wiping his nose as the attack eased. He was clearly suffering from the after-effects. Henri joined them.

"Don't invite me to look at your plants in that hot house again, Mr Green Fingers," snorted Grady, turning abruptly, and making his way back over to the house to retrieve his bicycle.

Darcy watched, surprised at his rudeness.

"I'm sorry," Henri remarked to Darcy, "I seem to have upset your friend."

"Don't be sorry, Henri. It wasn't your fault. Just ignore him!"

* * *

Rachel stepped over the threshold of the front door into the hallway, calling their golden retriever to follow. "Hurry up, old girl," she encouraged. Jess possessed two speeds – slow or stop; to hurry was not in her nature. Closing the door after the dog wandered in, Rachel made her way through to the rear lounge. She stopped and stared at the newspaper Tom was reading.

He looked up. "What?" he asked.

"Why are you reading 'The Times'?" she enquired. "You usually read The Journal or The Northern Echo – the local newspapers."

Tom dropped the broadsheet paper onto his lap.

"There's a reason," he replied.

Rachel sat down. It was mid-morning and Tom had recently returned from his errands in the town.

"A reason?" Rachel asked, staring at her husband who seemed lost in a world of his own.

"What? Oh, yes…I was chatting to Zac on the phone the other night, telling him the devastating news about Chantal's boyfriend and he mentioned something." Zac was Tom's lifelong friend. He lived in London and was an investigative journalist. He'd been very helpful when Tom was researching Rachel's family background, years ago. Tom continued.

"Zac indicated, because Sam has been missing for seven years, he will soon be declared 'officially dead' and a notice to that effect will be posted in a newspaper like The Times. So, I decided to begin reading The Times to see if I can spot it. It may be an obituary or a small paragraph. Of course, that's assuming his family want to declare him officially 'dead'."

Rachel raised her eyes. "Tom, it will be like searching for a needle in a haystack. The chances of it being reported, plus the chance of you noticing it …are very small!"

Tom sighed, looking intently at his wife. "I know – but it's June, right on the seven years since the ship sunk, so I figured it was worth combing the newspaper for a few weeks."

"What's right on seven years?" asked Darcy, entering the room, her sharp ears having picked up on the phrase.

Tom looked up at his curious daughter waiting for an answer. "There is a ruling which states …if a person has been missing for seven years with no indication of life during that period, then they are presumed to be dead. For legal and financial reasons, there is a court hearing. It's not an automatic process – the family must request it. Then it would be posted in a newspaper, like The Times."

Darcy was listening intently. "That's fascinating. So, you are thinking this Sam Carter's family might want to declare him dead, now seven years have passed…but why?"

Tom folded his newspaper. "Perhaps his parents have money or property to leave when they pass away. They will be elderly by now. Sam might have been their only beneficiary – so they would need to make another will or hold a memorial service to commemorate his life. It helps to bring things to a conclusion."

"But there's no body – so how can there be a funeral?" asked a perplexed Darcy.

"It's a legal formality, I have no personal experience of the process, but it gives the family an opportunity to say 'goodbye' to their loved one and maybe erect a memorial stone. They will also receive a kind of death certificate or whatever it's called. It will be legally recorded as a *death*."

Darcy was animated. "I want to become a journalist, when I leave school," she declared.

Her parents looked at her in astonishment.

"Get your Highers under your belt first, my girl," remarked her father. "I don't think journalism is a suitable job for a girl," he added.

"Dad," protested Darcy. "Girls can do loads of jobs which men do – the war proved that!"

Rachel felt sympathetic towards her daughter's idea.

"Come on, Tom, let her explore this idea," Rachel said to her husband. Then, turning to Darcy, added, "If you are interested in journalism, maybe you could talk to Uncle Zac, next time he visits."

* * *

Josh was devouring his bowl of porridge the following Saturday morning. "Can you take Henri up to Malsett today, to buy some new work boots, Josh?" asked his father.

Josh swallowed and shook his head. "Sorry, Dad, I can't. I'm playing cricket this afternoon," he replied.

"I'll take him," chirped Darcy. "Although I don't know the first thing about men's work boots, but I do know where the shop is located."

Rachel smiled. "Thank you, Darcy, that's most helpful. Your father and I are going over to Durham today, to visit some recently bereaved friends." She turned to Henri. "I'm sure Darcy will guide you around Malsett – it's a large town with an Iron Works, situated at the top of the hill. It will give you an opportunity to see the surrounding locality. Tom will give you some money."

"Non, non," objected Henri, "I have money, I will buy my own work boots but thank you for offering." Henri was not being employed by Tom, receiving board and lodgings in return for assisting Tom in his work.

It was the first time since Henri's arrival that the pair had spent time alone. The 'mistletoe kiss' frequently crossed Darcy's mind, but she felt at ease in the young Frenchman's company. Grady monopolised Darcy, whenever they were at the Youth Club events and although Henri, using Tom's bike, joined in the cycling trips, he tended to ride alongside Josh.

"Are you enjoying being in England?" Darcy asked her companion as they set off down the winding driveway.

"*Certainement, ma chérie*," Henri responded.

The French words brought a smile to Darcy's face. "Uh, uh! Henri. English please. You are going to speak the English language like an Englishman by the time you return to France."

Duly chastised, Henri continued. "I feel so at home with you all – you feel like my family."

Darcy was developing a soft spot for their French guest, but at the same time she was reluctant to be viewed as a sister or a cousin.

Taking their seats on the cream and red Venture bus, Darcy elbowed Henri. "I hope you and I can become more like friends than family, Henri."

He turned and gazed into her pale blue eyes. "I hope so, *ma petite fille*. I remember our little kiss at Christmas… it left me hungry for more."

Darcy blushed. "Henri Dukas…I think you are flirting with me!"

Henri raised his eyebrows. "I am, mademoiselle, but your boyfriend, Grady, he likes to keep you all to himself, *n'est-ce pas?*"

Darcy could feel the heat radiating from Henri's body as they sat closely on the narrow seat.

"I think Grady suspects you like me, Henri," she remarked.

Henri reached over, took Darcy's hand and squeezed it. "He is correct, Darcy, I do like you and I hope we can become good friends!"

The bus came to a halt in the main street in Malsett. The town was much larger than Malhaven – a long main street bordered by numerous shops, led down to the entrance of the Iron Works. Darcy showed Henri around the town, eventually arriving at the shoe shop. Boots purchased and errands run, the youngsters were making their way across to the bus station, when Darcy stopped.

"Let's walk back, instead of taking the bus – it's all downhill."

Henri agreed and they set off, taking a route which led them through the local park. The park stretched down the hill from Malsett to Bronhill.

"This is our local park. There's a bandstand, bowling green and some tennis courts in here," Darcy explained.

Henri's eyes lit up. "Did you say tennis? Do you play? It is my favourite sport!"

"Yes, I used to play often with my friend Chrissie, but she spends most of her time with her boyfriend these days." Darcy looked thoughtful, then asked, "Shall I book a court for us to play, one evening next week?"

"Yes, *ma chérie*, I will look forward to playing a tennis match with you. I will win, of course," he chuckled.

Darcy pursed her lips. "Don't be too sure about that, Monsieur Dukas. I am a good tennis player," she smirked.

They walked out of the park to Bronhill railway station and took the footbridge to the other side. They continued, down the hill to Malhaven, situated in the valley.

"This is quite a long walk," commented Henri.

Darcy chuckled. "That's why we took the bus, because it's a long climb up to Malsett." Henri stopped and crouched down. "What's wrong?" asked Darcy.

"Nothing is wrong, *ma chérie*, everything is well. Just look at this little plant."

Darcy looked down at the tiny daisy which had caught the Frenchman's attention. "It's a weed, Henri...a daisy... what's so special about it?" she enquired, mystified.

"Non, non, Darcy. See how it strives for life, it pushes up in the gap in the path...it is resilient."

Darcy stared at Henri. "You are just like my dad. He was always showing Josh and I various plants when we were little. You have a fascination with detail. I can see how you two will make a good partnership with his new project."

They resumed walking.

"I sometimes feel like that little plant. It strives for daylight and pushes through, overcoming obstacles."

Darcy was curious to know more about Henri's childhood. "Did you have problems in your childhood, Henri?"

"Not problems, *ma chérie*, more like obstacles. That little plant cannot reach the light unless it pushes through the gap – it finds a way around the obstacle which is blocking its path. A bit like the hazards on the obstacle course – you need to find a way to navigate them. My life has been like that, but you do not want to hear about it."

Darcy reached out and put her hand on Henri's arm. "I do, Henri, I'm interested to hear about your life, please explain."

Henri looked pensive, then spoke. "My parents wanted a large family, but my mother lost three babies, then I came along and survived. She was a fighter and encouraged my father to set up his own shop. He repaired clocks as a hobby and worked in a factory during the day. She pushed him to start his own business – we moved into the flat above a workshop. She walked the streets, handing out leaflets to advertise his business. Soon, he gained a good reputation as people came to the shop. Sadly, she became ill and couldn't walk. My father was busy, so I was needed to help with the household tasks." Henri paused.

"Even though my mother was confined to a wheelchair, her spirit and mind were strong. She handled the accounts and inspired me to work hard with my schooling and to be a sportsman. She taught me to always look for a way around a problem. 'Look for a way to succeed, Henri,' she used to say. When The Occupation came, my father's business continued. Even German soldiers need clock and watch repairs. My mother was the backbone of our family and when she died, I needed to support my father. So, Darcy, I admire resilience...even in a little plant."

Darcy felt choked – Henri had opened his heart to her, telling her about his childhood – she admired him.

Arriving home she made a snack for their late lunch. "Would you like to go to watch Josh playing in his cricket match?" she asked.

"Yes, I would like to learn about cricket – I did not play cricket at our school – it is more of an Englishman's game," he chuckled.

* * *

A sunny afternoon in June – the perfect backdrop for an English cricket match and the junior boys' cricket team were in action at The Spa in Malhaven. Darcy brought a rug and a hastily packed picnic basket. The match was underway, and the pair were soon enjoying watching Josh in action, looking splendid in his white attire.

Suddenly, a dark shadow loomed over Darcy and Henri. "I might have guessed," said a familiar voice with a disdainful drawl. Darcy looked up, shading her eyes from the strong sunlight. "I see your fancy Frenchman with the green fingers is enjoying your company," commented Grady.

Henri jumped up. "I am not a 'fancy Frenchman', and I do not have 'green fingers'," he retaliated angrily.

Grady and Henri eyed each other with animosity.

"I think you would like to become better acquainted with *my* girlfriend, monsieur, but take this as a warning... did you hear those words, Henri...*my* girlfriend...she is spoken for."

Darcy was incensed and stood up; aware the two young men were drawing attention to themselves.

"Grady, that's enough," she urged, keeping her voice low, "please be quiet."

Grady stepped over and placed his arm around Darcy's shoulders, smiling. "I am looking forward to our date tonight, Darcy, and I am somewhat disappointed. I thought you would be at home beautifying yourself in preparation, but instead I see you are entertaining this foreigner...tut, tut, it won't do. Shall I escort you home now?"

Darcy was seething. Grady was belittling Henri publicly. She squirmed her way out of his grasp. "Grady, leave us alone. We are here to watch my brother play cricket. If you can't be civil to my friend, then I think you should leave."

Grady tossed his head. "Oooo, all defensive, I see," he retorted in a 'sing song' tone of voice. "Don't worry your little head, my dear, I'm going. I'll see you later." Grady sauntered away.

Darcy and Henri sat down to resume watching the cricket match, but Darcy was upset. How dare Grady Forrester behave so rudely to Henri in public. Just who did he think he was?

Chapter 12

FRANCE

Rain lashed against the windowpane. The latch on the metal frame rattled and the wind howled. A summer storm – so rare. The air in her room felt warm and clammy. Chantal checked the bedside clock – it was approaching five o'clock. She sighed, hoping it would pass through before she set off on her morning rounds. She was weary. Disturbing images of Sam were producing numerous nights of disrupted sleep. Since her return from England a few weeks ago, these restless bouts of sleep had developed into a pattern. Her only experience of the sea was crossing the English Channel which was uneventful. But she knew living on the west coast of France, the havoc the sea could produce. The Bay of Biscay was infamous for its stormy, turbulent waters. Throughout her life she'd heard the tales of lives lost at sea as nature tossed the ocean-going vessels, testing their sea worthiness to their limits.

Was that Sam's experience? Had he been thrown into the clutches of the menacing seas as his ship was intercepted and attacked by an enemy battleship? She had no idea, but since receiving The Times newspaper account relating to the sinking of the vessel upon which her beloved Sam had served, her mind ran amok in the dark hours of the night.

Chantal was amazed when she had received the newspaper article, assuming it would be an unfulfilled promise on behalf of The Navy – but she was wrong, and Tom had forwarded it to her. It was a succinct account. HMS Precious was built during WW1. Her early days of service were spent in the Mediterranean Sea and the Indian Ocean. In the Spring of 1940, after undergoing a re-fit, she was deployed with the home fleet off Norway, to support the military.

During operations on the fateful night of 9th June 1940, the vessel was enroute in the North Sea to England, alongside other destroyers, when they were intercepted by German battleships. After a brief period of engagement, all three British ships were sunk. There were few survivors. Sam's name was listed as Missing in Action (MIA). The admiralty then listed the names of the casualties. Had it helped to see Sam's name listed this way? Did his name in black print on white newsprint paper finalise his life?

It certainly provided the answer as to why her beloved's letters had ceased in June 1940. When he penned the letter with the missing page – it must have been one of the last things he did before embarking on that fateful journey. Medical staff were deployed on warships to provide care for the crew if they became sick or injured. Serving on a ship, he would possibly have attended to many injured casualties. It was some comfort to picture Sam's days on board ship, he would have worked meticulously, tending to the needs of his patients. Had the attack been anticipated? Had it been sudden? Had he been on duty – midstream in administering a medical procedure? Her mind had explored many different scenarios since receiving the newspaper report.

Once the attack came...she shuddered, picturing chaos, klaxons sounding, the ship lurching. Had he been thrown into the depths of the waters of the cold North Sea – even in summer she knew the chances of survival would be negligible. The sea was perilous at the best of times. Was he wearing a life jacket? Could he have survived? Had he been rescued? Had he managed...somehow, to clutch at floating debris? It must have been chaotic. But amid this negativity, there was a tiny chink, a fragment of hope. She knew the chances of survival, given the circumstances, were slim. Repeatedly, she reminded herself that no body was recovered. The overriding outcome was stark...he was lost at sea. And yet...there was always hope.

There was little point in trying to sleep so Chantal pulled herself from her bed. She'd received a letter from Darcy the previous day, so she decided to reply. Darcy was such a dear girl and eager to support her. She was pleased she had reconnected with her niece – she must endeavour to maintain the correspondence. Darcy asked, in her letter, how she was feeling after reading the newspaper account. Had it helped her to come to terms with the MIA report. She asked if Chantal knew the area of Edinburgh where Sam's family lived. She would answer Darcy's questions.

After asking about the romance between Darcy and Grady, she wrote…

'The newspaper account has not altered my belief in the possibility of Sam's survival. However, I have endured many restless nights, envisaging scenarios where he could have been rescued without it being known officially. There is a 'faint glimmer of hope', Darcy.

As to Sam's family home – I only know it was Edinburgh. He visited his family twice a year – summer and Christmas. Consequently, we were unable to share holiday time together. His family details are unknown to me – he was a private person, and I hesitated to probe.

One thing I would like to share with you, Darcy, is the mystery of Sam's last letter…there was a missing page. He indicated he wanted to tell me something…I turned to the page, but it was missing.

I sense it was important and maybe one day I will know.

I am looking forward to visiting Malhaven in August and seeing you all again.

With love, Chantal x.'

She addressed the envelope and popped the letter in her bag to post later. As she began her morning routines her mind wandered to her young niece. As a child Darcy was so sweet, but as an adult Chantal felt a closer bond. She may not possess life experience with which to advise, like her mother Rachel could, but Darcy was fresh and enthusiastic about life. The girl seemed invincible, on the threshold of life. Chantal sighed, if only life could be predictable...

* * *

ENGLAND

"I've booked a tennis court again," Darcy informed Henri one morning in July. Since their first visit to the park tennis courts, the pair had played several matches. Henri was a competent tennis player, and they enjoyed a healthy rivalry.

"What's the score between you two?" enquired Josh, overhearing his sister's comment.

Momentarily, Darcy was thrown by her brother's remark. "Score?" she queried.

Josh laughed, following her line of thinking. "Tennis score, silly."

Darcy grinned. "You'll have to ask Henri – he's the one with the head for details."

Henri looked up from buttering his toast, pondered then replied.

"Equal – two matches each, but I'll probably win tonight," he added, winking at Darcy.

"Oh, sure of yourself, are you? Just you wait, Monsieur Dukas, I have some winning moves up my sleeve, which you have yet to see!" she retaliated.

"Up your sleeve?" Henri questioned.

Josh chuckled, he liked Henri, and he liked the fact his sister was spending time with him. He wasn't sure about Grady Forrester, but Darcy seemed 'gone' on him.

"She means she's got some tactics she has yet to play, moves she hasn't used yet, Henri – so watch out!"

Henri laughed.

"Are you and Grady going on the Cycle Club ride next Saturday?" Josh asked, drinking his tea.

Darcy looked up, grimacing.

"Oh, crumbs, I forgot to confirm it, and I've made other plans – he'll just have to go without me," she added, shrugging her shoulders. It was true, she had forgotten.

Her other plans involved visiting Durham with Henri. He'd mentioned to Darcy he would like to visit the cities in the North of England, while he was staying at Meckleridge. They had visited Newcastle two weeks ago and Durham was next on the list. To Darcy's knowledge, Grady was unaware of her visits to the tennis courts with Henri.

As Josh was clearing his breakfast dishes, she commented. "Are you cycling on Saturday?" Her brother nodded. "Well, if Grady asks where I am, just say I've gone to Durham, I'm taking Henri to show him the cathedral and the riverside, but don't tell him who I am with – I'm not sure Grady cares for Henri."

Josh smiled. "Your secret is safe with me, sis." Then he ambled out of the room.

However, Grady Forrester was already becoming suspicious. After telephoning Meckleridge House to speak to Darcy earlier in the week, he had been informed by her father, she was 'out'. Tom then forgot to mention this call to Darcy. Grady's suspicions were aroused further, when one of his friends referred to a French guy he'd noticed, playing an impressive game of tennis in the park. "French guy?" he asked his pal. "Who was he partnering?" The lad gave a vague reply – so, Grady decided to investigate.

Darcy and Henri were in full swing when Grady arrived in the park that evening. He viewed the pair from a distance. The little monkey, he thought to himself, observing the tall athletic Frenchman dressed in shorts, playing an energetic game of tennis with his attractive girlfriend. He grinned; Darcy was giving her partner the runaround. He cheered to himself when his plucky young sweetheart beat Henri. He wanted to walk over, lift her up in his arms and kiss her…but instead, he slunk away as the young couple exited the tennis court. He would plot his revenge and show Henri Dukas a bit of 'northeastern hospitality', when a suitable occasion presented itself.

* * *

"Did you know Chantal's doctor friend had family in Edinburgh?" Darcy asked her mother a few days later, entering the conservatory. Rachel shook herself from her daydreams.

"Er, yes," replied Rachel, "but Chantal wasn't asked to visit them. At the time, I thought it was puzzling because they were quite serious about each other. It's normal to take your girlfriend or boyfriend to meet your family, when a relationship becomes significant." Rachel was busy dusting and sat down to relax for a few minutes. "Chantal brought Sam here on many occasions. She asked him to accompany her to France to meet our mother, but he used his holiday time to visit his own family, so it didn't happen. We liked Sam Carter and got to know him quite well over those months."

Darcy was thoughtful. "I wonder why?" she asked rhetorically, wandering out of the room.

Tom was scouring The Times newspaper, which was becoming a chore – so far it was proving a fruitless task. "Dad...you know this newspaper announcement you are trying to find about Sam Carter," she began, as her father looked up. "I've been thinking. If Sam's family lived in Edinburgh – wouldn't it make more sense to look for an announcement in a Scottish newspaper?"

Tom stared at his young daughter in surprise.

"Darcy, what a brainwave – of course it makes sense. Why didn't I think of that! I'll telephone Zac tonight and ask which Scottish newspapers would publish those kinds of announcements."

Darcy was pleased with herself. "We could go to visit Edinburgh and if there is a newspaper office in the city, then maybe we could ask to see some old newspapers."

Tom looked at his daughter with admiration. She was trying so hard to be helpful and maybe her suggestion could be a possibility.

"Yes, Darcy. It's a good idea... although we would need to make an appointment to speak to someone and view archive copies. There may have been an announcement posted already." Darcy began twirling around on the floor, narrowly avoiding tripping over the dog. "Darcy, stand still – you'll make yourself dizzy," rebuked Tom.

"Dad," she muttered dreamily, coming to a standstill. "I've had a thought. Henri wants to visit cities in the north of England while he is staying with us. We could take him over the border into Scotland to visit Edinburgh. Have you visited Edinburgh?"

"Yes, a few years ago before the war - your mother and I took a train for a day trip. It's a beautiful city with a huge castle on a hill."

Darcy darted over to the writing bureau and pulled out a train timetable. After perusing the booklet, she jumped up.

"We could go next Saturday. There are a few trains throughout the day, and we could return later in the evening. What do you say, Dad?" she asked, looking enthusiastically at her father.

"Whoa, slow down, young miss, I need to consult your mother first and speak to Zac ...but it sounds feasible. It will combine some sightseeing and a possibility of finding a family connection for Sam."

Darcy was 'cock-a-hoop' with her suggestion.

* * *

The cathedral in Durham city loomed large as Darcy and Henri made their way through the streets. It had dominated the city for nearly nine hundred years. Admiring the sanctuary knocker on the large, studded door they stepped inside. Henri stood in awe, scanning the height of the towering structure. *"Magnifique!"* he exclaimed, resorting to his mother tongue. He was impressed by the splendour before him. "Look at that window," he declared, gazing down to the spectacular Rose Window at the bottom of the building.

"I love visiting this place," whispered Darcy, grabbing Henri's shirt sleeve, pulling him into a pew and sitting down. "Let's sit for a few minutes and absorb the atmosphere." Henri put his hand over his mouth to stifle a snigger. "What?" queried Darcy, with laughing eyes. Henri shook his head and placed a finger on his lips, but failed to stop the humour from reaching his own eyes.

Darcy gazed around the enormous cathedral, admiring the carved stonework and the colourful stained-glass windows, depicting various scenes. After a few minutes, she elbowed Henri to move back out into the aisle. Walking quietly, side by side, they listened to the dulcet tones of the choirboys practising their anthems, then joined other visitors visiting St Cuthbert's tomb. Slowly they made their way out into the cloisters, where Darcy leaned against the open aperture surrounding an inner grassed area.

"What did you find so amusing in there?" she enquired.

Henri put his hands on her shoulders and looked over her head. "You...*ma chérie*," he replied.

Darcy spun around to face him; his arms remained on her shoulders. She blinked, as he looked intently at her.

"Me? How was I amusing you?"

He moved his hand under her chin. "I was amused at the way you wanted to sit and absorb the atmosphere."

Darcy looked perplexed. "What was amusing about that?"

He grabbed her hand, and they began to walk around the cloisters.

"Darcy, you are so fully of activity – you rarely sit still. It seemed so strange to hear you wanting to sit and reflect," he chuckled.

Darcy was feeling playful. She knew his comment was truthful but decided to tease him. "Do you think I'm so boisterous, I am incapable of feeling a deep spiritual connection when visiting a place of worship?" she asked, pretending to look quite offended.

Henri pulled Darcy to a halt, then taking hold of both hands, he gazed adoringly into her pale, blue eyes. "I think, Darcy Smallwood, you are delightful. Your boundless energy and enthusiasm for life is so infectious. It makes me want to follow you everywhere. You set my life on fire."

Darcy stared at Henri, bewildered and swallowed before answering. "Henri," she gasped, "that's quite a statement...I feel flattered."

They ambled around the remaining sides of the cloisters in silence, but something had occurred...a connection, a turning point.

Darcy recalled Henri's words as she lay in bed later. Maybe he was just being French – weren't Frenchmen meant to be amorous with their words? She felt cocooned in a cloak of adoration. What did he mean by the words...

'you set my life on fire'? She could guess at hidden meanings…but they hardly knew each other. Perhaps he was relishing the companionship of being part of a family and it was his way of expressing himself? Yet, somehow, she sensed those moments in the cathedral marked a watershed in their friendship. In the two months since Henri Dukas had been residing in their home, she was becoming attracted to him. He was only twenty years old but compared to Grady Forrester – he was a man. Darcy was finding some of Grady's comments and actions to be more childlike, especially where Henri was concerned.

Josh approached Darcy before breakfast. "Just giving you a 'heads up', Darcy – but I think Grady's a bit curious about who you were with in Durham yesterday. He was on the cycle ride and normally he hardly acknowledges me. When Pete and I were a good way ahead of him, he came up behind to ask where you were. I told him you were in Durham. Later, when we stopped for a drink, he made a beeline towards me and asked what you were doing in Durham." Josh paused, as Darcy glowered at her brother.

"Of all the cheek! It's none of his business!" she exclaimed. "I could have been with Mother or Chrissie," she remarked adamantly. "What did you say?"

Josh shrugged. "Told him you were probably shopping, then I walked away, but not before I noticed a menacing expression on his face. So, be prepared, Darcy – I don't like his attitude."

"Thanks for warning me, Josh. I'll be ready for him, if he asks."

Josh's' comment about Grady weighed heavily on Darcy's mind that day. At school she went out of her way to avoid meeting him. Normally, she would hang around the areas he 'policed' as a prefect, to engage with him – but she was becoming uneasy about their friendship. He was leaving school at the end of term, then he would be going off to university in September – so in all probability their friendship would fizzle out, but it was two months away. Could she 'tolerate' him until then?

* * *

"I spoke to Zac last night," Tom announced as the family were taking breakfast a few days later. "He was very impressed with your ingenuity, Darcy." Tom smiled at his daughter, as she explained who Zac was, to Henri.

"He's an investigative reporter for a London newspaper," she whispered to the Frenchman.

Tom took a drink and continued. "Zac reckons Sam's family would be more likely to place a death notice in a Scottish newspaper, if they resided in Edinburgh." He paused, layering his toast with marmalade.

"Apparently, there is a Scottish edition of The Times published, but there's also another newspaper called The Edinburgh Evening News. It's a well-established publication and their offices are situated in Edinburgh, not too far from the station. Zac suggests we pick a date, not a Saturday, and I should write, informing them of the nature of my enquiry, rather than just turning up, unannounced."

Darcy was preening over her Uncle Zac's complimentary comment.

"What's all this about?" asked Josh.

Rachel filled in the background details for Josh and Henri's benefit.

"So…when can we go to Edinburgh?" asked Darcy excitedly. "Josh and I finish school next Friday for the summer holidays."

Rachel looked thoughtful. "Remember, we are expecting the Thibaults and Chantal to arrive for their August holiday," she remarked.

Darcy jumped up to retrieve the train timetable from the rear lounge.

"Right, Dad, that gives us a narrow window. We need to visit Edinburgh before the French visitors' arrival." She handed the timetable to her father, then addressed Henri. "This is partly for your benefit, Henri. You'll get to see another British city, the capital of Scotland, no less. It boasts an impressive castle on a hill, from what I've been told," she added, glancing at her father.

Tom smiled and shook his head, commenting to his wife, "Once our daughter gets her teeth into something, there's no stopping her!" he proclaimed.

Darcy looked around the table, hoping for support. "Does anyone have anything to say regarding the proposal?"

Josh raised his eyebrows; Rachel grinned, and Tom consulted the train timetable.

Henri spoke. "I should love to visit the capital of Scotland!" he remarked, with a huge grin on his face.

"Well. I need to check my diary," remarked Tom, "so will you, Rachel, but if we aim for the end of next week, it should allow time to receive a reply from the Edinburgh Evening News office...I'll write to them today." But as Tom spoke, he held reservations...what would they discover?

Chapter 13

The end of the academic year was being celebrated with a jamboree for the youth club members. It was an occasion for the youngsters to 'let their hair down' and have fun. The premises of the Cricket Club were hired for the evening, offering some outdoor space for the activities, if the weather permitted.

"Looks like a fine night for the jamboree," remarked Rachel to her daughter, when she arrived home from school, looking flushed.

"Gosh, it's soooo warm," Darcy replied, running the tap for a cold drink of water. "I felt as if I was cooking in the classroom today. It was a complete waste of time being at school. I know it was end of term, but we did absolutely nothing," she added, poking her head into the walk-in larder, searching for something to eat.

"Mmmm, they look yummy," she remarked, eyeing up some meat pies keeping cool on the shelf under a net. Rachel had spent the morning baking pies for the youth club party.

"Hands off, young lady," scolded Rachel. "Is Henri going tonight?" she enquired.

"Yep," Darcy replied, devouring a cookie.

Walking into the rear lounge from the kitchen, her attention was drawn to a photograph on the front page of the newspaper lying on a chair – she picked it up. "Aww, don't they make a gorgeous couple," she sighed, "they look so happy." The photograph depicted Princess Elizabeth and her fiancé Philip Mountbatten. News of their engagement had been announced a few days earlier.

Rachel walked up behind Darcy, drying her hands. "The wedding will be a wonderful event, just what the country needs after the gloom of the war years."

Darcy was still ogling the picture. "I would love to be a reporter writing about an event like that," she marvelled, wistfully. "It's what I want to do, Mother...I want to be a journalist. I know Dad favours me choosing a career like teaching, but being cooped up in a classroom all day is not my idea of a career." Darcy replaced the newspaper. "I'm going to have a bath," she announced, leaving the room.

Rachel stared after her ambitious daughter then remembered, "Darcy," she called along the hallway. "Your father received a reply from the Edinburgh Evening news office. He's got an appointment for next Thursday, so he's booked the rail tickets."

"That's great," responded Darcy, climbing the stairs.

* * *

The evening was balmy. Malhaven Cricket Club was situated in The Spa, a local beauty spot dating back to the Victorian days when gentlefolk travelled to the town to take the waters. Darcy was explaining the history of the location to Henri, as they walked with Josh to the venue. It was close to Meckleridge House, being situated over the road, down a winding track leading to a flat area near the river.

Henri was listening, but at the same time he was admiring his beautiful companion. Darcy looked so attractive wearing a full, floral-patterned skirt teamed with a crisp white short sleeved shirt. Her blonde bouncy curls were flowing loosely. She was gesticulating wildly with her hands. Henri loved being in her company. Since his arrival in England, he was slowly being captivated by her charms. Their daring kiss under the mistletoe at his uncle's home last Christmas had planted a desire… a desire to develop a romantic acquaintance with this feisty young woman. However, living under the same roof in a 'brotherly like' context, did not afford him any opportunities to further romantic notions.

Henri knew any move in that direction would be inappropriate, so he contented himself, spending quality time in Darcy's company and admiring her from afar. To add to his disappointment, he was frequently subjected to seeing her associating with Grady Forrester. The guy grated on Henri, and he was in no doubt the feeling was mutual. Several times Grady had referred to him in a derisory fashion. 'French geezer' was the most recent. He'd also overheard 'slimy French creep', spoken under Grady's breath. Henri was not one to be intimidated and felt sure it was only a matter of time before they confronted each another. Yet, once again he needed to consider he was a guest in the Smallwoods' home – his behaviour must remain circumspect – but it was becoming harder to maintain.

The jamboree was organised into three parts – games, supper and dancing. Henri and Josh participated in the sack race, howling with laughter as they jumped towards the finishing line. Darcy watched from the sidelines, cheering them on – but neither of them won. Then Darcy and Henri matched their skills in the egg and spoon race, with Henri winning.

"It's not fair," declared Darcy, indignantly, "your leg stride is much longer than mine," but her admiration for Henri shone through her teasing comments. A voice from behind startled her.

"He's obviously used to engaging in these ridiculous pastimes in his homeland – is that correct, *grand garçon?*" sneered the voice.

Darcy turned to face Grady, who until now had been absent from the proceedings. She glanced sideways at Henri – the disparaging reference to 'big boy' was unkind and riled her.

"Well, at least Henri is showing a sporting spirit by joining in the games, Grady," she remarked. "Where have you been until now, Mr Forrester?"

Grady refrained from answering and put his arm around Darcy, pulling her close. Josh nudged Henri and they walked off towards the refreshment table.

Grady looked cool and relaxed. He was smartly dressed in slacks, open necked shirt and lightweight jacket. He squeezed Darcy's shoulder. "I don't care for you fraternising with your French guest in such a public manner, my dear. My sources inform me you've been seen playing tennis with him in the park," Grady commented, snidely.

Darcy pulled free from Grady's grasp. "I'll play tennis with whom I choose, Grady Forrester. I object to being spied on and to your disdainful tone. And as for fraternising, Henri *is* a sort of brother to me. You are acquainted with his background, so try to show some empathy. He has joined our family for a few months, and I regard him as a brother...so keep your comments to yourself!"

Grady reached out, pulled Darcy close and placed a gentle kiss on her forehead. "Calm down, Darcy," he crooned with a velvety voice, "I'm only making an observation." He took her hand and guided her over to the refreshment table, handing her a glass of lemonade. Taking his glass, he gently clinked it against hers. "Friends?" he asked, placing his head on one side and raising his eyebrows.

Darcy nodded, reluctantly. Grady possessed the ability to win her round and make her feel special, but underneath she was troubled. She finished her drink.

Suddenly, he signalled to the games area. "Come on, this should be a laugh," he declared.

Darcy's short stature prevented her from seeing the preparations for the next game.

"What is it?" she shrieked, as Grady grabbed her hand.

"Three-legged race," he replied.

Soon, with two legs tied together, they were lined up to begin the race. Darcy noticed Josh and Henri securing a scarf around their legs. "Bet we beat you," called Josh as he and Henri grasped each other around the waist and hobbled towards the starting line.

"No way," retorted Grady, then whispered in his partner's ear, "Don't object when I lift you," he ordered.

"That's cheating," protested Darcy.

"Do as you're told, Darcy – it's called strategy!" he scoffed.

The race began and after much jostling and pushing, the pairs advanced towards the finishing line. Grady deliberately careered into Josh and Henri, knocking them sideways to pull his partner to victory. Josh was annoyed, feeling sure Grady had cheated by lifting his sister.

Supper was served, then the band – a local trio comprising an accordion, violin and banjo presented their offerings of popular music. Darcy danced with Grady most of the time, only sitting out once. Josh and Henri enjoyed dancing with a couple of young girls – classmates of Josh.

The atmosphere was jovial, as the youngsters of Malhaven revelled in the frivolities of the jamboree.

195

The school year was behind them and the long lazy days of summer stretched ahead. But eventually, the evening ended. "I'll walk you back home," announced Grady to Darcy.

"There's no need to do that, Grady, it's only a short walk. I can go with Josh and Henri, so you can get a lift," she added, knowing Grady would be in for a long uphill trek to his home in Malsett, after walking her to Meckleridge House.

Grady put his hands on Darcy's shoulders, staring into her eyes. "I will walk my girl home to ensure her safety," asserted Grady, taking her hand.

Darcy felt intimidated. There was something unnerving in the inflection of Grady's words.

"What do you mean by ensuring my safety, Grady? Who is about to harm me? I'd be with my brother and our guest," she protested.

"Exactly," taunted Grady, "I need to ensure your French guest keeps his grubby little hands off your body, Darcy. You don't see the way he looks at you. I've been watching him…watching you. You need to be wary. The French are known for their amorous ways – so, I'm warning you to be careful."

Darcy felt uncomfortable hearing Grady's comments but decided to let the subject drop as he escorted her home. His kisses on the doorstep were loving and lingering. She melded into his arms, enjoying his affections. He sighed in her ear. "Oh, I must let you go, dear Darcy. I could stand here for hours, kissing you goodnight, but I am a gentleman, and I must bid you farewell."

Grady turned and walked away, leaving Darcy in a state of bewilderment. Why did she fall for his charms?

Grady's actions and words during the evening bothered Darcy as she tried to sleep. The air of superiority with which he spoke, unsettled her. She was concerned at how he expected her to comply with his every demand. She was annoyed with herself, being so easily enticed by his charisma. Grady Forrester's behaviour towards her was unacceptable and yes…it was minacious. How could she handle the time before he left for university? She was minded to bring an end to their association, but felt intimidated at the prospect… it was a quandary!

* * *

FRANCE, JULY 1947

"*Bonjour,* Chantal, I have some sad news for you this morning," announced Madame Bolbec, when the *sage femme* entered the boulangerie. The proprietor retrieved a loaf of bread from under the counter. The older lady's action stirred a fear in Chantal's stomach. These days it was harmless, but old habits die hard. Madame Bolbec was the wife of the baker. The couple had owned this shop for as long as Chantal could remember – she recalled visiting it, with her mother, when she was a child.

Chantal offered her payment, and the older lady sighed. "*Merci,* Chantal. I regret to inform you Giuseppe has died." Chantal gasped, glancing furtively around the small shop – but no other customers were present. "His heart finally gave up – he was a very brave man," the baker's wife continued.

Chantal wiped her brow. "Indeed, madame – such a shock for his family, but he will be remembered for his acts of bravery," she replied. A customer walked into the shop and Chantal took her leave, stepping outside into the warm July sunshine.

For almost four years, Giuseppe had held the reins of their fragile network. Chantal doubted if Giuseppe was his real name – most of their contacts were known by pseudonyms – but the man was a stalwart. A giant of a man, with a gentle voice. Chantal recalled his hands – big and chunky, gnarled with sores. She clutched her shopping to her chest and sat down on a bench in the square. Nearly three years since the Occupation had ended in August 1944 and yet performing a simple act of sitting in a town square felt strange. It's over, she reminded herself...the war is over... relax and enjoy your surroundings. Yet, she felt nervous – why?

Hearing Giuseppe's name, mentioned after all this time, brought memories flooding back to her mind. Memories of acts of patriotism, in which she'd been proud to engage. She lifted her head and allowed the rays of sunshine to penetrate her face. She listened with pleasure, to the squeals of laughter from children chasing each other around the square. She sighed – no need for fear anymore, but her memories were aroused.

Following her first encounter with Cécile's husband, in the farmhouse, in the summer of 1941, she soon became involved in the Resistance network. As days turned to weeks and weeks turned to months, her role developed into a valuable link in the French Resistance work.

Chantal's daily routines provided legitimate cover, as she traversed the country lanes on her bicycle, carrying her midwifery bag. Some days she conveyed messages, written in code and carefully concealed. She varied her hiding places over those months. She smiled as she recalled one of them. She ingeniously secluded messages inside a maternity napkin – an innocent deception. More than once the contents of her bag were searched at checkpoints, but the delicate nature of the items frequently caused embarrassment to the young patrolling soldiers, which afforded Chantal's bag to be hastily repacked.

Yet, those messages passed on by her next patient, formed important links – lifesaving links. To this day, she was unaware just how important those messages were. She had played her part – a small, but vital part, in helping people to safety, buying time to allow others to confiscate items which would otherwise have fallen into enemy hands.

Chantal looked down at the loaf of bread she was clutching – a simple, everyday item – but it provided a conduit for messages during those dreadful days. Collecting her loaf of bread from the boulangerie was a daily task and most days it was as it seemed...a loaf of bread. But on other days a rough lump of dough somewhere on the loaf told her a message was concealed. On those days she would hurry home, slice open the loaf to reveal a roll of greaseproof paper. Unrolling the paper she would discover the coded message – sometimes letters; sometimes numbers; sometimes a mixture. Always she was ignorant of the meaning. But her task was to transfer the message via her midwifery bag to the various farmhouses.

Many times, she wondered how many pregnancies occurred among her patients to require her presence – that remained an unknown factor. Chantal felt she had played her part, albeit small, helping her occupied country. Her role was dangerous, but she'd possessed a strong determination and ultimately her actions remained undiscovered. Men like Giuseppe should have enjoyed a long life to reflect on the enormity of their cunning actions, but at least he had survived the ordeal of dying at the hands of the enemy.

Leaving the square, she made her way home and as if to celebrate the actions of her resistance counterparts, she resolved to cut two slices of her loaf of bread. She would spread them thickly with butter, lather them with fruit conserve and enjoy the taste, sitting in her lodgings, in her liberated country.

How long would it take for the memories to fade and the fear to subside? No-one... family, work colleagues or neighbours, knew of the role she had played during those war years – she was just an ordinary *sage femme*, attending to her daily work, assisting women to bring their offspring into a world, which she felt compelled to make a better place in which to live.

It was such a relief to walk the streets of Bordeaux again, in safety. The invading forces were attracted to the location because of its port and vital position. She recalled the enemy flags hanging from the buildings and some houses which were requisitioned. But…it was over, and she must press on…yet her own private quest was incomplete, inevitably tied to the same wretched war she'd been recalling. Only if her wildest dreams were fulfilled - and it was a massive hope…could she put the past behind and step into the future in peace.

* * *

SCOTLAND, AUGUST 1947

Screech…bang…crash…hiss…boom. Henri stood on the platform of Waverley Station in Edinburgh, absorbing the atmosphere. A train station was a universal place – its sounds, smells and sights. Henri marvelled – in recent months he'd stood on many station platforms and the sensations were familiar. People moving with determination, faces set, eyes searching.

"Hey, dreamer," a voice interrupted his thoughts. "This way, Henri," called Darcy, tugging at his sleeve.

"*Pardon*," replied Henri, "I was lost in my thoughts. I love the buzz of a station; the sense of purposeful movement; the excitement of travel."

Darcy stared at the young Frenchman. "You are very profound in your comments this morning, Henri," she remarked.

A smile spread across Henri's face. "A station is also the place of our first meeting, *ma chérie*," he winked at his young companion.

Darcy grinned.

"Henri...it's a station, a place where trains come and go," she teased.

He nodded. "I know where I am, Darcy, and its function – but just stop for a moment, appreciate the spectacle being played out before your eyes. Ask yourself... who are these people? Where are they going, where have they come from? What happiness do they hold? What sadness do they carry?"

Darcy was intrigued by Henri's ramblings.

Josh appeared at their side. "Are you two going to join us? We have more to do than stand on a station platform!"

The pair laughed and walked to join Tom and Rachel. The Smallwood family group exited the station.

Tom consulted his watch. "Right, folks – here's the plan. First, I suggest we find somewhere to eat, personally I'm starving. My appointment at the newspaper office is at 2.30pm, so perhaps we can visit the castle before then. While I'm at the appointment you can either stay at the castle or look at Princes Street and the gardens opposite. I'll suggest a meeting place before we part. We are aiming to catch a return train no later than 6pm... everybody happy with my proposition?" Tom noted nods of agreement from all except Darcy.

"I'm coming to the newspaper office with you, Dad," she objected.

Tom looked at his wife. He knew Darcy was keen to see the inside of a newspaper office.

"Makes sense, Tom – I've been here before, and have some idea of the layout of the place. I'll stay with the boys."

Fortified with food, the family made their way up The Royal Mile to Edinburgh Castle.

"What a position," declared Henri, as they stood on the esplanade outside the main entrance and gatehouse. Darcy was consulting a booklet she'd purchased about the castle.

"Hey, listen to this, everyone. The castle is over four hundred feet above sea level and is built on an extinct volcano...imagine that? There are rocky cliffs facing north, south and west and part of it is used as a military garrison."

The group listened with interest. For the next two hours they toured the various towers, churches, military museums, halls and siege guns. They stood to listen to the 'one o'clock gun' being fired. Henri and Josh were absorbed in the historical features, so Tom suggested Rachel and the boys remained at the castle while he and Darcy kept the appointment.

Excitement was rising within Darcy as they approached the offices. "I've made my mind up, Dad," she remarked, "I'm determined to be a journalist. Just imagine being able to write a report describing Princess Elizabeth's wedding."

Tom chuckled. "Darcy, it would be years before you would be given those sorts of opportunities – just ask Uncle Zac. I imagine even if you did land a job with a newspaper, it would involve filing, typing, running errands and tea making. Be realistic, it's a fanciful idea – you need to settle on a suitable career path like teaching."

"No, Dad, I want to be a journalist!"

Tom raised his eyebrows…his daughter's exuberance was evident.

Arriving at the newspaper offices, they were informed Mr McNab would be with them shortly and were shown into a small office. "Good afternoon, Mr Smallwood, pleased to make your acquaintance," said a tall, aging gentleman with a soft Scottish accent. He was attired in a dark suit. His hair was grey, and he wore spectacles.

Tom introduced Darcy. "My daughter is interested in pursuing a career in journalism, Mr McNab, so was keen to join me today."

The elderly man looked over his rimless spectacles at Darcy.

"Is that so," he remarked condescendingly, "most of the ladies in our employ hold a secretarial role rather than a journalistic role. We pride ourselves on producing a newspaper worthy of the city of Edinburgh. Our paper gives a balanced perspective on news events, local council, public notices and crime."

Darcy smiled sweetly at the elderly gentleman – one day the newspaper owners would value the work of female reporters!

Mr McNab stood. "Now, regarding your enquiry, we need to go to the archives... so follow me please. We will pass through one of our offices on the way to the archive department."

They followed Mr McNab through the loading bay. "You will notice an increase in noise levels, as we enter the next office – this comes from the printing machines and causes vibrations, we hardly notice it – but visitors are often surprised."

The thunderous sound of the printing presses only helped to enhance Darcy's experience as they were shown through the busy office. Typewriters clattering; telephones ringing and voices chattering, gave her a picture of a hive of industry – an industry which appeared tantalising to Darcy Smallwood.

Entering the archive room, Mr McNab sat down at a large desk and invited Tom and Darcy to sit opposite. He picked up Tom's letter, posted the previous week. "Now,

Mr Smallwood, your letter indicated you were interested to know if our newspaper had carried an obituary for Conrad Samuel Matthison Carter." He shuffled some papers, selecting one.

"I can confirm our newspaper featured such an article in our public notices section." He handed a single folded sheet of a broadsheet newspaper to Tom, who unfolded it. The date at the top said 18th June 1947. A section of the page was boxed with pencil. Tom and Darcy read it.

'It is with great sadness the family of Conrad Samuel Matthison Carter announce a memorial service to mark his presumed death. Mr Carter has been listed as Missing in Action, since June 1940. His parents John and Pauline, and his wife Evelyn, invite Conrad's friends to attend Saint Bartholomew's Church in Abbeyfield, Edinburgh, on Wednesday 2nd July 1947 at 2pm to celebrate his life.'

Tom and Darcy stared at each other in disbelief.

Chapter 14

It was past midnight, Rachel yawned and glared at the newspaper item. It wasn't an obituary as such, more a public notice. Tom had withheld their full findings at the newspaper office from the family group as they travelled home, deeming it unwise to discuss the revelation in front of Josh and Henri. He asked Darcy to keep the information confidential.

"It's not our business to share, Darcy. It raises questions. Did Chantal suspect Sam's marital status? Will she want to keep it quiet? No, I'll share the bare facts, saying there was a memorial service, two weeks ago to celebrate the life of Conrad Samuel Matthison Carter, Missing in Action since June 1940."

Darcy listened to her father's suggestion and agreed.

"Of course, I'll tell your mother…but not until we arrive home."

Darcy was itching to discuss their discovery, but in the end, it was tiredness which won the day, and the three youngsters all dozed off to sleep on the return journey.

"I can't believe it, Tom," Rachel remarked, having read the newspaper notice several times. "Do you think Chantal had an inkling?"

Tom shrugged his shoulders. "No idea, but this is a delicate issue. It's pointless sending a letter to France about it, when it's so close to Chantal's arrival. At least we can tell her face to face, and she'll be with us for a few weeks afterwards, which will help, I'm sure."

Rachel nodded, rubbing her eyes – she felt weary. "Oh, Tom, what a blow it will be for her. It's deceit... isn't it? He was unkind to allow their friendship to develop when he wasn't a free man to marry."

Tom climbed into bed and placed his hands behind his head. "Thing is, Rachel, we only know Chantal's side of the story. Maybe it was only a 'hope' on Chantal's behalf, a hope Sam would ask her to marry him. Also, it appears he was known as 'Conrad' to his family, not Sam – why did he use 'Sam' when he moved to Newcastle?"

Rachel extinguished the lamp, climbed into bed beside Tom and snuggled up to him. This visit had raised more questions than given answers – should they have left things alone?

"Hope seems to characterise Chantal's whole life. She *hoped* to return to live in England after our mother's illness; she *hoped* Sam would ask her to marry him; she *hoped* Sam would survive the war; she *hoped* she would be re-united with him...it all seems so futile, Tom...my heart aches for her."

"Yes, Rachel," he replied. "My father used to quote a phrase from the Bible – 'rejoice in hope'. Your sister's hope has been and still is, so real to her. But as I know from experience...sometimes hope is rewarded; let's enjoy our reward." He bent over and kissed his wife lovingly.

* * *

Darcy couldn't settle. As her dad would say she had 'the bit between her teeth'. The 'bit' was to track down Sam Carter's family home. Repeatedly, she assessed the situation. She agreed with her parents' decision to present the facts to Chantal face to face when she visited, but she was already formulating a plan – to find an address for Sam's family, before her aunt arrived in England.

She broached her plan to her parents two days after the Edinburgh trip. "I've got a suggestion," she announced when Tom and Rachel were relaxing in the conservatory after supper. Josh and Henri were out, dog walking.

"Now we know the names of Sam's relatives – it should be easy to find their address ...but it would involve another trip to Edinburgh."

Tom was shaking his head before Darcy finished speaking. "No, Darcy. It's not our place to investigate any further," he remarked emphatically.

Darcy pulled a face. "I disagree, I think we could be helpful by locating an address for her. Then it's up to her if she wants to visit Edinburgh when she's over here.

Perhaps she would want to send one of those letters you send to people after someone dies...what's it called again?"

Rachel stared at Darcy. "A letter of condolence," she answered, her eyes following Tom as he walked over to the window. "She's got a point, Tom. It would be helpful for Chantal to know the family address."

Tom remained thoughtful. "How do you intend to gain this information, Darcy? Your mother and I are far too busy to go traipsing off to Edinburgh again."

Darcy detected a chink in her father's armour. "Well, both Josh and I are off school now and if you could spare Henri for a day – he's a responsible sort of person. He's almost an adult – he'll be twenty-one in February." She looked pleadingly towards her father, who had returned to his seat. "The three of us could get the train up to Edinburgh and find telephone boxes. Then we could look in the directories."

Rachel's eyes widened and she sniggered. "Darcy, don't be ridiculous. Edinburgh is a vast city!"

But Darcy was not about to be intimidated. "I'm aware of that, but remember we know the area of Edinburgh and the name of the church where the service was held. That could be located on a street map, which we could obtain at the station. Once we suss that, we could take a tram or a bus or even walk to the church. Then we can consult a telephone directory!"

Tom shook his head and raised his eyebrows. His young daughter was a force to be reckoned with. But... it was plausible. It would mean divulging their findings about Sam being married, to the boys, but they were sensible lads, and he was sure they would treat the delicate information with respect.

"Okay, young lady...you win. I only hope I don't regret agreeing to this crazy plan of yours. But you must return on an earlier train than we did. I don't want you three travelling late at night."

Darcy ran over and gave her dad a hug. "Dad, what harm can possibly affect me when I have two strapping young men as my chaperones," she declared, blinking her starry eyes at her father.

Tom chuckled. "I think they might be the ones needing protection!"

* * *

Next morning Darcy was bursting to speak with Henri. She found him in the greenhouses before breakfast. Henri was so enthusiastic about his work; he often spent an hour in the greenhouse in the early morning. Darcy was always an early riser.

"Good morning, monsieur," she chirped, sneaking into the greenhouse. "Gosh, it's hot in here – how do you stick the heat?" she enquired.

"Good morning, *ma petite fille,*" he greeted. "What brings you here so early in the morning?"

"Well," Darcy began, poking around with a short stick in a plant pot filled with soil.

Henri tapped her hand gently. "Stop it, Darcy there's a little seed in there," he remarked.

She looked up and their eyes met. "Oooo, you sound all protective...sorry, little seed," she pouted, carefully smoothing over the soil.

Henri leaned back against the workbench.

"Is there something I can assist you with?" he enquired. Darcy fluttered her eyelids, enjoying the exchange and giggled. Henri's heart lurched – this girl was doing things to him – things he must subdue.

"Yes," she responded. "I want to give you some advance warning. Dad is letting me go back to Edinburgh to gain some extra information for Chantal, but of course I need companions, to protect me... I think. Anyway, he's going to ask you and Josh to accompany me."

Henri listened. "Extra information?" he queried.

"Dad will explain, but please say you will come – he won't let Josh and I go on our own... so you would be the one 'in charge'."

Henri grinned – he liked the idea of being 'in charge' of this delightful young girl for a day. "Sounds like a good plan and I'm happy to oblige."

Darcy reached up and gave Henri a peck on the cheek.

"Yippee, I knew you'd agree!" she exclaimed and bounded out of the greenhouse, pausing at the door. "Ooops, nearly forgot...I've booked a tennis court for seven o'clock tonight...hope that's okay?"

Henri nodded and waved.

Walking to the tennis courts after tea, Darcy discussed the 'plan of action' for the day trip to Edinburgh. "First, we buy a street map in the station, then we need to locate the Abbeyfield district. Once we've located that, we will take a tram, a bus or walk, if it's not too far, to this Abbeyfield place. We are trying to find the church where the memorial service was held. It might show up on a map, but if not, we'll need to ask in a shop or a post office or ask a pedestrian."

"Train stations in large cities often have an information office or desk," Henri remarked.

"I think telephone directories might give the address for Sam's family. The directories will be huge, but if the family lived in the vicinity of the church, it should be easy! We'll need to work methodically though, because we don't have much time."

"Why are we looking for the church?" enquired Henri.

Darcy shrugged. "Not sure really – just seems like a good starting place."

"You are full of ingenuity, *ma chérie*, I admire your strategies."

Darcy grinned. "Well, I see it like this – I've decided I want to be a journalist, so I'll need to take a secretarial course when I leave school to learn shorthand and typing. I'm hoping these skills will help me to get a job in a newspaper office. Embarking on an investigation of this nature will be good practice for me."

Their tennis game was active and quite prolonged as they matched each other with long rallies. Eventually, Henri won the deciding set. They were so focused on their game, they failed to notice a spectator beside the equipment hut... Grady Forrester. As they left the court, he stepped forward and began a slow handclap.

"Well done, monsieur. I see you possess excellent skills on the tennis courts and eventually managed to outplay my little star. My dear girlfriend proved a formidable opponent, but I suspect she will beat you next time, so you need to hone your skills."

The tone of Grady's comments rankled Darcy. "Grady...shut up, you are insulting my friend."

"Oh, he's graduated, has he? He was your 'brother' the other day! Now he has advanced to become your 'friend'," he sneered. "Insulting, you say, that is not my intention. I came along to watch your skills and to escort you back home. I was trying to be complimentary, my dear, that's all."

Darcy was annoyed, she'd had her fill of Grady's comments.

"I'm not 'your dear', Grady...so quit the charm. I made no plans to see you tonight, so sorry to disappoint you... but I do not need to be escorted home."

They stepped through the gate into the park. No-one spoke. Darcy felt her temper rising as Grady joined them on the path which would lead them to Meckleridge House. The park was deserted.

214

"Can't you take a hint, Grady Forrester; I said I had no plans to see you tonight," she repeated.

Without warning, Grady spun around and stepped in front of Henri, causing him to stumble. He reached out and grabbed Henri's arm, and with his other hand slapped the young Frenchman across the face.

"Keep your hands off my girlfriend, Frenchman," he snarled, then spat in Henri's face.

Darcy was incensed. She feared a retaliation or a full-scale fight, but Grady stepped back and grabbed Darcy's arm, roughly.

"Take that as another warning, *monsieur*. Next time… you won't get off so lightly," he growled, dragging Darcy along the path with a firm grip on her arm.

Henri wiped the spittle from his cheek, walked over to a bench and sat down – he was shaking; he needed to give them space; otherwise, his actions could be contentious. Looking up he saw Grady steering Darcy along the path. It was obvious she was agitated and upset with Grady, but he caught her words.

"Grady," Darcy squealed. "Let go of me now…or I'll scream. If I have any bruising on my arm, then I'm telling you…we are finished. I don't like your attitude towards Henri, and I resent your remarks about me. I think the time has come for us to part company!"

Grady stopped moving. Darcy was breathless…she was also scared. Grady's demeanour was threatening. They were in a deserted place. She'd hoped to avoid a confrontation with him, but he'd asked for it and she needed to put an end to their friendship...now!

Grady was seething. He released his tight grip on Darcy's arm and stepped back. Slowly, she pulled up the sleeve of her shirt...and there it was... a definite imprint of Grady's fingers on her arm. Now she possessed ammunition.

She stood tall and looked up at him, vaguely aware of movement at her side. They stared at each other – how had she allowed herself to fall for Grady's charms in the first place? He was controlling; he was deceitful; he was insulting – and the man was a bully!

She pointed to her arm. "See that, Grady Forrester – it means we are finished. Do not attempt to make excuses. No man will intimidate and treat me in that fashion. I could make this unpleasant for you...but I won't. Just go away and leave me alone...do you understand?"

"I am your witness, Darcy," interjected Henri, stepping forward, taking Grady by surprise. "I think you should go, Grady, and do as Darcy has suggested."

Grady looked uncomfortable, not realising the episode had been observed. Then recovering, he put his hands in his pockets and began to laugh.

"You, Darcy Smallwood, are a little cow. I wouldn't have you as my girlfriend if you decked yourself in pearls. You are welcome to her, Mr French Guy," he guffawed, turned and strode away, leaving Darcy trembling in his wake.

Henri reached out and took her in his arms. She sobbed, uncontrollably, into his chest.

* * *

EDINBURGH

"It's this way," pointed Josh.

"No, it's not," remarked Darcy, indignantly. "It's over there!"

Josh lifted his hands in resignation and muttered under his breath. Five minutes later, Darcy stopped, consulted the map and looked up.

Henri watched her… a smile spreading across his face. "I think your brother was right, Darcy," he suggested.

Darcy admitted defeat. "I was sure we were on the correct street, but obviously I was wrong…lead on, McDuff," she declared.

Henri looked between the brother and sister. "McDuff?" he queried.

Josh chuckled. "Just another whacky saying, Henri – not a real person!" The trio retraced their steps. Arriving back at the junction, they consulted the map together.

Henri was the first to spot the church. "There it is," he pointed on the map. "We need to go up that street and take the third turning on the right."

They agreed and set off, walking in silence.

Henri was surprised Tom Smallwood had given approval to the Edinburgh visit, after the fall out scenario in the park a few days earlier. He recalled the events. After comforting Darcy that evening, he had reluctantly released her from his arms. "Thank you, Henri," she sobbed. "I'm so pleased you overheard Grady's words. It's been brewing for weeks, but I didn't expect Grady to react in such a violent way towards you."

He touched his jaw still stinging from the slap. "It took a lot of self-restraints not to retaliate, Darcy. I am used to defending myself with physical force if required...but I figured it was the best course of action to take – it could have turned nasty, so I sat down and watched from a distance."

Darcy nodded and smiled weakly. "I feel honoured – two dashing young men fighting for my affections," she wiped her eyes, sniffling.

Henri had reached out and cupped Darcy's chin. "I do hold affection for you, Darcy...great affection. Until now you have not been free, so perhaps our friendship could be more, but only with your father's approval. I must remember I am a guest in your home." He dropped his hand and stared into her eyes.

A faint smile spread across her face. "I feel the same about you, Henri...but as you say, you are our guest, and it could be tricky if things didn't work out – so, let's leave it for now. I expect Grady will try to win me around, despite his parting words. Once he's gone off to university, I'll feel happier about taking our friendship further."

But Darcy's expectations were not fulfilled. Grady Forrester was conspicuous by his absence. Darcy was surprised and expressed her thoughts to Henri a few days later. "I felt sure Grady would come round to try to win me back and apologise to you."

Tom had overheard the exchange and wanted to know what had happened. Darcy and Henri gave Tom a brief outline of the episode, minus some details.

The three youngsters arrived at the church where the memorial service for Sam Carter had been held a few weeks earlier. They stood in the gateway and took in the large stone-built building. "Look," observed Josh, the church door is open."

Darcy felt excitement rising.

"That's not unusual for a Roman Catholic Church," commented Henri. "In my country, people often go inside to pray or to light a candle, during the daytime."

Darcy came to a decision. "Listen, you two have a wander around the outside and I'll have a look inside, maybe I'll light a candle."

Josh raised his eyebrows, as Darcy took off.

She approached the large, wooden door, which was standing ajar, and pushed it open, cautiously; she shivered...it was dark and eerie. A faint perfumed fragrance tickled her nostrils as she stepped into a large vestibule. Double doors stood to the right and left; half inlaid with panes of opaque glass. Darcy stared wide-eyed – what should she do? 'Go for it, girl', she admonished herself and reaching out, stepped across and pulled at the brass handle on one of the inner doors.

With a forcible creak, the door gave way, and she found herself at the rear of a large auditorium. She could hear voices as she glanced around – dust motes dancing in the sunlight, penetrating through stained glass windows. A wave of familiarity swept through Darcy, as she recalled her visits to the cathedral in Durham. Two figures were standing, staring at her, in the aisle between the pews.

"Welcome, my child," greeted the man, in a deep Scottish accent. Judging by his attire the man was a priest. "And how can I be helping you this day?" He smiled kindly.

Darcy cleared her throat. "I...I...wish to light a candle," she began, totally unprepared for this eventuality. Thinking quickly, she added, "For a friend who died."

"Of course," replied the grey-haired priest, pointing to a table at the side. A stout lady with a severe hairstyle, wearing an apron and holding a duster, pointed to a table.

"Over here, dearie," she remarked, in a Scottish lilt, then indicated the tray of holders and candles. Darcy crossed the tiled floor. As she approached the table, the incense smell became stronger. This was a first for Darcy, but she knew what to do. She took a taper, as the lady retreated, and lit a candle, placing it in the holder alongside other flickering candles. Instinctively, she bowed her head and made the sign of the cross.

"Sit awhile, reflect and pray for your friend," suggested the priest.

Darcy opened her eyes and noticed the priest standing beside a rear pew. She walked over and took a seat, closed her eyes and tried to remember the man for whom she had lit a candle. She'd met him – but her memory was vague. Did he attend this church as a youngster? Perhaps it was here he married the woman named Evelyn. She was aware of movement and a creak in the wooden pew. Opening her eyes she saw the priest sitting about two feet away.

"It brings comfort to our troubled hearts, to reflect on the life of a loved one," the priest remarked.

Darcy nodded and closed her eyes again. This priest may have known Sam Carter – dare she risk a question?

"I wonder if you could help me, please?"

"Yes, my child...if I can... I will. I am Father Quentin, priest in this parish. Now, tell me the nature of your query."

Darcy swallowed, here goes, she thought...

"Hello, Father Quentin. My name is Darcy Smallwood. I am trying to trace the family of a man whose memorial service was conducted in this church a few weeks ago, he went missing during the war."

The elderly priest pursed his lips.

"Would that be the memorial service for Conrad Carter?" he enquired, in his deep Scottish brogue. Darcy nodded. "Ah, yes, such a tragedy for his loved ones. The years of waiting and not knowing have taken a toll on his dear mother. Sadly, his final resting place remains a mystery...but at least, now, his dear family have a memorial to visit and remember him. Are you a friend of his daughter, Francesca?"

Darcy froze...had she heard correctly...his daughter... how should she answer?

"No, no...I'm making enquiries on behalf of my family who knew Dr Carter, when he worked in Newcastle – they recently learned of his passing and wanted to convey their condolences but had no address." The words tumbled from Darcy's mouth – had she given too much information?

The priest looked thoughtful and somewhat surprised. "Yes, Conrad worked away from home for some years before the war. Address? – why – that's easy, my dear...the family reside in Matthison Hall, in this parish."

Darcy noticed the lady she'd seen earlier, walking purposefully down the aisle.

"Father, you are needed..." she began.

Father Quentin stood and nodded to the lady, then turned to Darcy. "It has been a pleasure to meet you, Miss Smallwood, I'm pleased I could help you. Now, if you will excuse me, I have duties to fulfil."

Darcy expressed her thanks and left the pew.

Chapter 15

B right sunshine blinded Darcy's eyes as she exited the
church, still stunned by Father Quentin's comment.
Her brother and Henri were loitering on the steps.

"You took your time, what were you doing in there…
attending confession?" asked Josh, smirking.

Darcy hopped down the steps and flung her hands
in the air. This investigation was unearthing more
concerning facts…how could they tell Chantal… Sam
had a child?

"We found something interesting," remarked
Henri, walking up behind her. "It's around the other
side of the church," he indicated. Setting off, Josh and
Darcy followed.

The graveyard surrounding the church was extensive.
Many old headstones were perched at precarious angles,
and most were in disrepair. A large stone wall ran along
the perimeter. The youngsters weaved their way through
the graves. Henri stopped beside a large rectangular area,
marked out by weathered kerbstones – it defined a family
burial grave. A granite memorial stone stood at the head,

inscribed with the names of deceased people belonging to a family called *Matthison*. In front of the inscribed stone lay a collection of wilting floral tributes, and a small wooden cross. Henri stopped and pointed. Darcy pushed past her brother. The temporary marker bore a brief inscription:

'In loving memory of Conrad Samuel Matthison Carter. Missing in Action, June 1940. RIP'

Darcy crouched and fingered the words on the memorial cross. No doubt Sam's family would add his name to the granite headstone at a future date. The once attractive wreaths looked sad and limp, withering under the August sunshine. A lump formed in Darcy's throat…it was so final. Family death had not invaded her young life, yet – she had been a young child when her grandparents died.

Absentmindedly, she read the black edged cards attached by wires to the circular wreaths. Some were indecipherable, having been exposed to the elements. Two larger offerings were placed immediately in front of the cross. One, with drooping white roses now tinged with browned edges read:

'To our beloved Conrad, forever in our thoughts, Mother and Father'. The other, containing pink carnations, was smudged, but Darcy could just make out some words…

'May you re.t in peace. Lo..ng me..ries, wife Ev..yn and dau.hter, Francesca.' Seeing the name in print jolted

Darcy. She beckoned to Henri and moved to enable him to read the inscription.

"Oh, gosh," gasped Henri, in surprise, "poor Chantal." He motioned for Josh and swapped places.

Josh's eyes widened. "A wife... and a child!" he exclaimed. "Do you think Chantal knew?"

Darcy stepped between the graves, until she reached the gravel pathway, then turned to the boys. "No, I doubt if she knew. Come on, let's go."

They retraced their steps, making for the gateway. Once out of the confines of the church yard, Darcy rested against a wall and sighed.

"I'm beginning to wish we hadn't made this trip. How are we going to tell Chantal about the daughter?" She consulted her watch. "Look at the time...we need to hurry."

"Why...what else do we need to do, apart from find some food...I'm starving!"

Darcy glowered at her brother – he was always thinking about his stomach.

"Chew on some gum, Josh...we need to find a place called Matthison House," she declared indignantly.

Henri pulled out the map. "Matthison, as in this guy's name?" he asked.

"I presume so, I got the impression the priest expected me to know where it was...any joy?" Henri's eyes scanned the map with no success. Darcy leaned in to take a closer look, while Josh moaned about his stomach rumbling.

"Oh, for goodness' sake, Josh...stop being a pain. Let's see if we can find a corner shop – feed you and ask for directions." The threesome wandered back to the main junction, where they had taken the wrong direction earlier.

An elderly man was walking on the opposite side of the road. Darcy crossed over and chatted to him. He gesticulated with his hands, then Darcy re-joined her companions. "Jackpot!" she exclaimed. "There's a shop on the next corner – follow me." Ten minutes later, the howling beast in Josh's stomach was being quashed, as he devoured some fruit and biscuits. The threesome sat on a low wall, as Henri and Darcy also satisfied hunger pangs.

"Now, to business," declared Darcy, "we have just over an hour before we need to head back to the station. My friendly old gentleman tells me Matthison House is situated near to St. Bartholomew's Church – so we need to return there."

Josh let out a moan. "Darcy... why do we need to look at the house, if we have the name and the district of Edinburgh, surely Chantal's correspondence would get there?" he pleaded, hoping to deter his sister from another pointless walk.

"I'm going to look at this house, Josh Smallwood. I suspect it might be rather grand, with a name like Matthison Hall, so, let's get moving, we've no time to waste!"

"She should join the army; she'd make an excellent sergeant major!" Josh mocked, as he followed in his sister's strident footsteps.

Henri sniggered – he loved the banter between Darcy and Josh.

However, finding Matthison Hall proved a hard task. The map was useless, giving no hint of a large house in the vicinity of the church. They felt they were going around in circles until Henri noticed a lane running up the side of the graveyard wall.

"I think we should try up there," he suggested. "On the map it indicates open space...so why is there a lane leading to an open space?"

"Last try," commented Darcy, sounding defeated, as they set off up the lane.

"Wow!" Darcy exclaimed, rounding the bend at the top of the lane to be confronted with large double gates. On one of the gateposts was a sign – *Matthison Hall.* The trio peered through the bars on the gates. An imposing driveway, lined with trees, gave way to a substantial residence, whose outline was only just visible through the trees.

Henri let out a low whistle. "That looks impressive...I guess Chantal's doctor friend belonged to a wealthy family!"

Darcy was silent...why, oh, why did Sam Carter keep his family background so secretive?

"What now, sis?" asked Josh wearily.

"Home," replied Darcy bluntly. "We tell Mother and Dad what we have discovered. Our role is over...for now."

* * *

It was late afternoon, five days after the Edinburgh expedition. Rachel and Tom were on their way to collect Chantal from the train station. Rachel was still struggling to come to terms with the news of Sam's child.

"I feel so sorry for my sister, Tom. It's one blow after another. She's lived with hope for years and all our findings are doing is pulling everything down for her – Missing in Action, then learning about a wife and now compounded by this final revelation…a child!"

Tom had listened to this same conversation for five days now. He was a patient man, but his wife could be trying. "Rachel…please let it rest. Going on and on, is not going to alter the circumstances – it is a disturbing turn of events, but we must accept it."

"Should we even tell her about the child?" Rachel looked pleadingly across at Tom, as they travelled the road to Durham. "I wonder how old this Francesca will be – she could be older than Darcy."

"Rachel, that's speculation. Yes, we inform Chantal of the facts. Remember how undisclosed truth, almost denied us a chance to find love? Chantal must be told the truth – we won't withhold any details. Once she's let it sink in…she can move on with her life. Look at it this way – the reality of war brought an end to what could have been a tricky situation for your sister."

"Oh dear," Rachel sighed, anticipating difficult days ahead.

CHAPTER 15

Henri was mulling over the same events as he lay on his bed. He'd returned from the greenhouse, taken a bath and was relaxing. Supper was delayed tonight to accommodate Chantal's arrival. He'd enjoyed the return trip north of the border and was looking forward to re-connecting with his uncle, aunt and cousins, but a telephone message the previous evening brought a change of plan. The Thibaults were unable to travel as planned, and hoped to follow in a few days, so it was only Chantal who would be arriving today.

A piercing scream resonated along the corridor, causing Henri to jump off the bed in alarm. The noise was coming from Darcy's room – he had no idea of Josh's whereabouts. The scream sounded again, and Henri flew out of his room and along the landing to the young girl's door.

"Darcy, Darcy...what's wrong?" he called through the closed door, as the screaming continued.

"I...I...can't move," a high-pitched voice replied.

"Can I come in?" he asked frantically, conscious of being the only person around. Without waiting for an answer, he opened the door to behold Darcy standing barefoot, on a chair beside the wall. At the sight of Henri, she stopped screaming but looked terrified.

"What happened?" he asked in panic, scanning the room for some clue to her distress.

"S...sp...sp...i...der," she articulated with shallow gulps of breath.

Henri placed his hands on his hips, tried to hold back a smirk and shook his head. "Where?"

"Sh…sh…shoe," blurted the traumatised girl.

Henri glanced down at the small white pumps lying askew across the floor beside the bed. He picked up the shoes, peered inside then walked over to the open window. Reaching out he tipped the offending creature from the shoe and tapped it against the window ledge. Closing the window, he returned the shoes to the bedside.

"Oh, my hero!" exclaimed Darcy, relaxing.

Henri observed Darcy – she looked so adorable standing on the chair. "Can I help you down?" he offered, grinning.

Darcy held out her hands. The chemistry of the moment was too much for Henri. He lifted the trembling girl into his strong arms, lowering her gently to the floor. Their faces were inches apart and their eyes were transfixed on each other. Henri could resist no longer. Slowly he brought his lips to meet hers. The pressure was light at first but intensified as Darcy eagerly responded. Pulling back, Henri brought his hands to her face, tenderly caressing her cheeks, before kissing her lightly on the forehead.

"You are intoxicating, *ma chérie*," he uttered." I am sorry if I am out of order, but you are so adorable." He trailed kisses from her forehead down her nose until he found her lips again.

"*Je t'aime, ma chérie,*" he whispered softly. He placed his hands around her waist, and she rested her head on his shoulder. "Say something, Darcy… please."

Darcy was savouring the moment, pleasurable tingles pulsating through her body. She was dizzy with delight. "Oh, Henri…that… was… so special," she stuttered. "Again?"

Henri required no second bidding and placing his hand on the back of Darcy's head, he drew her into a tight, loving embrace, combing his fingers through her blonde bouncy curls.

"Anyone at home?" shouted a voice from downstairs, causing the young couple to pull apart. It was Josh.

"Quick," whispered Darcy, "I'll go downstairs. You go back to your room, hopefully Josh won't notice."

Henri grinned. "Your cheeks are flushed, *ma chérie,*" he remarked. Darcy went downstairs. If her brother noticed her tousled hair and flushed cheeks, he passed no remark. Henri returned to his room.

"Thank God for that little spider," he said to himself under his breath, feeling smug.

* * *

Weariness filtered through Chantal's body. The journey had proved arduous, exhausting and lonely. She missed the companionship of Peg and Pierre, and their family's playful exchanges when conversing. She'd arranged to meet them in Paris, to make the onward journey to northeast England – but a message the previous evening had informed her of their travel delay. Now she was here. She loved staying at Meckleridge House – it was her home before the war, while she studied and worked in Newcastle.

"I hope the Thibaults will join us soon," commented Darcy, to no one in particular, as they sat in the conservatory after a delayed supper.

Chantal yawned; tiredness etched on her face. "Oh, excuse me please, everyone. It was an early start, and I didn't manage to sleep on the journey."

Tom glanced questioningly at Rachel, trying to convey to her they should leave imparting their findings to her sister, until the next day.

But Chantal possessed an acute awareness, and her eagle eyes noticed the look passing between them. "You know something else…don't you? What is it?"

Rachel stood, walked over to her sister and knelt on the floor beside her. "Yes, Chantal, we do have more information – but you are too tired, I think it can wait until you are rested. I suggest you have a good night's sleep, and we will talk tomorrow," she appealed.

Chantal sat forward; her senses alerted. "No… tell me…I want to know," she urged.

Rachel sighed and sat on the arm of the chair, placing her arm around Chantal.

Tom looked across at his sister-in-law – she was an attractive young woman, so like his dear Rachel in looks. "Chantal, we wanted to help you regarding Sam and tried to ascertain some further information. We hoped it would assist you in laying to rest the devasting news of the MIA report you received. To that end, we visited a newspaper office in Edinburgh. My friend Zac, a journalist, suggested that after seven years Sam's presumed death, would possibly be recorded, and notification given...for legal purposes."

A sound emitted from Chantal's throat, almost inaudible. Darcy stared at her aunt.

"If...there is no body – how can they record a death?" Chantal groaned.

"It's a formality, Chantal," Tom explained. "After seven years without proof of life, a family can request a presumption of death – meaning the missing person's assets can be dispersed, wills re-written, etcetera."

Chantal stared blankly across the room. Rachel squeezed her shoulder reassuringly.

"It was a long shot," Tom continued. "I searched The Times newspaper each day. Then Darcy had inspiration, suggesting we approach an Edinburgh-based newspaper, as you indicated it was where his family lived." Tom paused. He felt he was dragging out his explanation but wanted to set it in context.

"We visited the Edinburgh newspaper and saw the public notice. It gave details of a memorial service to be held at a church in Edinburgh, to commemorate the life of Sam, or Conrad, as I think he was known. Darcy, can you fetch the newspaper excerpt, for Chantal, please."

Darcy jumped up and ran off to the bureau in the rear lounge, returning with the notice. She gave it to her father.

"Before I hand it to you, Chantal, I am sorry to inform you…but we learned more facts about Sam."

Rachel felt her sister stiffen, as she whispered.

"Say the words, Tom…he was married, wasn't he?"

Tom gawped at Rachel – had she known? Rachel stared wide-eyed and clasped a hand to her mouth.

"Yes, Chantal, he was married. Did you know?" Rachel asked.

Chantal shook her head. "No, he didn't tell me, but he was always so vague about his family. He once mentioned he was brought up to be a Roman Catholic but had walked away from the church, because of their viewpoints over certain issues. I asked him to explain, but he changed the subject. I was aware of the Roman Catholic teaching regarding divorce, and I guessed it was a possibility."

Darcy was looking perplexed. "Why couldn't he divorce his wife?" she enquired.

Rachel shook her head at Darcy's bluntness.

"The Roman Catholic Church have strong viewpoints regarding divorce, Darcy, it is only permitted in exceptional circumstances." Tom handed the newspaper notice to Chantal.

Rachel watched as her sister's trembling fingers unfolded the sheet of paper. The room fell silent. It felt icy, matching the sombre mood of its occupants. Chantal read the stark, chilling notice, without comment, then refolded the paper. Tom nodded to Darcy. She moved over and sat on the floor in front of her aunt. "We are all here to support you, Tallie, but there is something else you need to know."

Chantal looked up at her niece, puzzled. "Something else...what do you mean?"

Darcy balanced on her knees and reached out for her aunt's hands. "A week after our first visit to Edinburgh, Josh, Henri and I returned to locate the church and try to find an address for the family – just in case you wished to make contact," she explained.

Chantal began shaking her head. "No, no, I won't do that," she uttered. "What is this 'something else' I need to know?" Chantal's gaze penetrated her niece's eyes.

Darcy was shaking; she squeezed Tallie's hands. "I'm sorry, Tallie...but there is a child. Sam had a daughter called Francesca. I talked to the priest, and he mentioned Sam's daughter – he thought I was her friend...so, she could be my age, or older."

Chantal pushed Darcy out of the way, shrugged her sister's arm from her shoulder, then ran out of the room. Rachel attempted to follow her distraught sister, but Tom grabbed her arm.

"Leave her, Rachel," he ordered. "Let her be alone in her grief. It's been overwhelming for her – but there was no easy way to relay our findings. It will take time for her to come to terms with her loss coupled with these revelations."

* * *

Opening the back door, Darcy slipped out into the early morning mist. It was thick and gloomy, and she shivered, but suspected another delightful summer's day was in store, once the mist cleared. Darcy loved early mornings – those magical hours before the buzz of the day began. Most of her friends liked to lie in bed and struggled to get up in time for school, but not Darcy. It was five days since she'd conveyed the distressing news concerning Sam's family, to her aunt. In the intervening time she'd seen little of her, as she was only joining the family for mealtimes, then excusing herself to return to her room.

"We've got to do something to cheer Tallie up," Darcy remarked to her mother. "She'll go into a depression if she stays in that room much longer. I think we should suggest taking her up to Edinburgh so she can visit Sam's memorial...it might help."

Rachel was doubtful but indicated she would seek a suitable opportunity to mention it.

Meanwhile Darcy was harbouring a little secret. The day of Chantal's arrival was the day Henri Dukas had declared his love for her! It felt like a little treasure she was holding in her hands. The 'spider' incident was so innocent, but its impact on Darcy was electrifying. Her insides melted whenever Henri was close. He was so devastatingly handsome – she'd been aware of it previously, but now...oh...she was walking on cloud six, seven, eight and nine!

Every time he looked in her direction his eyes seemed to caress her features, sending ripples of anticipation running through her being. She was desperate to seek him out and continue their appreciation of one another, but finding Henri by himself was challenging – almost as if he was avoiding her. This morning, she was acting on a hunch – she knew he worked in the greenhouse in the early morning. She entered the large glass structure and noted movement in the bottom corner. She tried sneaking up quietly, but to no avail. He was standing with his back towards her. "I'm not deaf, Darcy Smallwood – what are you doing here?" he asked turning.

Darcy stared. Henri was looking unusually 'rugged'. His dark hair was uncombed, his clothes creased and his beard unkempt. Beads of perspiration stood on his brow. "Darcy – leave me alone. I need to wash and change before breakfast. I look bedraggled, so please go away."

Darcy grinned – she rather liked his rough appearance. "It doesn't bother me, Henri. I just wanted to be alone with you again. Have you been avoiding me?"

Henri sighed. "Yes, I have... we must put distance between us, Darcy. What happened the other day was delightful…but untimely. I cannot show you the affection I feel, without your father's approval. I risk my work here coming to an end and I want it to continue – so do you see my dilemma?"

Darcy pulled a face. She'd already guessed how Henri would view this 'thing' between them. "I know, I know but can't we meet sometime and enjoy a little more of what we experienced the other day? Tennis perhaps?"

Henri turned to resume his task. "Perhaps," he said in resignation.

Darcy clapped her hands. "Yippee…I'll book a court," she responded, and walked quickly towards the door.

"Stop!" called Henri. "Come here."

Darcy turned and cautiously approached the young Frenchman. Within seconds she was enveloped by two large arms. His kiss was rough, deep and possessive. Darcy melted into his intense embrace. Then he pulled away. "Go, Darcy…I am struggling to control my emotions. Please forgive me." Darcy turned away.

"Nothing to forgive, *monsieur*," she replied, stepping out into the cool morning air.

Chapter 16

Anticipating precious time with his sweetheart, who was tantalising his every waking moment, was soon dashed. As Henri and Darcy stepped out of the door, to go to the tennis court after supper, Chantal ran after them.

"Do you mind if I tag along?" she asked, following them down the drive. "My dear sister is stifling me, and I trust you two not to interrogate me! Apart from that, I want to see your skills – I suspect you two are fiercely competitive on the tennis courts – am I correct?"

The young couple were surprised how light-hearted Chantal appeared as they walked to the park. Once the match was underway Chantal let her cares slip away as she enjoyed the ups, downs, twists and turns of the youngsters' antics. But just before the final set finished, with Henri in the lead, he stumbled and grasped his leg, unable to complete the game.

"What's wrong?" called Darcy, running to his side.

"I don't know...my hip seemed to lock...it's easing now. I don't think I can continue, so you can claim victory and add it to your tally." He grinned.

Chantal joined them, asking what had happened.

"Have you sustained an injury?" Chantal enquired, but Henri dismissed the incident and after a brief rest they walked back to Meckleridge House.

"Any thoughts about a future career?" Chantal asked Darcy, as they walked.

"Yes, Tallie. I want to be a journalist."

"Oh, my...how have you arrived at that decision?"

Darcy was keen to share her recent experiences in Edinburgh but was unsure how her aunt would view her involvement.

"I would love to write an article for the forthcoming royal wedding – from the princess's viewpoint. How she feels; how she reacts; what she sees. It's just an idea ...for now. But I also found researching our Edinburgh trips fascinating. I loved visiting the newspaper offices."

"What appeals to you about journalism?" Chantal continued, sensing how animated her young niece was with the subject.

"Discovering new stories – I like the aspect of detective work associated with story backgrounds, scratching beneath the surface to reveal facts. I'm hoping my ability to speak French will help – I might get some overseas assignments!"

"Was it your idea to visit the church where Sam's service was held, Darcy?"

The young girl felt her cheeks flushing and nodded. "Perhaps I should have left things the way they were. If it hadn't been for me, you would not have known about Sam's wife and child."

Chantal reached out and took Darcy's hand. "No recriminations, Darcy. It's better that I know. Now, here's a suggestion – shall we visit Edinburgh, so you can show me what you investigated?"

Darcy's eyes lit up; perhaps her research was being valued after all.

For the third time in a month Darcy, Josh and Henri visited the Scottish capital – this time accompanied by Chantal.

"I think you will make a splendid reporter," remarked Chantal on the train journey north. "I can just see your name at the end of a newspaper article...written by our foreign correspondent, Darcy Smallwood. It's got a ring to it...go for it, Darcy, follow your dreams!"

Henri beamed across the carriage at Darcy.

Arriving in Edinburgh, Chantal treated the three youngsters to a hearty meal, much to Josh's delight.

"You've made a friend for life, Tallie. Feeding my little brother before we set off to the outskirts of the city was a sensible idea, otherwise he would nag us."

Josh gave his sister a dirty look as they set off for Abbeyfield. The mood turned sombre as the group approached the church. The friendly Father Quentin was nowhere to be seen as Darcy and Chantal entered the building. The weather was dry, but dull, and the place felt cold and uninviting, without the sun shining through the stained-glass windows. After sitting for a while, they re-joined the boys outside. Darcy kept quiet. Her mother had advised her to let Chantal have space. 'Give her time to reflect, Darcy... don't chatter all the time,' she'd warned.

The floral tributes were no longer in evidence. Only the stark wooden cross, devoid of sentiment, bore Sam's name. Darcy, Josh and Henri remained on the path after indicating the memorial marker. Surprisingly, Chantal spent only a couple of minutes staring at the cross before she rejoined the young people. Darcy searched her aunt's face expecting to see tears...but none existed.

Chantal noted the look on the young girl's face. "It's only a piece of wood, Darcy," she exclaimed. "It doesn't mean Sam's dead. Now, show me this house then we can go back into the city."

Darcy was flabbergasted. They walked the short journey from the church to the residence – Sam's family home. Again, Chantal showed no inkling of emotion as she peered through the gates. She only made a brief comment. "Well, well, so that's where he grew up."

Darcy was puzzled as they walked back into the city. She'd expected an outpouring of grief, yet her aunt showed none of the normal reactions to viewing a loved one's grave and former childhood home. Having left the church and house, she decided to talk to Chantal.

"So, Tallie, this brings your years of hope to a conclusion – has it helped to see Sam's final resting place?"

Chantal kept walking. "Darcy, I still believe Sam is alive. No service or memorial marker bearing his name will convince me otherwise. Thank you for all your hard work researching the church and house – I appreciate your efforts. I understand his family would need to sort their affairs – they couldn't continue without legalising things – a house like that will need to be bequeathed to somebody, but if there's a daughter...she will no doubt inherit it."

They walked in silence for a few minutes.

"I knew Sam, Darcy...I loved him...he loved me. There must be a good reason why he chose to leave his family. I continue to hope."

The group returned to the city centre and after looking at the shops, they took the train back to Durham. Chantal engaged Josh and Henri in conversation, but Darcy remained quiet – she was dumfounded by her aunt's reaction to the day's events.

* * *

"Oh, Peg...that's so disappointing. We were looking forward to a repeat of last summer. But we understand. He has new responsibilities now."

Rachel was hovering in the hallway, listening to the one-sided telephone conversation. She mouthed to Tom, 'Christmas?' Tom nodded.

"Peg...Rachel is standing beside me and is asking if you can visit at Christmas?" Tom listened to his sister's response. "Good." He continued: "So, it's a possibility – let us know and enjoy whatever time you can manage to spend, having holiday with the family. Give our love to everyone." He ended his call.

"What's up?" queried Darcy, descending the stairs.

"The Thibaults are unable to be with us this summer," Tom replied, sighing. "Uncle Pierre has been promoted in his work – he's the equivalent of a chief inspector in the police force now. Unfortunately, he cannot be out of the country, so his leave will have to be taken in France. However, they might be able to come here for Christmas."

Darcy pulled a face. "Aww, that's a shame. I was looking forward to seeing Jonty and Sylvie," she commiserated.

Over supper Rachel shared the news with Chantal, Josh and Henri, who were equally disappointed. It meant Chantal would be travelling solo again, when she returned to France. "How long are you staying, Henri?" she enquired, unsure of the young Frenchman's plans.

Henri looked over at Tom.

"Well, initially it was for six months," Tom explained, sitting back in his chair. "It was something I intended discussing with Peg and Pierre. The six months will be up in November, but if you would like to extend your time, Henri, I am happy for you to continue. Considering this news from France, you could stay on until Christmas, then travel back with the Thibaults when they return."

Henri's face lit up at the suggestion. "Yes, Tom, that arrangement appeals to me!" he declared.

Darcy was helping with the dishes. Chantal had retired to her room, complaining of a headache. "Has Tallie talked to you about the Sam Carter issue?" Darcy asked her mother. "I get the impression she's avoiding talking about it with me," she remarked – it was a week since they had visited Edinburgh.

"Only briefly," replied her mother. "She's adamant she won't be sending a condolence letter, which I understand – his parents are most likely unaware of her existence. But she is still convinced Sam is alive."

Darcy rattled around the kitchen, putting crockery and cutlery in cupboards. "Honestly, Mother, I think she's living in a false world. It's as if this feeling she has, that Sam is still out there, is somehow going to make him appear – just like the genie in the bottle appearing when you rub the lamp! Mother, she is totally disillusioned. Her reaction in Edinburgh showed me this…no emotion whatsoever. I might as well have been showing her some sightseeing attraction." Darcy pulled out a chair and sat down opposite her mother.

"It's there in black and white in the obituary. It's reported in the newspaper account of the ship sinking and his name is on a memorial cross in a graveyard. He's gone… he's dead…end of the trail! I'm beginning to lose patience with her," Darcy exclaimed in exasperation.

Rachel looked at her daughter – she was so full of life and vigour. On the threshold of a new career and exciting relationships. It was hard for her to relate to Chantal's viewpoint.

"I know, Darcy, I see your point, but she's only here for another week so let's make it a good one for her. I suggest we refrain from discussing it with her anymore. Once she's back in France maybe she will come to accept the situation. Our task is to help her enjoy the remainder of her holiday. I suggest a shopping trip to Newcastle; maybe a day at the coast and an outing up to Trespershields, if I can persuade your father to go."

Shopping in Newcastle was such a treat for the three ladies, although clothes rationing affected their purchases. Rachel, who possessed a keen eye for fashion, was wowed by the 'New Look' which was launched earlier in the year. The full skirt styles appealed to the ladies. Rachel studied the garments; she was adept with her sewing machine and took note of the designs, hoping to replicate them if she found some suitable material. Tom had encouraged Rachel to spend the clothing coupons. Chantal was a cautious buyer, preferring to stick with the utilitarian styles worn during the war, but was persuaded to buy a new day dress. Darcy was fascinated with shoes and bought a new pair.

"I'm exhausted," exclaimed Rachel, as they returned home.

Tom made a cup of tea after collecting them from the station.

"Are we being treated to a fashion show this evening, ladies?" he asked mischievously.

"Perhaps," replied Rachel, fluttering her eyelids at him.

"Oops, I'd better take my cuppa with me, I've got an appointment," Tom declared, consulting his watch, then disappeared off to his office. His appointment was with Henri. He was unsure as to why the young Frenchman was asking to speak with him privately, but they'd arranged to meet at six o'clock, half an hour before supper.

"Come in," Tom responded to the tap on his office door. Henri was freshly groomed and looking smart after a day working in the gardens. "Now, Henri, I hope this is a positive request. I'd miss your assistance and contributions if you were to return to France early." He waited until Henri was seated.

"No, Tom, I am loving my work here in England and I wish to repeat the situation next summer...if you'll let me return. My botanical studies are intriguing. I'm so grateful for this personal tuition – you are a great teacher. I'm excited to see the outcomes of our experimental work."

Tom felt flattered and assured the young man the opportunity would be there next year.

Henri fidgeted in his seat for a few seconds, then began his well-rehearsed speech. "The reason for this meeting, Tom, is to ask something personal. Over the months I have lived here," he paused and coughed, "I have developed a fondness for your daughter. Until recently I was unsure it was reciprocated, but since Darcy has ended her friendship with Grady, I have conversed with her in a more meaningful way, and I believe the feeling is mutual."

Tom raised his eyebrows somewhat surprised, as Henri continued.

"However, I realise my residing in your home could theoretically make a liaison between Darcy and I... rather awkward."

Tom smiled; he needed to put Henri at ease, before the young man tied himself in knots.

"Henri." He smiled across his desk. "Excuse me for interrupting, but I suspect you are wanting to take my daughter out on a date and wish for my approval...am I correct?" Henri sighed audibly.

"*Oui,* monsieur...I mean...yes, sir, I would."

Tom stood, walked around his desk and patted Henri on the shoulder. "Of course you can ask her out, Henri. You are a fortunate young man to have caught her attention. Just let me know where and when, so I won't be sending out a search party to look for her."

The relief showed on Henri's face, as he left Tom's office.

* * *

The North Sea coast always brought excitement for the Smallwood family. Darcy loved visiting the beach. From being a small child the pleasure she derived from splashing about in the waves, building sand creations and searching for sea creatures, amounted to hours of fun. Even teenage years brought new experiences for her.

"Race you," she called to Henri as soon as the older generation had settled themselves in some deckchairs. Darcy flew off at speed, shoes abandoned. Josh had remained at home as the others squashed into Tom's car. Living in northwest Durham afforded a choice of seaside venues but Whitley Bay, just over an hour's drive away, was their favourite rendezvous.

An array of shells caught Darcy's attention as she bent to pick them up, allowing Henri to catch up. "Here," she called, throwing them to him. "Put them in your pocket. I always take a collection home with me."

Henri rubbed the sand away and admired the tiny shapes. Since his *tête-à-tête* with Tom, he'd been hoping for an opportunity to ask Darcy out on a date. They paddled in the sea, chatting generally about the location and seaside adventures.

"Darcy, I spoke to your father concerning our friendship," Henri began.

"Oh, Henri...surely not...I mean it's such an old-fashioned thing to do, these days," she admonished. "What did he say?"

The sea was encroaching the shore, and they jumped to avoid getting wet.

"Yes, I know it's not the way to go about things these days, but I wanted our friendship to be acceptable to him, because I live in your home. Your parents have been so kind to me, and your father is teaching me so much. I would love to return next year, so it seemed only right to seek his approval. Good news is…he's happy about it!" Henri chuckled, as Darcy reached up and gave him a peck on the cheek.

"Oooo – you are so gallant, Henri Dukas!"

Their eyes connected. Henri was so pleased he had paved the way to court this beautiful young woman, even if his actions did appear 'old-fashioned'.

"So, *ma chérie*…where can we go to celebrate our first date?"

Darcy looked thoughtful. "I would have suggested the local cinema, but there's a possibility we could bump into Grady Forrester…so perhaps we could take a train into Newcastle one afternoon, if Dad would let you finish early, then we could go for a meal and visit the cinema afterwards. But I think we should wait until Tallie goes back, okay?" Darcy deliberately splashed Henri.

"Oh, you want to play games, do you?" he laughed, as Darcy ran off. Henri soon caught up as they continued to splash the water with their feet.

"Stop, stop," called Darcy, breathlessly. "No more – I have no dry clothes with me," she squealed.

Henri reached out, took her hand and brought it to his lips.

"You are so delightful, *ma chérie*." They sauntered back, hand in hand, to join the family.

* * *

The following morning at breakfast, Chantal made a request. "Can we squeeze in a visit to The Bungalow before I return, please?"

Rachel put down her toast and motioned to her husband. "See, I told you Chantal would want to visit The Bungalow before she went home!" she exclaimed.

Chantal looked perplexed. "Is there a problem?" she enquired.

Rachel shook her head. "The only problem is inside Tom's head. The place needs repairing, and my dear husband has been full of good intentions all summer – none of which have materialised."

Tom scowled. "Give me a break, Rachel. I've been occupied elsewhere. It's not that bad, Chantal, but I admit we've let things slip during the last couple of winters. Last winter's prolonged snowfall has compounded the problems."

Chantal looked sheepish. "Oh dear, have I stirred something? I have such happy memories of Trespershields and even if we don't go inside, just to have a walk along the riverbank would be pleasant."

Rachel smiled. "Of course we'll go to The Bungalow, Chantal. I'm only having a go at Tom, because when I suggested visiting, he said it was a ridiculous idea because the place will be a mess."

"The place needs to be pulled down, if you ask me," muttered Darcy, buttering her toast.

Tom was on the defence. "Nobody is asking you, Darcy Smallwood, so keep your opinions to yourself. It was a haven for us during the hotel years, and you and Josh enjoyed many happy hours of play up there."

Darcy rolled her eyes. "Yes, Daddy, but we've grown up now, we're not little kiddywinks anymore," she mocked. "The place is surplus to requirements – so demolish it and stop renting the field!"

Tom was annoyed and scowled at his daughter. "When I want your opinion, I'll ask for it, young lady. Your mother and I have no plans to part with The Bungalow. Now the subject has been raised, I say we go up tomorrow – all of us, and assess what needs to be done. Perhaps you," he pointed at his daughter, "and Henri can cycle up to 'Green Pastures' to join us!"

Darcy pulled a face at her father.

"This bungalow…you have another residence in the area?" asked a bewildered Henri.

Darcy almost choked on her toast. "Don't hold your breath, Henri…wait until you see it…it's a mess on stilts!"

* * *

A wave of nostalgia washed over Chantal as Tom brought the car to a halt in the field at Trespershields. This place was always the backdrop to her happy memories with Sam.

A particular weekend in the autumn of 1938 had been a defining moment in their relationship. The rarity of having a weekend free from work, and Rachel's suggestion they spend time by themselves, had proved magical. Time stood still, as they spent an idyllic day and night away from interruptions and distractions and expressed their love. It was the last significant occasion they had spent together. After that weekend, their time off was limited. They only managed to snatch a few hours together at the end of a shift, but it was always tempered by the weariness, stress and strains of their demanding jobs. At Christmas, Sam had spent his dutiful two weeks with his family and at the start of the new year Chantal was required to return to France...it was nine years since that sublime weekend.

Chantal felt a tear trickle down her cheek and realised she was sitting alone in the car. The others were inside the wooden structure lovingly referred to as The Bungalow. They can't pull it down, thought Chantal, as she left the car and walked up the rickety steps onto the veranda, which ran along the front of the building. She fingered the plaque bearing the name 'Green Pastures'.

A cacophony of noise invaded her ears as the family surveyed the damage. "This place smells damp...just look at the state of that...we've had another leak." The comments were flying thick and fast as Chantal stepped inside.

She surveyed the small living room which included a sink, cupboard and a small stove. Yes, it was in disrepair.

The smell of dampness pervaded her nostrils, mingled with mustiness. In one corner daylight was evident through a hole in the ceiling. It was downtrodden...but to Chantal it was a haven of love. Tom was looking at the damage, muttering to himself. "I might have guessed that repair I did last year, would give way under the weight of all that snow."

The water penetration had caused damage, rendering the soft furnishings useless. Chantal walked across to the bedrooms – two of them, both tiny, leading off from the living space. It was a basic structure. The dividing walls between the rooms were made from thin wood and provided limited privacy. She opened the door to the bedroom overlooking the rear of the property – the door squeaked and jerked, shaking the thin walls. The double bed filled the room with barely space to walk around it. Limp curtains, sagging in the centre, hung on a wire suspended above the window. A dark grey blanket was strewn across the mattress and pillow.

"Tom," gasped Rachel, from behind Chantal, "I think we've had some uninvited guests." Tom appeared, peering over the ladies' heads. "Look at that blanket," she added, pointing. It was an army issue blanket – rough and grey. "That's not ours – it's disgusting." She turned and stepped back into the living room, colliding with Darcy who had just arrived; Henri was standing in the doorway.

"What's disgusting?" asked Darcy, having overheard her mother's comment.

"Looks like we've had a tramp taking shelter in here over the winter."

Tom added, "There's only one thing for it...a bonfire. Bundle that blanket, pillows, curtains and cushions, towels – any soft stuff, and take it outside. Josh, Henri... find some wood and lay a fire out front."

Between them they carried the mildewed items outside. The boys soon had a fire going and bit by bit the items burned. As they watched the flames licking around the soft furnishings, Darcy turned to her brother. "Can you cycle back with me and let Henri ride in the car?"

"Why?" asked Josh.

"Henri had a problem with his leg on the way up, we needed to stop until it eased."

Chantal overheard and looked over at Henri. "Was it the same sort of problem you experienced playing tennis?"

Henri nodded. "Similar... I'm fine now, but I'll accept the offer of a ride home in the car, thank you."

Darcy nudged Henri. "Well, and what do you think of our country residence...posh, isn't it?" she jibed.

"Just you wait," sneered Rachel. "New curtains, cushions, pillows, bedding, towels and I think I'll replace the crockery and cutlery...provided Mr Smallwood attends to the repairs. We have plenty of surplus items from the hotel days. All the place needs now is a good scrub and a fresh lick of paint!"

Henri smiled. "I think you have *'une belle maison'*, *mes amis*!"

Chapter 17

C hantal sighed as she relaxed in the conservatory, after supper. Tomorrow she would travel home to France. "I always feel as if I leave a piece of myself here in England when I return to France. Thank you once again for having me to stay and making me feel so welcome." She looked at Tom, Rachel and Darcy – the boys had gone to their rooms. "Time seems to stand still in Malhaven, unlike my country, where signs of the war are still apparent."

"Did you have much contact with the occupying forces, during the war, Chantal?" asked Rachel.

So far, Chantal had avoided talking about her wartime experiences. She looked pensive – should she tell her family?

"Unfortunately, I did," she replied. "It was unavoidable – they were everywhere. Often my midwifery duties involved night visits – babies do not always oblige by being born during daytime hours. My bag was searched at checkpoints on many occasions, even though I carried papers explaining my reason for travelling at night."

Darcy stared at her aunt in disbelief. "You mean a German soldier searched your bag while you watched?"

Chantal nodded. "I was fortunate, they did not find anything."

Darcy was curious. "But why would they search a midwife's bag – it was an unlikely place to be carrying anything suspicious?"

The colour drained from Chantal's face and Rachel noticed. "Oh, Chantal…did you…were you?"

Chantal looked down and fidgeted with her handkerchief, pulling it tightly. "Yes, Rachel, I did. I helped my country in whatever way I could, which involved me being a vital link, in a chain for the French Resistance." She raised her eyes. "I'm telling you this in secret…you are the only ones who know outside of our network."

Darcy was sitting on the edge of her seat. Tom was staring at his young sister-in-law in disbelief. Rachel reached out and grabbed Chantal's arm.

"It's all in the past now, but it was real at the time… and frightening. I was involved in passing messages via the local boulangerie. I 'ate' a lot of bread in those days… supposedly." She smiled…but it was an empty smile. "I took the coded messages to my patients' homes, under the cover of attending to the mothers – there were many 'false alarms' in those pregnancies, necessitating my attendance."

"Oh, Chantal, you must have been so brave, and to do it without any family to support you. I feel honoured to have a sister who would risk her life to help others." Rachel squeezed her sister's hand.

"You do what you must do, Rachel. War makes people inventive. It causes them to step outside their comfortable places. I look back now and wonder how I was so brave and confident...but I don't regret it. I like to think I helped others to escape or to be warned of a raid. I know no outcomes, I was only a link in a chain, but I felt I did my part to help to win the war."

Darcy listened in amazement. Stories like this belonged in books or films...not with your aunt – a humble midwife.

The atmosphere was taut. Everyone seemed lost in their own thoughts.

"It's a relief to talk about it, but please, everyone, respect my secrecy...it is for your ears only," Chantal remarked.

Tom smiled at Chantal. "Thank you for sharing your experiences, Chantal. You have our word...we will keep your confidence. Now, you have an early start in the morning."

Darcy yawned. "Yes, I think I'll go to bed. It's been great to see you again, Tallie. I hope all the information we found for you about Sam, will help you to come to terms with what happened."

Chantal stood and walked over to the fireplace, resting her hands on the mantelshelf. She looked deep in thought. Then she turned and directed her words at her young niece.

"Darcy, hope is an active ingredient in my life. The more hope I have the more real it becomes. I'm not about to 'come to terms' with what happened. I've thanked you for uncovering the information. It's a setback, yes, to learn of Sam's marital state and the existence of a child... but setbacks toughen me. Hope helps me to keep going. I live and breathe *hope* in finding Sam...I will not give up!"

Darcy stood and shook her head. "Tallie...you are lying to yourself. All this 'hope' talk...it's futile...face the facts and move on. I've tried to help you, but you just keep burying your head in the sand." Her voice became more agitated as she eyeballed her aunt.

"Darcy, that's enough," urged Tom, but aunt and niece were locked in their words.

"Accept it, Tallie. It's the truth – Sam Carter is dead... he's gone...he's not coming back. I want to shake you and pull you out of this ridiculous belief you possess. You've just told us how you risked your life serving your country. Face facts, Tallie...black is black...white is white, but you are living in a bubble of grey and I can't agree with you!"

"Darcy, stop it," yelled Rachel.

Tom raised his eyebrows and motioned to his wife to stop interfering.

Chantal stiffened. "Well, you've made yourself very clear, Darcy Smallwood. Life does not always go according to plan. One day you may realise what an active role hope can play in someone's life. We are going to have to disagree over this...now I think I'll go to bed. I have

a long day of travel ahead of me tomorrow. Goodnight!"
Chantal left the room.

Rachel eyed her tempestuous daughter. "Darcy, you
must apologise to your aunt before she leaves."

But Darcy was resolute. "No way, Mother...she's a
fool, living in a false world. The sooner she accepts it the
better it will be. You and dad are not helping her." Darcy
stormed out of the room.

* * *

SIX MONTHS LATER,
SPRING 1948

"Darcy...post for you!" shouted Tom, flicking through
the recently delivered pile of letters. He blinked as a vision
of loveliness skipped down the stairs to take two letters
bearing her name. Tom swallowed – his daughter was no
longer a child. She was blossoming into a beautiful young
woman, so similar in looks to his wife...but different
in habits.

"Remember, miss – used envelopes go in the bin.
Do not leave them lying around for others to tidy!" His
daughter had not inherited Rachel's fastidiousness.

"Mmmm," came the distant reply, as Darcy opened
an envelope. "Golly, I can't believe it...I've done it. Dad...
look. I've won that competition...it's incredible." Darcy
was staring wide-eyed at a typewritten letter, bearing the

heading DAILY SKETCH YOUNG JOURNALIST COMPETITION.

Tom looked over her shoulder and read the contents.

'Dear Miss Smallwood,

It is with great pleasure we announce the judge's decision of the Young Journalist of the Year competition for 1947. Your entry 'Behold the Beauty' has been awarded first prize. We wish to offer you, our congratulations. You are invited to attend our offices in London, on Tuesday 4th May at 11am where you will be presented with your certificate and a cheque for £10. An invitation is extended to you and a companion, to tour our offices and printing works on that occasion. Please sign the enclosed receipt accepting our offer and return it at your earliest convenience.

Yours sincerely,

Frank Thompson, Editor.'

Tom hugged his excited daughter. "Congratulations, Darcy. Well done. It's a great achievement. I guess this shows you could be a journalist after all," he chuckled.

Darcy was beaming. "Dad, there's no *could be* about it. I *am* going to become a journalist. This is proof I have talent. I've already made enquiries about taking a secretarial course to learn shorthand and typing."

Tom nodded; he knew this, but still hoped his daughter would choose a more suitable career.

After sharing her news with her mother and brother, Darcy wandered upstairs to the privacy of her bedroom to read her second letter...a letter from France.

Ma Chérie,

I count the days, no I count the hours until I can hold you in my arms and kiss your sweet, inviting lips. My heart pounds with anticipation. Oh, my darling, these weeks without you have been unbearable. My sleep is peppered with sweet dreams of your graceful figure; your beautiful blonde curls; your enticing smile; your beguiling manner; your mischievous comments and those adorable lips. Je t'aime, ma chérie. How I long to whisper those words in your ears. But back to reality...

Your father will be pleased to hear I have completed the reading programme he outlined for me. Now, I am ready to put into practice what I have learned in theory. My ticket is purchased; my suitcase is packed; my financial tasks are complete, and I will be with you on 1st April. Au revoir, ma petite fille – not long now,

Your beloved, Henri xxxxxxxxxxxx

Darcy held the letter close to her chest and sighed. It was almost three months since her beloved Henri had returned to France. Her aunt, uncle and cousins had spent ten days over the festive season in northeast England. The house rang with laughter and good cheer, but for Darcy the festivities heralded her parting from Henri.

From making their courtship official, the pair had become inseparable. Darcy was madly in love with the young Frenchman, who was celebrating his twenty-first birthday in February 1948. It was necessary for him to be resident in France at that time to complete the legalities of his inheritance from his parents. From that date Pierre was no longer his legal guardian. He was a young man of independent means and received guidance about investing his assets wisely. On his return to England, Henri Dukas would have healthy financial prospects. This year Tom was making Henri an employee at the Meckleridge Estate, rewarding him for his work, minus his living expenses.

During their separation Darcy had celebrated her eighteenth birthday. She held the anticipation should Henri propose to her during his summer stay, then maybe her father would approve a long engagement. To wear Henri's ring would be such a joy and let everyone know of their betrothal...but this was all speculation on Darcy's behalf.

Yet one issue remained unresolved – her estrangement from her Aunt Chantal. The morning after their disagreement last August, Chantal had returned to

France. Aunt and niece did not say goodbye. Darcy knew the time of Chantal's departure but made no attempt to bid her farewell.

Only one item of correspondence had passed between them in the intervening months and Chantal was unable to join the families for the Christmas holiday. Frequently, Rachel would mention the situation to her headstrong daughter, but she refused to apologise. Likewise, Rachel pleaded with her sister in their regular letters, to reach out as the senior, to attempt to resolve the matter. Chantal also maintained a steely resolve, *'Darcy may be young, Rachel, but she expressed her views clearly. She cannot accept that hope is my waking dream. I live and breathe hope in a reunion with Sam and until Darcy accepts my viewpoint we will remain at odds.'*

It saddened Rachel – life was too short to harbour ill feelings. "Why can't Darcy and Chantal agree to disagree over the issue and move on?" she commented to her longsuffering husband.

Tom held Rachel tightly. "It's because they are too much alike, Rachel…they are both strong, determined women. What Chantal did during the war gives credence to her strength and we know how immovable Darcy can be, once she sets her mind to something. Your place is to be there for both as a sister and as a mother. Don't take sides. I'm sure, given time, the situation will resolve itself – you must be patient."

* * *

Darcy and Tom stood on the platform awaiting the arrival of the London train. Tom was watching his daughter's agitation. She was walking up and down, straining her neck for signs of the train, then returning to Tom's side, stepping from one foot to another and consulting her watch. "Relax, Darcy – all your anxiety won't make the train arrive any sooner."

"But, Dad, I can't believe I'm going to see him, touch him, kiss him again. These three months have been like torture – you don't understand."

Tom chuckled. "Oh, yes, I do. I know what it's like to be separated from the person you love. You seem to forget your mother and I were young once!"

Darcy stared at her father…how could he possibly know how she felt?

Tom emitted an audible sigh. This friendship between Henri and Darcy was consuming. He'd expected the weeks of separation would cool the ardour between the pair, but it seemed to have intensified their feelings. He'd envisaged Darcy going off to college, establishing an academic career then after a few years meeting her future life partner. But typical of his spirited young daughter, who wanted to live life at full speed – these possibilities were not on her horizons. This summer could raise all sorts of problems if Henri and Darcy's relationship were to accelerate. He must ensure Rachel gave Darcy a comprehensive talk about how to conduct themselves. Living under the same roof could present compromising circumstances.

Seconds after Henri stepped from the train, the young couple were locked in a tight embrace, heedless of the public nature of their location.

Tom coughed loudly. "Excuse me...please remember where you are," he rebuked them sharply. "Welcome back, Henri," he added, shaking the young Frenchman's hand, when they released each other. Tom felt invisible as they travelled the twelve miles from Durham to Malhaven. The young couple clung to one another in the back seat of Tom's car and after a few failed attempts at conversation, Tom resigned himself to his role as a chauffeur.

While Henri was unpacking, Tom spoke to his wife. "Rachel, about Henri and Darcy...we could have a potential problem on our hands."

Rachel grinned. "Young love, Tom...it's beautiful, isn't it? So free from the cares of the world – let them enjoy this blissful time."

Tom sighed; his wife was as bad as they were!

"Rachel, I'm being serious. They are so besotted with each other...it's dangerous...she is too young...you know what I mean. Please speak to her and warn her about the consequences."

Rachel placed her arms around Tom's neck. "Have you considered the possibility it might be 'the real thing'... and if it is, we can only advise."

Tom kissed his wife and squeezed her tightly. "I know all that...but I feel responsible. I was the one who offered for him to work and reside here. I admire him, like him and I would love to see them settle down together…but it's too soon…about five years too soon." They pulled apart as Josh came into the kitchen.

"Where's Henri? I haven't seen him yet," he asked.

"Oh, you'll see him at supper time, Josh, that is if he can pull himself away from your sister!"

Josh grinned. "Like that, is it? I take it the two lovebirds are re-united!"

* * *

Suppertime was full of chat, catching up with the news from France. Jonty was studying at university in Paris; Sylvie was excelling in her school subjects and her mind was set on becoming a veterinary surgeon. Pierre was finding his new role at work demanding, and Peg was holding everything together with her organisational skills.

"Have you told Henri about the writing competition?" asked Rachel.

"Yes," replied Henri. "I have received all the details – she's wonderful, isn't she?" remarked Henri, looking adoringly at Darcy.

Josh rolled his eyes.

Rachel then outlined their plans to visit London.

"You're coming, Henri," Darcy informed him. "I want you to be my companion when I tour the offices and printing works."

Rachel looked surprised; she'd assumed Tom would perform the role.

Tom read Rachel's mind and interjected. "Time enough to discuss the arrangements – it's a month away. Back to the present. Josh, Henri would you both be willing to set aside a couple of hours on Saturday, to help me carry out some repairs at The Bungalow?" Both young men nodded. "I haven't been up since doing a temporary repair last summer. Hopefully, it was enough to keep the rain out and the place should have dried out. But I need to do a proper repair, and I need assistance. I'm determined to get the place sorted for this summer."

Darcy accompanied the menfolk when they went to Trespershields on Saturday. Rachel stayed behind, planning to make new curtains in readiness for the makeover. Darcy bounded out of the car, and up the steps onto the veranda, followed by Henri.

"Can you reach up there?" she said, indicating the hiding place for the key – a groove set into the top of the door frame. Carefully she unlocked the door, ever mindful of an incident years ago when a bird had become trapped inside and flew into her face when she opened the door. She scanned the room before stepping inside. "Looks better, and smells better," she announced, as the others followed.

"Yes, that damp problem seems to have resolved. Now, lads – I need one of you up on the roof with me; the other will need to pass the tools when required." Tom scrummaged under the wooden structure to retrieve a ladder, then positioning it, climbed up followed by Henri. Slowly and carefully, Tom manoeuvred the new tarpaulin into position with Henri's help.

Thump! Thump! Thump! The hammering resonated on the roof. Darcy was mooching around inside. Her mother had issued instructions for her to pull the furniture and cupboards away from the walls and sweep the place thoroughly. She was about halfway through the task, when something caught her attention – an apple core. Sweeping it onto the shovel she observed the offending item – strange, she thought…it isn't mouldy. Surely if her dad had dropped it when repairing the roof last year, it would be mouldy by now. Senses on high alert, she opened the rear bedroom door and froze. She knew the curtains, along with the soft furnishings, had been destroyed in the bonfire last year, but hanging from the curtain wire was a rough piece of material – a makeshift curtain! She bounded outside to deliver her news.

"Dad, looks like that tra…" She stopped and stared up to the top of the ladder where Josh and her dad were carrying Henri down to the ground. "What's happened?" she shrieked, panicking.

"Oh, it's nothing, just that hip locking thing again. I'll sit for a few minutes then it will pass. I haven't experienced it for months. I probably twisted myself, climbing onto the roof," Henri explained, dismissing the incident.

While Henri was sitting on the veranda steps, Darcy showed her father the makeshift curtain and the recently discarded apple core.

"Yes, it looks like we have a regular vagrant enjoying our hospitality. Don't tell your mother. It's not a big deal – The Bungalow is bare at present, but once the new drapes and furnishings are replaced, I'll need to change the lock."

* * *

Receiving the prize for the competition afforded an opportunity for the Smallwoods and Henri to spend a long weekend in London.

"Tell me about your winning entry, Darcy," Henri asked on the train journey south. Darcy was still revelling in the excitement of it all.

"Well, you know Princess Elizabeth and Philip Mountbatten were married last November. They make such a lovely couple. I went to watch the newsreel of their wedding a few times. I was captivated by it all. I saw the competition advertised in dad's paper, so I wrote this article from Princess Elizabeth's point of view... how she felt...what she saw. I sent it off and forgot about it. I didn't think they would consider it, let alone choose me as the winner!"

Henri was impressed.

Sightseeing in London, in post-war days, was a sad experience for Tom and Rachel. Their memories of visiting the capital before the war, were marred by evidence of the bombing and rebuilding work. To Henri, it was a wonderful opportunity to view the capital, having only been inside the stations. Two full days of sightseeing were accomplished. On Tuesday it was the visit to receive Darcy's prize.

On Monday night, as they were leaving the restaurant, Henri suggested to Darcy they should take a walk along the embankment. Rachel, Josh and Tom went back to the hotel. The air was balmy, the sun was setting, casting its golden glow over the river and the Houses of Parliament. They walked hand in hand and stopped to admire the view. Henri stood behind Darcy cradling her in his arms.

"This trip has been so special. It's been a delight to spend holiday time with your family." He turned her around to face him. "I didn't plan to do this tonight, but I want to ask you something." He reached out and stroked the side of her face sending shivers through her being. "*Ma chérie,* I love you so much...will you marry me, Darcy?"

She gasped. Henri looked so handsome, wearing a dark blue lounge suit, white shirt and blue tie. His dark hair and beard were neatly trimmed.

"Oh, Henri...*oui*...yes...I will."

Their lips met – his kiss was sweet and gentle.

"I should be down on one knee giving you a beautiful ring, but I did not anticipate this enchanted evening."

"I love you, Henri," she said, and he kissed her again.

"Of course, I must speak to your father... I expect he will want you to wait until you are twenty-one, *ma chérie*... but I hope he will give his consent to our engagement." Darcy nodded. "I want this to be the moment...the real moment, when I proposed to you. It will be our secret betrothal." Darcy's eyes were sparkling, as tears filled them. Henri gazed at her. "What's wrong?" he asked, concerned.

"Nothing, Henri, they are tears of happiness. My father will say I am too young, and we should wait until I have some life experience. Oh, why does age matter so much? I know it's a big step...but he can't take this moment from us. On the banks of the river Thames, we pledged our love to each other...we are engaged, Henri – even if I don't have a ring."

Henri pulled her into a loving embrace – it was a defining moment.

The presentation at the newspaper office was an informal event. Darcy met the runner up – a young man, who wrote his article from the perspective of the horsemen accompanying the entourage at the royal wedding. A photograph was taken as she received her certificate and cheque. Darcy was elated as she and Henri were given the tour along with the runner up. Once again, the sights and sounds of a busy newspaper office excited her. Meeting up with the family afterwards, they enjoyed a celebratory lunch.

"Make sure you order a copy of The Daily Sketch for Saturday," Darcy remarked to her father.

"We'll do better than that, Darcy...we'll have it framed!"

Chapter 18

"Look, Rachel," Tom nudged his wife. "Watch Henri...do you notice anything?" The family were walking into the station to catch their train north. The youngsters were walking in front.

"Er...I'm not sure what you mean," mumbled Rachel.

"Sometimes he limps," observed Tom. "I've noticed it a few times now. I think we should make an appointment at the doctors for him."

Rachel was puzzled. "Why? It's not our responsibility to do that, Tom. He's an adult."

"I know, but as his employer, I can suggest it. When he was helping me with the roof repairs up at The Bungalow, he called out in obvious pain – Josh and I had to help him down the ladder."

"Oh, yes, and I remember that time last year, when he couldn't cycle back home from Trespershields. I hope it's nothing serious – he is such an attractive, athletic young man, who seems destined to become our son-in-law."

Tom swallowed. "Come on, Rachel...that's a leap – Darcy's only eighteen!"

"What's age got to do with it," Rachel chuckled.

Darcy's euphoria from the journalist award soon evaporated. After the article appeared in the national press, she received letters of congratulations from friends and family. The local weekly newspaper carried the story, along with another photograph. Uncle Zac sent a bouquet of flowers, saying she'd taken her first step towards her future career in journalism. But Darcy's exams were looming, and she needed to spend her time studying. Even her free time with Henri was curtailed. He found his own work absorbing, so it was easy to keep occupied and Josh was encouraging him to learn to play cricket.

One morning, walking over to the greenhouses, Tom raised the subject he'd mentioned to Rachel. "Henri, I hope you won't take offence at this...but have you considered discussing your hip problem with a doctor?"

Henri was embarrassed. "No, Tom. It's an intermittent problem and it passes. During the three months I was in France, it didn't trouble me at all."

"How active were you during that time? Did you play any sport, go cycling?"

Henri looked thoughtful. "No, it was winter. Jonty was away at university, and I spent my time reading and sorting my financial affairs."

"It's just a suggestion, Henri, but I could make an appointment for you with our family doctor, if you would like to seek medical advice."

"That's kind of you, Tom – I'll consider it and let you know," he replied.

The young sweethearts contented themselves with a walk around the Meckleridge House grounds each evening after supper. They held hands, wandered and chatted about their days.

"Your dad suggested I seek medical advice concerning my hip problem," Henri informed Darcy. "What do you think?"

Darcy pulled a face. "That sounds a bit serious, Henri. Describe your leg problem – how do you assess it?"

Henri looked thoughtful. "It appears to be related to physical exertion, like that night playing a strenuous tennis match; the long cycle ride to The Bungalow and clambering about on the roof a few weeks ago at Trespershields. Yet, I'm playing cricket with Josh, and I've had no occurrences."

They stopped; Darcy snuggled into Henri's arms. "You're young, fit and athletic – is it painful?"

"When it happens it's a sharp pain, then it's more like stiffness in the joint, causing me to limp a bit but it eases when I rest." He bent down and kissed Darcy, lovingly.

"Perhaps, you should have it checked, Monsieur Dukas – I want a fit, able husband!" she jibed.

"Guess who I met today?" remarked Henri to Darcy, at the weekend. Darcy shook her head. "Your former boyfriend, Grady Forrester."

Darcy was shocked. "Never...where? I thought he was at university in York."

"Well, I told you I was learning to play cricket with Josh. He arranged to practise with a few of his friends this morning and let me join in. When we were finished, I was walking back into the pavilion when I bumped into him."

"What did he say?" enquired Darcy, remembering the last time the pair had met.

"Well, the look he gave me was deadly. He glowered at me and passed some pert comment about me having other sport to enjoy and didn't think I'd have time to play cricket."

"Did he mention me?" Darcy asked.

"Yes, said something about me keeping you entertained with my amorous French ways...but I ignored him," Henri replied.

"That guy is cheeky and impertinent. He's trouble, Henri, always trying to goad you. You did right to ignore him. He must be visiting his family for the weekend."

"Oh, changing the subject...I've got an appointment with your family doctor next week."

* * *

The long-promised makeover of The Bungalow took place the next weekend, but Darcy stayed at home studying. Rachel set to, giving the rooms a fresh coat of paint. Tom and Henri repaired some broken glass panes and replaced the lock on the door. Josh began clearing rubbish and debris caught under the wooden structure. The Bungalow was suspended on wooden supports, so it was a substantial task, which was long overdue and required another bonfire.

After helping Tom with the repairs, Henri wandered around the back of The Bungalow to clear more debris, while Josh attended to the fire. Something caught his attention. "Tom," he called, "does this belong to you?"

Tom went around the rear of the building to find Henri retrieving a large sack-like bag, pushed underneath the building. It resembled the kind of kit bag, used by servicemen in the forces.

Tom shook his head. "No, it doesn't belong to me, but let's see what's inside." The bag was constructed from substantial material and contained a tin plate and mug; cutlery; a towel; washbag and shaving items. There were a few articles of clothing and a blanket. Tom perused the contents.

"Oh dear," he remarked, "looks like our vagrant is still around. I'd hoped he'd decided to move on when he noticed we'd started tidying the place, a few weeks ago."

"Do you think he's an army man?" Henri asked, studying the items.

Tom shrugged. "Maybe...I can't help feeling sorry for the chap. For many men the war was devastating, but it's three years since it ended... so this guy must have a problem returning to his former life." Tom looked thoughtful, then replaced the items.

"Should I put it on the bonfire?" Henri asked.

Tom shook his head. "No, put it back, Henri. I don't intend to confiscate this chap's earthly possessions. I hope he takes the hint and moves on. Don't mention this to the ladies...let's keep it to ourselves."

By the end of the day, Tom and Rachel were satisfied with their work.

"All spruce and tidy," Rachel commented. "Next time, I'll hang the new curtains and replenish the cushions, pillows and bedding. This summer we are going to *use* The Bungalow," she announced, triumphantly.

Henri visited the doctor on Monday and mentioned it over supper that evening. "The doctor gave me a thorough examination today and couldn't find anything dislocated, but as a precaution he's advised me to see an orthopaedic consultant in Newcastle. It will take a couple of weeks before the appointment comes through."

"That's a sensible suggestion, Henri, but do you realise it will cost you financially?" Tom indicated.

Henri nodded. "Yes, a few guineas, I expect, but hopefully it will put my mind to rest."

Rachel looked pensive. "There's this new National Health Service being launched; remember we got a letter about it from the government. All medical, dental and nursing care costs are to be covered. It starts this month I think, but I doubt if it covers private consultations, like Henri's," she remarked.

"Yes, I've been reading about it in the newspaper. It's a brilliant idea," added Tom. "Let's hope it succeeds, but I think you're right about private consultations, you'll still need to pay for them."

Darcy scraped back her chair. "I've got another half hour's study to do, then I'll meet you, Henri," she announced and left the kitchen. Darcy's exams had started, and she was taking no chances.

"She deserves to get good results," Henri remarked in her wake.

* * *

TWO WEEKS LATER

"I can't believe I've finished school forever." Darcy was so relieved, as they made the journey into Newcastle for Henri's hospital appointment. She was driving – Tom having entrusted the car to her. "I'm free until my three-month secretarial course begins in September, so I'm going to enjoy the next two months. Uncle Zac has promised to speak to someone he knows at the Northern Echo and I'm going to write to the Newcastle Journal, and the local weekly paper, to see if they have any job opportunities."

"It will be so good to spend quality time with you again, *ma chérie*, now your exams are over," Henri commented. "And all sounds promising for your future career in journalism. All we need now is good news from this consultant," he added.

Understandably, Henri was nervous. His experience of hospitals was grim, having lost both his parents in recent years. He'd always been active where sports were concerned – even during The Occupation he'd managed to play tennis and football at school. Riding a bike was part of his everyday life and swimming was another activity he'd enjoyed regularly. The prospects of curtailing an athletic lifestyle, due to a physical problem, filled him with dread, but he must remain positive.

Darcy opted to wait outside the hospital. Henri followed the receptionist's instructions and was soon shown into a consulting room. After describing his problem, he underwent a lengthy examination involving various physical tests. The orthopaedic consultant was joined by a younger doctor, and both carried out individual assessments. Then he was asked to wait outside the room. He sat on a wooden form, in a long-tiled corridor – an antiseptic odour filled his nostrils. The enormity of the examination and the anxiety of the findings, weighed heavily on Henri's mind. His thoughts were punctuated at intervals with the echoing feet of a nurse or porter making their way along the high-ceilinged corridor. What if? Why? How? A range of scenarios panned out in his mind. He'd been asked repeatedly if he'd sustained any injuries to his leg or thigh. He'd combed his mind. Yes, he'd taken the odd tumble; been kicked; landed heavily during the various sports he'd engaged in...but nothing significant to his knowledge. The door opened and he was invited back into the consulting room.

Fear gripped Henri as he observed the consultant's face. "Monsieur Dukas," the man began. "Are you sure you want to hear my diagnosis without a relative present?"

The muscles in Henri's stomach clenched. "I have no relatives in England. Both my parents are deceased, and I have no siblings. I live in northeast England with my employer and his family. Please explain your findings," Henri replied.

The two doctors exchanged ominous glances, then the older man continued. "It is our combined opinion, Monsieur Dukas, that you are suffering from a condition called *osteonecrosis* which has affected your right hip joint. *Osteonecrosis* is a degenerative bone condition caused by an interruption to the blood supply," he paused. Henri felt his throat tightening. "This condition is often associated with a joint injury such as a dislocated hip, which damages the blood vessels surrounding the hip joint."

"I...I... can't remember a specific injury... but I have played a variety of sports all my life," Henri stuttered, as the doctor listened.

"Your symptoms – a locking hip with sharp pain, leading to stiffness which can affect the way you walk, sometimes causing you to limp, are all conducive to this diagnosis. However, you are young. In my experience this condition is usually prevalent in males aged 30 – 50 years of age – so at twenty-one you are young. With this early diagnosis you will be aware of the condition and can adapt your lifestyle."

Henri was stunned and shocked into silence. He wished now he'd asked Darcy to accompany him for support. He cleared his throat. "Is surgery an option?" he asked.

The younger doctor spoke. "Maybe…in the future. There have been experimental attempts at hip replacement for the condition, but it is a procedure which is yet to be approved."

Henri swallowed; he was struggling to concentrate. The young doctor offered him a welcome glass of water, as the older doctor continued.

"We are looking at managing your condition, Monsieur. You will need rest and immobilisation when the condition is evident. You may need to avoid weight bearing on the affected joint – this would be achieved using crutches."

Visions of wounded soldiers using crutches flashed before Henri's mind.

"We recommend a programme of physiotherapy at your local hospital. This will provide gentle, strengthening exercises. In summary, we advise gentle strolling. Try to avoid smoking, drinking alcohol and walking excessively – avoid squatting or sitting in a cross-legged position." The doctor looked at the athletic young man and rubbed his chin.

"You must learn what brings stress to the joint and avoid it – so we recommend no sporting activities. I am sorry to deliver such a difficult diagnosis to an active young man. Your physiotherapist will supply you with crutches, which you must use when you experience pain, but as you have already learned, rest brings relief. Do you have any questions?"

Henri was dumbfounded. Questions? The diagnosis had turned his young life upside down! This was unbelievable...too much to assimilate.

The doctor seemed to read his mind. "Monsieur Dukas, do you have someone – a friend or your employer – who could accompany you on another appointment next week? This is a serious condition, and you will need time to fully understand its implications. If we arrange another appointment for you for next week, please bring someone with you. Write down all your questions and we will try to answer them. In the meantime, I will arrange your physiotherapy and monitoring appointments, along with a fact sheet which I will give you on that occasion."

Henri nodded, barely taking in the consultant's words.

"I will write to the doctor who referred you, and it would be wise to make a future appointment with him. You must also consider your work implications – can anything be done to assist your physical movements?"

Henri watched as the older man stood, signalling the end of the consultation.

The younger doctor stepped forward and shook Henri's hand firmly. He looked only a few years older than Henri. "I am hopeful, Monsieur Dukas – medical procedures are advancing every day. If your condition is in its infancy and you can manage it…you may be able to undergo surgery in the future, which will enhance your lifestyle. Always remain hopeful."

Those words rang through Henri's head as he made his way out to the car park and the woman he loved.

Henri's devastating diagnosis was tangible in the Smallwood household that evening – it oozed from the walls. After relaying the doctor's diagnosis to Darcy on the return journey, Henri then disclosed it again to Tom, Rachel and Josh when they arrived back at Malhaven. Everyone was in disbelief. Each time Henri repeated the doctor's words, he felt the traumatic experience afresh. It was like a thunderbolt ripping through the house and their lives. All the family felt its effects. Josh would lose his cricket partner; Tom his protégé in his infant business enterprise; Rachel experienced the motherly instinct wanting to smother him with kindness, affection and protection.

But for Darcy…words could not describe Darcy's feelings. If it were possible… she fell deeper and deeper in love with the young Frenchman. It wasn't sympathy, it was a profound admiration for the man she adored and a desire to support him whatever it entailed. Thoughts of a life without him were unthinkable. No one had dared to mention the word *prognosis*…would his life expectancy be cut short? Thoughts in this direction only served to make Darcy determined to spend their lives together at all costs – such was her devotion for Henri Dukas.

"The young doctor said I must remain hopeful – medical advances are happening all the time – he indicated surgery may be an option in the future."

Darcy squeezed Henri's hand as they sat side by side on the settee in the conservatory.

"Then that's what we must do, Henri…we must stay positive…we must remain hopeful!"

The irony of Darcy's words struck a chord with Rachel, but she remained silent. It was later as she was lying in bed, she passed on her observation to Tom.

"It's ironic, Tom – did you hear Darcy's words to Henri…*'we must remain positive, we must remain hopeful'.*"

Tom was perplexed. "I'm not following you, Rachel – ironic?"

Rachel sighed. "In the light of this devastating diagnosis, Darcy and Henri are being told to remain hopeful that one day, in the future, surgery may be an option. For Chantal, she's spent ten years of her life holding on to hope. Darcy has fallen out with her because of it!"

Tom considered his wife's comment. "Yes…I see the comparison, but I'd say Henri's hopeful outlook has more going for it than poor Chantal. The object of her hope has not been seen for years and has been declared dead."

They lay in silence, each lost in their own thoughts.

* * *

Along the landing Henri was struggling to sleep. His diagnosis was life changing in all respects. Perhaps he should return to France – his homeland. It was unrealistic to expect the Smallwood family to continue their hospitality to accommodate his physical needs. He must return to Lyon – possibly find accommodation near to his aunt and uncle. Surely there would be work of a sedentary nature he could do – this diagnosis would not affect his ability to use his mind.

But as he reasoned with himself, he felt the wrench of the prospect of being separated from Darcy. He loved her with all his heart – she was his reason for living. He loved his work in England. He was sure adaptions could be applied to allow him to carry out his work from a sitting position. The physical side of gardening – stooping, crouching, kneeling, digging – perhaps with some assistance...? His mind trailed off. It was his future with Darcy, his beloved Darcy which was tearing him apart.

It was unfair to expect her to align herself to a man with an unsure future. She was so full of vitality – he could not ask her to take on the restraints of spending her life with...with...he swallowed as he articulated the word aloud...'*a cripple*'!

Tears streamed down his face as he sobbed into his pillow. The future which only a short while ago looked so beautiful – a future with his adorable Darcy, but now it was bleak. He knew...he must...release her from their secret promise to marry.

* * *

The car was stocked with soft furnishings, as Tom and Rachel prepared to visit The Bungalow. Newly made curtains in floral prints – former drapes from the windows of Meckleridge House, altered to fit the small windows of their country retreat. Freshly stuffed cushions in an array of patterns, a new carpet rug, blankets, sheets, pillows, tablecloths, towels.

"Rachel...that's enough," called Tom, as his wife continued to bring stuff into the hallway to be packed into the car alongside new crockery and kitchen items.

"I said we'd renovate the place, Tom...and that's what I'm doing!"

"Well, I hope our visitors appreciate it," he chuckled. "We're off," he called to the empty hallway. "Bye."

No-one heard Tom's farewell. Henri had spent the morning working in the greenhouse, free from any pain. In those moments the diagnosis seemed impossible to believe. Darcy was in her bedroom writing an article for a women's magazine. She'd convinced herself if she could prove her worth as a journalist, it would help with her desired occupation. She was taking real life issues to produce interesting articles. She was currently working on an idea about women who stepped in to fulfil men's roles during the war. Some were now being sidelined as the returning servicemen took up their jobs again. She'd spoken to two ladies in the town who'd experienced this situation. She was sure it would make interesting reading. Just before lunch, she went over to find Henri, in the greenhouse.

"How are you?" she asked sympathetically.

Henri turned and spoke sharply. "Darcy, I'm fine. I do not want or need your sympathy. I am not an invalid and please don't treat me like one!" Darcy was astounded by his angry retort. She'd not heard him speak in such a manner before. "It's a diagnosis, that's all...miracles do happen. It may not turn out the way the doctors expect – on the other hand it could." He stopped and flung down his trowel on the workbench – a frustrated action.

Darcy gasped.

"We need to talk, Darcy, after lunch. I've got lots on my mind so leave me alone. Get out of here, now!"

Darcy felt her lip quivering. Words like this, coming from Henri's lips, were alien. She felt snubbed. She turned and left him to his work. 'It's shock,' she told herself, trying to make excuses for him.

Lunch was a silent affair, at least for Henri and Darcy, as they listened to Rachel describing her plans for The Bungalow. Josh was full of energy as he discussed his tactics for his cricket match that afternoon. And now the house was deserted. Darcy sat in the conservatory in trepidation, awaiting Henri's arrival. He entered the room and sat in the chair beside the fireplace, opposite Darcy. The atmosphere felt tense and unreal. She'd expected him to take her in his arms and apologise for his earlier behaviour towards her – but he didn't.

"Darcy, I spent a restless night thinking about us and our future…eventually, I came to a decision. I hate saying this, but I must release you from our secret promise to marry. You are a bright, energetic girl. You are the light of my life, my reason for living, but because of this…" He stopped and tapped his thigh. "I cannot expect you to entangle yourself with me. I would hold you back. You have dreams – dreams to become a journalist…dreams to travel." He paused and Darcy opened her mouth to speak, but he lifted his hand to silence her.

"Don't interrupt me, I have more to say," he uttered. "I must return to my homeland, find accommodation near to my aunt and uncle, and seek a sedentary occupation to accommodate my condition. It will be the end of my horticultural studies – but I will need to adapt." He paused, rubbed his brow and sat forward.

"You must forget about me, Darcy. I will always love you…but I cannot hold you back, our relationship is at an end, but we can remain friends. I will stay on until the end of August and return to France with my relatives."

Darcy stared at Henri in disbelief – how could he speak such words; think such thoughts; make wild decisions. "Henri," she whispered, "I love you. I want to spend my life with you. When I accepted your proposal, it was genuine – it was like saying "I do" in a wedding ceremony. I will love you for better or worse, for richer or poorer, in sickness and in health!"

Henri shook his head. "Stop! Stop! Darcy – you don't know what you are saying. I lived with a disabled mother; I saw firsthand the restraints my mother's condition brought to their marriage. I could never expect you to live like that."

Darcy stood and walked over to where Henri was sitting and knelt in front of him.

"I'm not a quitter, Henri Dukas. I'm going to stand by you. I will be there for you and encourage you. I won't wrap you in cotton wool – I promise, but if you need help, I'll be there for you. Forget about my career ambitions. I won't give up on us, Henri I love you too much!" She was shrieking, tears pouring down her face. She flung herself forward and sobbed into his lap.

But Henri remained silent. He refused to touch her, knowing it would weaken his resolve. Minutes passed and her sobbing abated. She lifted her blotchy face, and their eyes met – hers full of love and devotion…but Henri's were hard and steely.

Chapter 19

THREE WEEKS LATER

"Jess, come here, now!" Darcy called to the dog. A rabbit, she thought. Their usually laid back, twelve-year-old canine, had dived into the hedgerow and disappeared. She waited patiently. Stupid dog, one of these days she'll injure herself, thought Darcy as she walked the length of the hedge, shouting her name. Darcy gave up and flounced down on the grass. She picked a tall blade of grass and used it to waft the flies. She felt miserable.

Tears no longer brought her relief. She felt defeated. She'd tried all ways to break down the barrier Henri had created between them. Oh, he was pleasant towards her, talking in a friendly manner at mealtimes…but there was nothing between them – a big, fat… nothing!

The day of his outburst he left the room, leaving her, sitting on the floor, totally shocked and bewildered. It was so out of character for him. She waited for an hour, then stood outside his bedroom door and asked if they could go for a walk. He obliged and they strolled around the grounds, making 'small talk'. He made it clear the subject was closed – he'd shared his heart and there was no more to be discussed. She'd stopped and pleaded with him. Many men had returned from the war with life sustaining injuries, but their families had learned to adapt. "We can adapt, Henri," she beseeched him.

"Darcy, forget we were ever sweethearts. I want to remain your friend, and I will value your support, but our physical relationship cannot and must not develop. It is futile. I am wrong for you. You must pursue your career and look for a new boyfriend."

A pattern developed. Each evening after supper, Henri and Darcy took a walk in the grounds. There was no physical contact between them. Darcy recalled reading somewhere if you adopt a habit and keep it going for three weeks, then it becomes the norm. She doubted if anyone in the family suspected their 'estrangement'. On the surface they were still a couple... but underneath a vast chasm lay. If it was raining, they didn't walk.

Tantalising reminders seemed to rear up, reminding both Henri and Darcy of his changed lifestyle. Josh frequently talked about his cricket. The season was in full swing. He encouraged Henri to spectate at the local matches and he agreed. Darcy accompanied them – but she could sense his frustration. Chrissie invited her to play tennis – her romance had run its course, and she was keen to occupy her time. Darcy apologised to Henri – she couldn't keep their usual walk, because she was off to play tennis… then the cruelty of her words hit her, but it was too late to take them back. She went on the Cycle Club outing over to Blyhope, reminiscent of the first day she'd befriended Grady. She was with Chrissie…but her mind was elsewhere – back home with Henri Dukas.

The Youth Club Summer Jamboree took place to mark the end of term. Henri accompanied her, they sat and watched the games, cheering Josh on, as he tumbled around in the sack race. They sipped lemonade, and Darcy joined in the egg and spoon race, but failed to win.

Reminders were everywhere, but the pinnacle of Henri's exasperation arrived in the form of a young man, called Fred, who knew Darcy from school. Henri watched, jealousy gripping his being, as Darcy and Fred bopped around the dance floor to the beat of the local trio – she was enjoying herself.

Henri had returned to The Infirmary the week after the diagnosis. Tom accompanied him, as his employer, to talk through the restraints of his condition. Darcy listened at the supper table to further details. His condition was to be monitored, regularly, by the hospital. His weekly appointments with the physiotherapist were arranged and he'd been back to see the family doctor. Tom offered to accommodate, making adaptions to his working position.

It was the resigned acceptance of the issue which rankled Darcy the most. Some days she wished he would shout at her; throw something at her; take off back to France and totally ignore her...but he remained polite and friendly and...devoid of emotion. A rustling in the hedgerow, signalled the return of Jess, twigs hanging from her golden fur. She wandered over to Darcy wagging her tangled tail.

"Silly girl," muttered Darcy, removing the debris from the dog's coat and tail. The pair sauntered back towards the house.

* * *

Rachel closed her bedroom door and walked along the landing. It was mid-afternoon. She felt refreshed, having taken a snooze after lunch – hopefully her threatened headache had passed. She stopped and listened – what's that? A quiet muffled sob was only just audible – she continued to listen, but it was unmistakeable.

"Darcy," Rachel spoke, quickening her step until she reached her daughter's room. The door was closed. She paused, hearing anguished moans before tapping and gingerly opening it. "Darcy...what's wrong?" she uttered, closing the door behind her.

Darcy was lying face down sprawled across the top of her eiderdown. Her blonde curls looked unkempt, adhering to her face. Her body was heaving as she continued to sob into the counterpane covering the pillows.

Rachel sat down and placed her hand on her daughter's shoulder. "Darcy, whatever is the matter? Can I help in any way?" she enquired.

The sobbing eased and Darcy rolled onto her side. Rachel was shocked to see her daughter looking so distressed. She stood and took a handkerchief from the dressing table drawer, passing it to Darcy. After wiping her face, the young girl spoke.

"It's personal, Mother, I don't want to talk about it so leave me alone," she responded.

Rachel sat down again. "I'm not going anywhere until you tell me the reason for your distress," she commented.

Darcy sighed and rolled over away from her mother. But Rachel continued to sit and watch. She yearned to comfort the girl – but she was stubborn. As a little girl Rachel had soothed Darcy by singing to her – the words and music seemed to pacify her, but that was all in the past. The fractious tensions caused by teenage tantrums had forced a wedge between them. Without thinking, Rachel began to hum the tune to *Frère Jacques* – an old French nursery rhyme. She hummed the tune a few times then began to sing the words, softly.

The song transported Rachel back to the days when she soothed her baby daughter on her shoulder. Tom could hum or sing the same tune to the troubled baby with no effect…yet in Rachel's arms, with her sweet voice, a calm would descend on their fretful offspring. As she grew it still worked, and in time Rachel taught Darcy to sing the words in a round. When Josh was born, he was more likely to respond to his father's baritone voice.

Rachel's mind was so caught up in the memories, she was startled back into reality as Darcy joined in the song. They continued to sing in a round. Feeling close to tears herself, she reached over and clutched Darcy's hand. "*Ma chérie,*" she uttered. The phrase was so poignant. It was a regular utterance in the days when Chantal had lived with the young family, but to Darcy those words encompassed all she had lost in her estrangement from Henri. She felt like a lost soul.

Darcy took her other hand and clasped her mother's. Rachel swallowed, almost choking. It was years since they'd contacted physically in an emotional way. The troubling trials of teenage years had ripped apart the once tight bond Rachel and Darcy had shared. It was like a spring uncoiling as the pair wrapped their arms around one another. Tears streamed down both their cheeks as they rocked to the silent rhythm of the old rhyme, which was no longer audible, but provided the simultaneous movement. "Ssh," comforted Rachel, as Darcy slowly settled in her mother's arms. They sat in silence.

Darcy sat up, pulled away and fixed her gaze on the sky outside. "I've made a decision, Mother," she stammered.

Rachel stared at her beautiful daughter...a decision... about what? So many issues were threatening her young daughter's mind...which one was prevalent? Darcy slipped off the bed and walked over to the window. Rachel remained still and silent, fearing any words spoken by her could rip through and break this fragile truce in their relationship.

Decision could mean one of a few things, Rachel mused. Darcy's career choice – Tom was determined his daughter should abandon this journalism idea, replacing it with a sensible career such as teaching. But Rachel knew Darcy was not 'teacher material' – she lacked patience, so she avoided having any discussion with her on that subject.

Her boyfriend choice was another area of decision. Since Henri's diagnosis, Darcy was carrying a huge burden. Rachel was perceptive. She knew the relationship was struggling – and so did Tom. Her daughter's body language gave the vibes – the deep love the pair shared... and Rachel knew it was deep, was being tested. It was something they needed to work out. Tom was adamant she would 'get over it'. "If there's a rift between them, it's for the best, Rachel. All this talk about standing by him and hoping for a cure is admirable... but a lifetime commitment to a disabled man is no small undertaking. She's too young and vulnerable...too scatterbrained. She needs to get away, go to college and move on from this infatuation with Henri." But Rachel knew Darcy was in it for the long haul. Her love and devotion for the young Frenchman was far more than a compassionate response to the nature of his diagnosis – it was born out of an intense love.

Yet, there could be a third area of decision for Darcy – her relationship with her aunt. They were family and this rift was all Darcy's making. From the outset Tom and Rachel had refused to take sides and eventually it ceased to be mentioned. It was almost a year since this unpleasant situation began and now Chantal's summer visit was imminent.

Rachel blinked...which was it? Slowly, Darcy turned, and Rachel joined her daughter by the window.

"I've decided to seek Tallie's forgiveness, Mother, but I don't know if she will forgive me. I wrote to her after our disagreement."

Rachel gasped – she was unaware of that fact.

"I... wrote a forthright letter reiterating what I'd said and told her not to write back to me. I said our friendship was dead. Oh, Mother, I regret what I did, and I must try to make amends. So much has happened since I spoke those harsh words."

"I think that's a wise decision, Darcy – I'm pleased to hear it. I was in a similar situation many years ago. I wronged someone...greatly. I doubted if the person would or could forgive me. I struggled for many months about making my approach, but the more I thought about it, the more I knew I needed to try. It was like a canker, gnawing away at me and I couldn't move on with my life. I knew I faced rejection, but I had to try to seek this person's forgiveness."

Darcy turned and looked at her mother. "Was it serious stuff...I mean serious, like those awful things I said to Tallie?"

Rachel sighed. "Yes, Darcy – it was so serious...it went to a court of law."

Darcy's eyes nearly popped out of her head. "Mother, I'm not following you...say that again."

Rachel stood on the edge of a precipice. Should she impart important information from the past, which could affect her relationship with her daughter? How would Darcy react? Yet, she'd always known this day would come. Tom wanted their hidden past kept quiet and she'd always agreed...but somehow, this seemed an appropriate moment.

"Let's sit, Darcy." They sat side by side on the edge of the bed. Rachel reached out and took her firstborn's hand. "I'm telling you this, Darcy, because... if I had not sought forgiveness, you and your brother would not exist." Rachel swallowed and Darcy gasped. "It was something I needed to do face to face, I needed to see the reaction. I could have tried writing a letter, but written words were not an option."

Darcy stared in bewilderment – this sounded serious. "Tell me, Mother."

Rachel took a deep breath and began.

"Many years ago, I wrongly accused someone of a crime. I was a troubled soul in those days. My childhood was difficult. I was abandoned by my parents and brought up by my aunt – our relationship was 'thorny'. I wanted to blame someone for the lot life had dealt me. Then I lost a close friend in a tragic accident. I wanted to retaliate, hit back at someone...and the person I chose... was your father."

Darcy gulped and clasped her hand to her mouth. "What did you do?"

Rachel removed her hand from Darcy's and sat up straight. "I accused your father of pushing his brother, causing the accident which led to his death."

Darcy's jaw dropped and her eyes widened. She recalled hearing how her uncle had fallen at a local beauty spot and died from his injuries months later.

"I am ashamed to say...it wasn't the truth. I was distraught, because at the time your father's brother was my boyfriend. Thankfully, the court found your father 'not guilty'."

Darcy was shocked – how could her parents have married after such a betrayal?

"I was so relieved at the verdict, but I couldn't live with myself. I was tormented and needed your father's forgiveness. Prior to my friendship with your uncle, I was courting your father, and I knew he loved me...but we fell out and grew apart." Rachel stopped, lost in her memories. "Love is a powerful emotion, Darcy...I think you know what I mean. It can transcend the cruellest of knocks. Months after the trial I arranged to meet your father, told him how sorry I was and begged his forgiveness. At that point, he couldn't forgive me – he was still grieving and in shock...but he held out a ray of hope...and offered to meet me a year later." Rachel looked at Darcy and smiled. "I think you can work out what happened."

Darcy nodded.

"Your father is a wonderful man. Receiving his forgiveness a year later, I was overwhelmed with relief. We renewed our friendship and married six months afterwards. Bystanders were shocked, said it was preposterous and scandalous – how could Tom Smallwood forgive his accuser? But it wasn't preposterous, Darcy… it was love – deep, true love… unconditional love and I didn't deserve it."

They sat in silence. Rachel was drained by the resurfacing of emotions recalling the events from twenty years ago.

"Now, back to the present, Darcy. Chantal loves you… but you must seek her forgiveness, say you are sorry for your harsh words and actions. I can only offer advice based on my own experience."

Darcy flung her arms around her mother's neck. Then Rachel stood and walked towards the door.

"Thank you, Mother, for sharing your experience… but can I ask you something? Does the subject crop up when you and dad have a disagreement?"

Rachel shook her head. "No. He loves me and holds no grudges. His love is unconditional. He told me it was as if it never happened…because love conquers all. In his eyes I am totally forgiven. I admit it's hard to accept. Others no doubt think it's implausible… but your father's love for me was more powerful than my act of betrayal – and love won!"

Darcy stood. "I'll speak to Tallie when she's here in August. I must seek her forgiveness."

* * *

"I did something today, Tom, something I hope will meet with your approval," Rachel commented, snuggling under Tom's arm, as they lay in bed later that night.

He squeezed her shoulder. "I'm waiting."

"Darcy was upset. I could hear her crying upstairs, when I came out of our bedroom this afternoon. Amazingly, she let me enter her room. I sat for a while, imagining it was related to Henri – then she shared what was troubling her. She has decided to seek Chantal's forgiveness when she arrives in August."

Tom looked down at his wife. "That's good, but what do you mean about my approval?" Tom felt Rachel stiffen.

"Oh, Tom…I told her about us. About me accusing you and it going to court. We agreed we wouldn't tell our children, but it seemed like the right time to tell her."

Tom was silent. Yes, they'd decided not to share this blight on their relationship with their offspring. He'd come close to telling Josh a couple of years ago, but it passed without further revelations.

"You're angry with me…aren't you?"

Tom raised himself on his elbow and gazed at his wife. "No, Rachel, I'm not angry… surprised, yes. But I guess we were foolish to think our children would never hear about the episode at some point. I'm pleased Darcy heard it directly from you, free from the tittle tattle of gossipers, like Josh experienced. What was her reaction?"

Rachel felt tears rising to the surface. She blinked them back and pulled her lips, her voice was quivering. Tom was watching her and lifted his hand to wipe the stray tear. "She...she...was grateful for me telling her and wanted to know if it was still there between us." She gulped. "I told her it wasn't."

Tom caressed Rachel's face. "Rachel, I love you so much. You have given me years of happiness – how easily we could have missed the deep love we share. If I had harboured unforgiveness, it would have led to bitterness. Forgiveness is hard to understand, we naturally want people to suffer for their wrongdoing...but forgiveness is profound. I am thankful every day of our lives, that we grasped it and twenty years later we are still bearing testimony to the miracle of forgiveness." Tom Smallwood gazed adoringly into his wife's eyes, then kissed her and loved her with intensity and passion.

* * *

Tom walked into the greenhouse, carrying a high stool with a backrest. "Look what's just been delivered, Henri, your new stool has arrived."

Henri looked up from his work as Tom placed the item in front of the young man. Following the hospital appointment, Tom had commissioned a local joiner to make a stool for Henri. The joiner took measurements, and the newly designed stool had been delivered earlier. Henri positioned it and sat down.

"That's great, Tom. I won't use it all the time, but it will give me a chance to rest and still be working."

Tom nodded. It was only a small gesture but hopefully a useful one. Tactfully, Tom began discussing the progress of the various propagation experiments Henri was monitoring. It was a detailed process – Tom would have been lost without Henri's help. The young man was meticulous in his record keeping, noting dates of growth signs. He organised various experiments, grafting stems from different rose plants and watching their progress as they fused together. He was investigating using differing locations and conditions. Tom admired Henri's devotion to the task.

"Henri, you are gifted in this area. I'm so pleased to have you working alongside me – I could never have accomplished all this without you. Now, if there are any other adjustments you would like me to make, just say the word. I think we'll see hopeful signs in these little plants in two to three months, so keep at it!" Tom turned and walked away.

Henri sat down on his new stool. Tom was kind in arranging the item to be made. But he felt guilty. If he carried through with his plan to return to France at the end of August, when the Thibaults' vacation ended, the stool would be wasted. So far, Tom was ignorant of Henri's plans.

He looked around at the plants he was nurturing – another two to three months was needed to see if these early experiments were working…and they were his *babies*, he would struggle to walk away from Meckleridge House at the end of the summer. He would be devastated to leave all this…and to leave Darcy.

He blinked and told himself to think sensibly. A little voice tickled in his ear: '*do the right thing, Henri Dukas. Go back to France and forget about propagating plants and Darcy Smallwood*'. He sighed – was he about to make the worst decision of his young life?

He felt isolated. There was no-one with whom he could share his concerns. Josh was too young; Tom was his employer; Darcy was too close to him. He'd tried to disassociate himself from her …to no avail. He longed to spend that blissful hour in her company each evening – it was a healing balm to his soul. They conversed so well, even allowing for the huge gulf in their relationship. She was so understanding, taking a keen interest in his work, discussing current affairs, keeping him updated on her writing projects and all the while not referring to his *condition*. She was proving to be a supportive friend – so why walk away?

Chapter 20

Tom turned off the country road onto the lane. The remnants of dusk were fading. Stars were pricking the darkening skies. The eerie moonlight was casting its beams across his path. As the car began to descend the incline, Tom turned off the engine and lights. He allowed the car to 'free wheel', thankful for the receding fragments of daylight guiding his way. It was just after nine-thirty on a balmy evening in early August, and Tom Smallwood was on a mission.

This was the third time he'd performed this assignment – if he was unsuccessful tonight, he would make it his last attempt, accepting it was not to be. He patted his pocket, checking if he'd remembered his wallet. Carefully, he steered the car as it propelled itself towards his destination. As the road began to level, the car lost momentum. Tom turned the steering wheel and pulled up onto the grass verge. He secured the handbrake, picked up his torch from the passenger footwell and climbed out of the car, securing the door with a gentle click...so far, so good.

An owl hooted, giving him a start as he walked with trepidation across the bridge. Ahead lay the field at Trespershields where their bungalow was situated. There was an uncanny, ghostly aura surrounding the wooden building as he scaled the gate and stealthily wove his way through the meadow of wildflowers and bracken. The moon caused shadows to be cast in curious forms. It was a stark contrast to the usual scene of peace and tranquillity associated with summer daylight hours.

Surreptitiously, he tiptoed onto the veranda and reached above the door frame for the groove which concealed the key...it was empty! Having recently changed the lock, a spare key was in his pocket but first he tried the door, turning the handle – it was unlocked. Carefully, he pushed the door inch by inch to avoid creaking noises. He waited before entering, listening in case the trespasser was alerted.

Silence pervaded the room, and he stepped over the threshold, closing the door without sound. His nose detected a faint odour of food – but nothing distinguishable. His eyes adjusted to the dimness, and he noted the rear curtains were open, allowing slivers of moonlight to penetrate the space. His eyes scanned the scene – nothing appeared out of place. Cautiously, he flicked on his torch and let the beam continue the search. He halted as the beam picked up a shape lying on the floor near to the sink – it was an object he'd seen recently...an army kit bag, devoid of its contents.

Suddenly, he was aware of a shuffling sound originating from the rear bedroom – he stiffened and waited. Then another sound...a gentle purring...it was the unmistakable tone of human snoring – his mission was successful!

Tom eased himself into a chair, in a corner on the far side of the room facing the bedroom door and extinguished his torch...what next? Since hatching this plan to discover the tramp, he'd not envisaged how he would deal with the culprit. This was his property, and the man was an intruder – he was within his rights to investigate. But should he accost the stranger? Stride into the bedroom, shine the torch in his face and startle him? He would then have the advantage. But what if the perpetrator was armed with a knife – or worse, a gun? If, as he suspected, the man was an ex-serviceman, he would have no quibbles about defending himself.

No-one knew about Tom's late-night mission. He frequently stayed up late, after the family retired for the night – working in his office or reading in the conservatory. He doubted his absence would be noted before morning – Rachel was a sound sleeper. He continued to sit and think through his course of action. In essence, Tom only wanted to be helpful. Seeing the kit bag stowed away under the rear of the building had struck a compassionate chord within Tom. He sensed the tramp was a troubled soul. He wanted to talk to him, maybe advise him, perhaps offer him some money and send him on his way.

Oh...he hadn't thought this through properly. What if the man was a drunkard – he'd spend the money on alcohol, but then...Tom sniffed – there were no telltale smells of spirits. The only odour he detected was... yes, a faint whiff of fish. Should he have reported the presence of the vagrant to the police? No, he had dismissed that option – why, he was unsure. Empathy for the guy, he guessed. He'd been so blessed to live out the war in the comfort of his own home – so, if this visitor had partaken of shelter under the roof of The Bungalow...well, Tom was at ease with that. There were no signs of damage...share your blessings, Tom reasoned. He glanced at his watch, nearly eleven o'clock. He continued to sit...and think... and wait...and eventually doze.

A noise startled him. He blinked, momentarily unsure of his whereabouts. Realisation kicked in as he recalled where he was and what he was trying to achieve. It was difficult to decipher the time on his watch, but it was still dark outside. Creaking and shuffling sounds caused a tension within Tom, as the bedroom door jerked open to reveal the silhouette of a tall man framed in the doorway!

Tom held the advantage – his presence obscured from the man's line of vision. The intruder walked slowly to the front door and stepped outside – to relieve himself, Tom guessed. Returning, he sauntered towards the sink area and poked about in the kit bag. Tom watched as he picked up a jug, filled a basin with water and performed his ablutions. He rummaged in the kit bag, retrieved a towel and dried himself. Oblivious to Tom's existence, the man then proceeded to clean his teeth!

Something was out of place – a tramp... having a good wash...cleaning his teeth? Glimmers of dawn were materialising, helping Tom note his guest was barefooted, wearing a vest and trousers, with braces hanging loose. Convinced the man was unarmed... Tom spoke.

"Good morning, sir, I trust you slept well."

The interloper froze, then slowly and cautiously turned. The light was still dim. Tom flicked on his torch, shining it directly into the vagrant's face. Tom gasped audibly and jumped out of his chair in disbelief...before him stood a man he recognised; a man who'd been a guest in his home; a man he admired; a man who was supposed to be dead!

"S...S...am?" he exclaimed. The man was shielding his eyes from the glare of the torch – Tom switched it off. "Good grief, man – what are you doing here? You are supposed to be dead!"

The man straightened. Tom stepped forward, offering his hand. The startled man shook it with a firm grasp.

"I'm...s... sorry for trespassing in your property, Tom. Please... forgive me and let me explain," the man stuttered in a cultured Scottish accent.

Tom walked over and pulled back the front curtains, allowing light to penetrate the room. The dishevelled man sat down. Tom watched then returned to his seat. Now he could see Sam Carter, he realised he looked much older than he remembered. His once thick head of brown hair was now receding and greying. There was a scar above his left eye. He wore a bushy beard and appeared weather beaten but toned. His build looked broader, filled out and his arms were muscular – he resembled a manual worker – not the dashing young doctor Chantal had brought to their home before the war.

Sam was sitting forward, staring at the floor. "I don't know where to begin," he mumbled.

"The beginning, Sam. Where have you been?"

Sam sighed and looked up at Tom. He noticed his eyes were glazed and furrows etched his brow.

"I don't know what you've heard about me…you said I'm supposed to be dead?" he questioned Tom.

"What I know, Sam, is that a few weeks ago I saw an obituary notice in a newspaper inviting friends to attend your memorial service. I also have a sister-in-law who refuses to believe it and is convinced you are still alive."

Sam's eyes seemed to brighten. "Chantal?" he uttered. "Is she living with you again?"

Tom shook his head. "No, she's lived in France since before the war. I made enquiries, on her behalf, and discovered you were Missing in Action since June 1940 and declared officially dead in July 1947."

Sam rubbed his forehead. "I see," he muttered, thoughtfully. "My family didn't waste any time having me declared dead."

312

Tom waited. Sam was obviously unaware of this development. After a few minutes' silence, he looked at Tom.

"What else does Chantal know about me?"

It was a leading question – was it Tom's place to disclose his sister-in-law's knowledge of Sam's marital status? But she did know... so he may as well tell him.

"Sam... Chantal has recently learned you are married and have a child."

Sam Carter lifted his eyes towards the ceiling, as if seeking for inspiration. He began to shake his head.

"What a mess...what a mess," he added, looking utterly dejected and defeated. He stared straight ahead, avoiding eye contact, making no attempt to give an explanation.

Tom was a patient, sympathetic man by nature, but right now he was feeling somewhat agitated. Sam shifted on his seat and stared at the floor.

"My ship was torpedoed off the Norwegian coast. I was rescued by a small fishing boat after clinging to floating debris, but I sustained a head injury." He touched the scar above his left eye, which Tom could now see was about two inches long. "My injury caused concussion and memory loss." He paused. "The fisherman's elderly parents cared for me, but I have no recollection of those months – only what they told me."

Again, he stopped, frowning. "Anders and Hilde lived on a remote farm. When my physical injuries healed, I did manual farm work for them, answering to the name Ivan. They told me about the war and how I was found...I had no recollection of the event. Time passed but my memory did not return. One day, Anders sustained an accident to his leg. Some instinct prompted me to assist him. I was able to save his badly injured leg. I started to have flashbacks, relating initially, to medical matters."

Tom listened carefully.

"The family suspected I might be a doctor. My memories were spasmodic – I recalled Chantal's face – but no name; a large hospital – but where? Time passed and the war ended. I knew I must leave Norway. I was a doctor with a Scottish accent and a beautiful woman belonged in my past, but I possessed no documents and no name...I was a displaced person."

What a predicament, thought Tom.

"So how did you get back to England," he asked.

"Anders' son arranged travel for me on a fishing trawler to the North Sea port of North Shields. I was given refuge in a Fisherman's Mission Hostel. My plight was not unusual – there were other displaced persons staying there. I was cared for and given basic personal items. I was also asked many questions – which triggered more memories and slowly full recollection returned."

Tom nodded. "Did you try to contact your family?"

Sam shook his head. "No. I did not want to return to my family. My wife and I have been estranged for many years, long before I met Chantal – but she refused to divorce me. I left the hostel and took to the road. I wasn't thinking straight...I needed to work out what I was going to do... I could not return to my former life."

"When was this, Sam?"

The man looked bewildered. "I still struggle with dates and times, Tom. This is the second summer I've stayed here, so – a year last Spring?"

"How did you find this place?" Tom asked, curiously.

"I was used to farm work, so I worked as an itinerant labourer. Many farmers, especially those in isolated areas seek seasonal workers and don't ask for paperwork. They also pay 'cash in hand'. I bought a bike and kept moving on. One day I saw a signpost to Blanchland, remembered this place and the times I spent here with Chantal. When I found this bungalow, I felt so close to her. It appeared deserted and unused. I have returned here many times over the last year. I work locally, and it pays well." Sam looked drained. "What time is it?" he asked, returning from his reminiscences.

Tom consulted his watch. "It's five o'clock – what time do you leave for work?"

"I start at six, so I must be going. I wanted to find out about Chantal before...before... I faced the consequences... dare I ask about her – is she married?"

Tom pondered his answer. "No, she's single – do you want her to know you are alive?"

Sam buried his head in his hands, then replied. "Yes, Tom, most certainly I do. She is the reason I have stayed around here. The only way I could contact her was through you and Rachel."

Tom stood – he also needed to be on his way. "You are fortunate, Sam. Chantal is due to arrive for her annual holiday with us. She will be here for about a month."

A glimmer of a smile spread across Sam's face. "That's amazing Tom...how can I see her?"

Tom rubbed his weary brow. "I suggest we give her a chance to settle in, then I'll seek an appropriate time. If you are continuing to stay here, I'll bring Chantal to visit...if that's what she wants. Of course, I can't be sure."

Sam pursed his lips. "Yes, she may not want to see me...now she knows about my family."

"It sounds like you have a great deal to sort out, Sam. Chantal deserves an explanation... but one step at a time. Welcome back."

They shook hands and Tom left The Bungalow. He returned home, sneaking into his bed just before 6am. Sam's return from the dead was good news, but Tom needed to tread carefully and talk to his wife. He also needed to seek legal advice for Sam Carter who appeared reluctant to undertake this of his own volition.

* * *

Tidying the dishes after supper, Tom's mind drifted to Sam – he must be so lonely...when was the last time he had enjoyed a home cooked meal, he pondered. Perhaps he was fed at the farms where he worked. He carried the dishes into the kitchen where Rachel was filling the sink. "Rachel, I need to talk to you," he commented.

"Yes, Tom, but can it wait, I still have loads to do before our guests arrive tomorrow," she objected.

Tom placed the dishes on the table. "No, it can't wait...it's important."

Rachel sensed the urgency in Tom's voice. There was certain tone which Tom used, and when he did, Rachel knew not to argue.

"Okay, the dishes can wait, I'll grab a cardigan, and we can walk."

The grounds surrounding the house were extensive, giving them privacy. The dog sauntered along behind them.

"Over the last couple of weeks I have visited The Bungalow late at night," Tom began.

Rachel looked aghast. "Really? Why?" she enquired.

"To track down that tramp, who has been using our property. My intention was to offer him some money in return for him vacating the place."

Rachel was surprised. "Gosh, you were brave...he could have attacked you. Were you successful?"

"Yes...but I made an unbelievable discovery. Our guest was known to me. It was a shock and I'm still recovering. The tramp, Rachel...is Sam Carter...alive and well."

Rachel ceased walking, froze and faced her husband, in astonishment. She began to tremble.

"What? Tom, are you sure? How? Why?" The questions tumbled from her lips. They resumed walking as Tom outlined his nocturnal visit, his unbelievable discovery and Sam's explanation.

"Tom, that's incredible...I can't believe it," Rachel exclaimed, as their steps crunched along the gravel pathway. "How is he?"

"He is physically well, but his appearance has changed – he's not the handsome young doctor we remember. I suspect he's struggling mentally. I got the impression he will take some persuading to face up to reality. Sam Carter is procrastinating – he's been back in England for over a year and is happy to keep quiet about his existence."

"It raises so many questions. Will he be treated as a criminal...or worse... a deserter?"

Tom put his arm around Rachel. "Quite frankly, Rachel, I have no idea. I would like to delve into the legalities of it all. He seems content to live *under the radar* and he's done well to do that so far – but it can't continue. If he wants to reconnect with your sister, he'll have to declare himself alive. The longer he waits, the more likely it is someone will ask probing questions."

A breeze picked up and Rachel shivered. "Poor man – he must have stayed at The Bungalow hoping to discover if Chantal was living here and if she had married."

"Yes, I think it's a fair assumption Chantal and her whereabouts were the reason he's been lying low."

"Perhaps you could make inquiries at our solicitor's – anonymously?" Rachel suggested.

"Yes, I intend to do that, but first we have to get our heads around telling Chantal – she won't take kindly to us keeping the information from her."

Rachel was deep in thought. "We need to give her a couple of days to settle in – and hopefully Darcy will sort her problem with her aunt. Should we tell Chantal in advance…or just take her up to The Bungalow?"

"Again, I don't know. There's a lot going on, Rachel. It's going to be traumatic for Peg and Pierre learning about Henri's condition. Let's take one step at a time. Sam is busy working – it's harvest time on the farm where he's labouring, so a few days won't make much difference."

Rachel couldn't sleep. Everything was heading towards a crunch point at the same time – Darcy and Chantal; Henri's future with his diagnosis; Sam's 'return from the dead' and its implications; and Darcy and Henri's relationship – the latter was unspoken, but her mother's instinct told Rachel the young couple were at variance.

She was struggling to come to terms with Sam's return – yet his explanation was believable. She'd read of similar incidents in the press. The world war had created havoc and even after three years – pieces of human jigsaws were still being found, Sam Carter being one of them. But she worried for her sister – Sam was still a married man so, what future did they have? Weariness eventually took over and Rachel fell into a deep, troubled sleep.

* * *

Within an hour of the French visitors' arrival, Darcy knocked on her aunt's door. After being invited into the bedroom she stood in the middle of the floor, feeling like a naughty schoolgirl about to receive a punishment. Sheepish and Darcy were not words to be put together, but Darcy was slowly learning her attitudes to certain subjects needed refining.

"Tallie," she began, "I want to apologise for my outburst and subsequent behaviour last year. I was stupid and childish and I'm seeking your forgiveness." She sighed inwardly, her pent-up emotions finally finding release.

Chantal remained silent but opened her arms. Darcy ran into them, and aunt and niece hugged. Tears ran down Chantal's face. "Of course I forgive you, Darcy, we are both adults and are each entitled to our own viewpoints. Let's agree to disagree over the subject. You know my belief in hope – I cling to the tiniest fragment, vestige or splinter and I won't be sidetracked. But I accept you are young and see things differently."

Darcy pulled back and stared at her aunt. "No, no, Tallie... I've changed. Something has happened and I'm learning how life can throw things at you when you least expect it. The events of the last few weeks have made me realise how important it is to possess *hope*...even the smallest iota. I won't say anything else just yet, you will understand what I mean later."

Chantal raised her eyebrows. "I'm curious, Darcy...is it about your friendship with Henri?"

Darcy wanted to tell Chantal but hesitated. "After supper, Tallie, you'll hear about it then. Come on, let's join the others."

The atmosphere around the supper table was buoyant as general news was shared. During the final course, Rachel noted how mature Jonty was becoming – he was entering his second year at university in the autumn. The boy was gone – he was developing into a sensible young man. Sylvie was growing into an attractive young woman, her mannerisms so like her mother, Peg. Even Josh had left childhood behind. Rachel felt nostalgic watching them all ...if only Darcy and Henri could overcome their problems. She was pulled from her reverie by Tom.

"We'll see to them, won't we, Rachel?" Rachel was miles away. "Rachel?" Tom prompted. "I was saying Pierre, Peg and Henri need to talk by themselves," he repeated, for his wife's benefit.

"Oh, yes, of course they do...the rest of us will see to the dishes."

Henri relayed the devastating details of his diagnosis and its implications, to his aunt and uncle. They listened carefully then asked pertinent questions.

"How does this affect your work here in England?" Pierre enquired.

Peg regarded Henri – he looked older. It was only four months since he had left Paris, yet his conversation was

controlled, and he'd expressed himself without emotion…
she was concerned. Henri appeared resigned – where was
the fight? Where was the young man's determination to
face the future with positivity?

Henri answered Pierre's question. "I am going to
return to France – but Tom doesn't know yet; I was
waiting until I'd spoken to you. I can't impose on Tom
and Rachel's hospitality any longer and it seems pointless
staying on. I will of course look for my own apartment and
seek sedentary work to support myself. It's disappointing,
but I must adapt."

Peg was about to give Henri a 'pep' talk, when Tom
entered the room.

"It's a lot to take in, isn't it?" Tom remarked, taking
a seat. "Rachel and I are more than happy for Henri
to remain at Meckleridge. His work here is valuable,
helping with my horticultural project. I have organised
a specially designed chair to assist him when working in
the greenhouse. It also means he can continue under the
care and monitoring he is receiving from The Infirmary
in Newcastle. On that note, there is an appointment for
you to speak to the consultant next week. It will give you
an opportunity to ask whatever questions you may have."

Peg stared at Henri, willing the young man to speak.

"That's kind of you, Tom. You are being so
accommodating, and Peg and I want to thank you both,"
Pierre commented.

Peg continued to watch Henri, then spoke. "Henri… what do you want to do…I mean… really want to do?"

Henri looked defeated. "I…I…don't know, to be honest. I feel confused. My head tells me to return to France, but my heart wants to remain in England. I don't want to be a burden to any of you. Tom and Rachel have been so kind to me, accepting me into their family and I love the work I'm doing. Yet, I'm an independent man, with financial means… but I'm in a quandary."

Peg jumped out of her seat and went over to hug her nephew. He was only twenty-one and life had dealt him bitter blows.

"We're your family, Henri, on both sides of the channel. You are in no state of mind to make decisions. All this leg stuff is overwhelming for you. My suggestion would be to stay here, for the foreseeable future, knowing if it doesn't work out for you…you can always come back to France. We will stick together and support you whatever your choice. Don't think you have to make any decisions at the present time."

Peg looked at her brother who nodded his agreement.

"Sound advice, Peg. You always manage to put into words what others are only thinking. Now, Henri, your cousins and Chantal need to know about this development, so I'll fetch them."

Chapter 21

Rachel blinked and opened her eyes. The early hints of dawn were penetrating the gap in the curtains. She snuggled up to Tom. An arm made its way across her body as he made a soft moan. "Are you awake?" she whispered.

"Mmm...what?" he muttered.

"It's got to be today, Tom...it must be today."

Tom sighed. "What time is it?" he asked wearily, lifting himself up to view the bedside clock. "It's too early, I can sleep for another hour – what's so imperative?" he groaned.

"The Sam and Chantal meeting. It's got to happen tonight...do you agree?"

Any thoughts of returning to the land of slumber were whisked away from Tom. Since discovering Sam's existence a few days ago, he'd envisaged various scenarios in his mind. Should they inform Chantal, see her reaction and let her decide how she wanted to meet him? Should they take her up to The Bungalow and let them meet 'by accident'. Nothing seemed appropriate. Rachel wriggled and he kissed the top of her head.

"Here's a suggestion," Rachel began, "after supper tonight, ask Chantal if she fancies a run up to The Bungalow with you, because you need to check on something."

"That's a bit vague," Tom objected, "she'll want to know why her...why not Pierre or Peg?"

Rachel was thoughtful. "Well, I don't know – just think of something, Tom Smallwood... but get her up there! If they meet...then...don't sit over them...give them space."

Tom squeezed Rachel and chuckled. "Give me some credit, Rachel. I'm not daft. I can remember how it feels to reconnect with the love of your life."

Rachel sat up. "Be flexible, Mr Cupid. We haven't got a plan. We are only facilitating the uniting of two people who love each other. Now, I'm off for a bath while the house is still quiet. We have a busy day ahead!"

* * *

"My, my, Darcy Smallwood, you are famous – congratulations!" Darcy entered the hallway to her aunt's adulation. True to his word Tom had arranged to have Darcy's newspaper article and prize winner's certificate framed, and now they took pride of place on the wall in the hallway. "Your mother failed to mention this accolade in her letters."

Darcy smiled as Chantal hugged her. "It seems so long ago now, Tallie. The day I received the prize I felt invincible. Henri and I thought the future was bright and then *poof* – it all vapourised with his diagnosis."

Chantal pointed to the conservatory. "Time for a quick chat before breakfast?"

Darcy nodded. Her early morning rendezvous with Henri was a thing of the past and their evening walks were becoming intermittent, as Henri often said he was retiring early for the night.

They sat beside each other on the settee. "How are things between you and Henri?" Chantal asked.

Darcy's eyes filled with tears. "There is nothing between us anymore, Chantal. The day after his diagnosis, he told me he couldn't pursue a future with me, because it would be unfair to ask me to align myself to a man with his condition." As Darcy spoke the tears flowed and Chantal reached out and embraced her niece. "I told myself to be patient. I knew he was in shock, and it was probably a natural reaction. But nearly six weeks have passed and if anything, he's become more distant."

"Does he speak to you?"

"Yes, we are still friends. At first, we met for a walk in the grounds each evening – it used to be our regular pattern. We talked about everything... except us. But there was no physical contact. However, even those walks have become less regular. Oh, Tallie he's so resigned to it all. You would expect him to be angry or hopeful for a cure, but he's ...so...complacent and I think he's going to return to France with the Thibaults and turn his back on Meckleridge. Dad will be so disappointed – he likes Henri and values his work."

"How do you feel about Henri, now you know about this *osteonecrosis*?"

"I love him, Tallie, and I want to stand by him, encourage him to think positively. He once told me his mother taught him to overcome obstacles when he was a youngster...yet look at him, being so resigned. It makes me want to shout at him 'don't give up hope'!" Chantal patted the young girl's hand.

"You have changed, Darcy. Hope isn't easy, it comes with risk, it goes against the odds. Henri's condition might not develop the way the doctors expect. Perhaps a medical procedure will be available soon. Love needs hope. Love also needs faith because faith is the confidence we have in our belief. Your love for Henri exists because of love and faith. Do you follow me?"

"I don't think I've thought about it like that, Tallie. But I already know hope can bring strength to the situation. Persuading Henri not to give up on our love, is the problem. I'm prepared to be there for him and help him to navigate the hurdles and hope for a medical breakthrough... because I love him."

Chantal squeezed Darcy's hand. "Hope is my lifeline; it must be yours also, Darcy. Keep on hoping. Hope for your future with Henri and hope for a medical cure."

Darcy smiled at her aunt. "Yes, Chantal. It's all about hope...*hope on hope*!"

Sylvie burst into the room. "Breakfast's ready!" she called.

Rachel's busy day flopped. She was on tenterhooks. Peg and Pierre had opted for a quiet day – reading and pottering around. After lunch, Sylvie and Darcy chose to play tennis, and Tom went over to the farm to discuss accounts with the farm manager. The weather was perfect – a blissful summer's day. Chores finished, she went outside with her book, wondering where Chantal was hiding. She found her lounging in a deck chair. "You look as if you are relaxing," she commented to her sister.

"Yes, it's so peaceful and pleasantly warm. I rarely relax at home, there's always something to do. I'm supposed to have two days off per week, but it doesn't happen that way. Margot, my landlady, has heart problems, so I spend my free time helping her with household tasks."

They chatted about Chantal's work, then Rachel jumped up.

"I'm going to prepare some strawberry cream scones. I picked some beautiful strawberries this morning."

"Can I help you?" Chantal asked her sister.

"No, Chantal, it's your holiday…why don't you take a bath and have a snooze, while everybody's doing their own thing. I'll see you later." She wandered off, hoping Chantal would follow her suggestion. As she entered the front door she bumped into Jonty.

"Where's Henri?" he asked.

"Greenhouses, I imagine, Jonty – he's dedicated to his work."

* * *

Jonty entered the greenhouse and found Henri sitting on a high stool, in a corner beside an open door. The cousins greeted each other and conversed in their native tongue. Jonty watched as Henri took a rose plant, cut a diagonal slit in the stem and joined it to another plant, secured it, fusing the two together.

The two young Frenchmen shared many interests, including their flirtations with young ladies.

"How's the female scene at university, Jonty…anyone caught your fancy?" Henri asked, grinning.

Jonty was popular with the girls and found no difficulty moving from one brief encounter to another.

"Oh, you know me, Henri Dukas. I appreciate the female species, add in brains and I'm hooked. I've enjoyed many liaisons since we last spoke, but I try not to get too involved with a particular girl. How about you? When we were here at Christmas, you and Darcy were an item. Is the romance still going?"

Jonty watched as Henri laid down the delicate rose plant and turned to face him.

"Jonty, I'm unsure what to do. I'd value your advice. I find it difficult to talk about this subject with Josh and there's no one else. I love Darcy…I think you already know that, but how can I continue a relationship with her, when I have this medical condition? She's young, full of life and vigour. She thrives on action. I would be a handicap to her, holding her back. She wants to be a journalist – that would involve travelling. How can I travel about with this handicap?"

Jonty listened. "The sensible thing would be for me to return to France and separate from her...but I enjoy my work here – I'm passionate about it. I've told myself It's the best way forward. Find an apartment near to your folks, get a sedentary job and forget about the girl I love."

Jonty regarded his cousin carefully. They were close in age, almost like brothers. But Henri had always been the 'sensible' one. The mature one, the one who made the right decisions. It was ludicrous to have Henri asking him for advice. Henri picked up another rose, repeating the same procedure as before.

"Hey, this is a first...me giving you advice," Jonty chuckled. "I thought you had found your life partner, Henri. You are devoted to her and from what I observed last Christmas, she was besotted with you. I know she's young...but wow, she's a stunner, bet she'll be fun – in *every way*!"

Henri sighed. "That is my problem, Jonty. I want to be a proper husband to her...how can I ask her to marry me, when I can't be sure how things will turn out with this...thing!" he patted his thigh.

Jonty grinned. "Henri...you love her...she loves you...why make yourselves miserable by parting? Love can overcome difficulties. I've just been watching what you're doing with those roses. I don't know anything about horticulture, but am I right in thinking you are uniting two plants with that delicate process?"

Henri grinned. "Yes, it's called grafting. You take healthy stems from the current season's growth – two roses you like. You cut a diagonal slice, fuse them together and secure them. Then you nurture them, keep them shaded and protect them, inspecting regularly. The hope is they will grow, combining their attributes, drawing strength from each other and resisting disease. Tom hopes to cultivate a new species in the future."

"Have you told Darcy how you feel?"

"Yes, it didn't go well. She can't understand my logic. We've ceased to be involved with each other, but we are still friends."

Jonty sensed Henri's dedication to his work...but something else struck him. He continued to watch as his cousin used growth hormone and potted the plant in a gritty compost mixture. "Henri, I'm not one for being philosophical, but something tells me you should reconsider your decision to walk away from Darcy. I've just watched you do something practical, and I see it as a representation of your potential future with my beautiful cousin." He followed Henri as he took the pot to a new position.

"Look at what you are doing with those plants... bonding them together. Those two rose stems are going to do something together, which they can't do by themselves…gain strength. Their combined attributes will produce something strong and sturdy."

Henri looked at his cousin questioningly. Jonty slapped Henri on the back.

"My advice is don't let cautious thinking steal your future joy and blessings! Think about it. I'll let you get on…see you later." Jonty left a bemused Henri in his wake.

* * *

In the end, Tom and Rachel's fretfulness proved fruitless. Tom was busy scrubbing a pan in the sink after supper when Chantal walked in, carrying dishes. "Did you refurbish The Bungalow, Tom?" she asked. What a leading question!

"Yes, we did, Chantal… which reminds me…I need to pop up to check on something. Do you fancy a ride up there before it turns dark? You'll be able to see what we achieved – it was mostly your sister who did the work."

"Yes, I don't mind a ride out. I've been sitting around all day – something I'm not used to doing."

Tom couldn't believe how Chantal had paved the way so easily. He informed Rachel as she walked into the pantry. "We're on for tonight," he whispered to her.

She smiled and nodded.

Half an hour later, Tom was manoeuvring a series of sharp bends enroute to Trespershields. Chantal was relieved to hear her sister and brother-in-law's decision to keep the country retreat. "When I was here last year you were unsure if you were going to keep the place – what changed?"

Tom drummed his fingers on the steering wheel. "Sentiment, I think. Weighing it up, we realised how many happy memories we made at The Bungalow as a family. It was a haven for us away from the hotel. We reckoned with a re-vamp, it could be a retreat again."

Chantal smiled to herself – she was pleased.

"Changing the subject, Tom. About Henri and Darcy... Henri is struggling to continue his relationship with your daughter, thinking he will be a burden to her in the future. But from what I understand, they are in love...and I think it's the real thing. He's talking about returning to France with the others at the end of August – in my opinion, that's a big mistake. I hope you don't mind me mentioning this, but...perhaps you could bring a bit of wisdom into the situation."

Tom was silent for a few minutes, causing Chantal to think she'd spoken out of turn.

"Darcy is far too young to be settling down, Chantal, but I would miss Henri's contribution to my work. On the other hand, a break, away from Darcy, might not be a bad idea."

Oh dear, thought Chantal – that wasn't the reaction she'd expected.

The fading embers of sunlight slid below the horizon as Tom pulled alongside the gateway to The Bungalow.

"I'll leave the car here, not worth taking it into the field at this late hour. I've got a torch." He climbed out and went around to open the passenger door. On his way he glanced over the field and noted the curtains were drawn. What should he do? Should he leave it to chance or prepare Chantal? Carefully they picked their way through the wildflower meadow.

"Chantal…I need you to brace yourself. You are about to receive a shock." Chantal was concentrating on where she was stepping, trying to follow the beam of the torch.

"A shock?" she asked, bewildered.

As she spoke the door to The Bungalow squeaked open. A hazy glow from a paraffin lamp silhouetted the outline of a male figure stepping onto the veranda. Tom instinctively placed his arm around his sister-in-law's shoulder. He felt her tremble as she stopped walking.

"S…S…Sam?" she whispered, so quietly Tom doubted Sam would hear.

"Go on," Tom urged.

Sam reached the edge of the veranda and slowly descended the steps. Chantal was frozen to the spot, as the object of her devotion, the pinnacle of her long-held hope, walked towards her in the flickering torchlight. He opened his arms and enveloped her. Chantal's body was like a statue – her arms refusing to move. Tom stepped back.

"I'll go for a stroll, and let you have some privacy," he indicated.

Chantal was motionless. Sam scooped her up in his strong arms and carried her up the steps into the wooden structure, kicking the door closed behind him. Slowly, Sam lowered the trembling woman to the ground, then gently propelled her towards the settee.

"You are in shock," he said, walking over to his kit bag to retrieve a hip flask. "Take a sip," he encouraged, unscrewing the lid.

Chantal took a gulp as Sam held the flask. The foul-tasting liquid trickled down Chantal's throat, causing her to cough and splutter. Sam sat down beside her, wrapping his strong, sturdy arm around the woman he loved.

"H...h...ow?" Chantal tried to formulate a question.

Sam reached out and stroked the side of Chantal's face.

"Ssh, my dear girl," he soothed, as she rested her head on his shoulder. "Ssh...all in good time," he pacified, as deep, heaving sobs engulfed her. His tight grip and the comforting beat of his heart gradually alleviated her overpowering emotions. Slowly, Chantal lifted her head. Sam cupped her face with his free hand and brought his lips to hers. The sensation she experienced ignited sparks of joy, mingled with relief.

"Oh, Chantal my love, I never thought I would taste those sweet lips again." He whispered into her ear as she leaned in close. "Let me explain briefly – the details can be filled in later.

"I was a medic on board a ship in the North Sea which was attacked. Few survived. Miraculously, I was found clinging to some floating debris, wounded and unconscious." Chantal reached out and took Sam's hand. "My rescuer was a Norwegian fisherman, who found me shelter with his parents on their farm. My wounds healed, but not my memory." As he spoke, he lifted Chantal's hands to touch the scar above his left eye. "I worked on their farm, oblivious to time and world events, which my hosts relayed.

"When Anders, the farmer, sustained a serious leg injury, I instinctively knew what was required. My quick intervention saved his leg...and his life. Images from my past slowly returned – you, my darling, amongst my earliest. When the war ended, I knew I must return, but my memory was patchy. I suspected I was a doctor. My accent told me I was Scottish, and there was a beautiful woman in my life – but I knew no names." He rubbed his thumb along Chantal's knuckles.

"My friends arranged a passage on a trawler to the River Tyne in northern England. I was given hospitality, along with many others in a similar predicament, in a mission home for fishermen. Slowly, my brain processes returned...and I remembered who I was." Sam was holding Chantal tightly as if she would vanish if he let her go. "Questions were being asked – I knew I needed to disappear. I did odd jobs, bought a bike and sustained myself with manual farm work – sleeping in barns and deserted outbuildings. A signpost to Blanchland reminded me of this place. I first stayed here last summer."

Chantal sat up and spoke. "I was here last summer. We found an old blanket and burned it."

He smiled. "I moved around, not too long in one place, but I returned here frequently, hoping to find a way to you. I needed to find out where you were, if you were married. I reasoned staying here, I might meet your sister. I couldn't move on until I had those facts, but... I was frightened to make myself known. Then last week... Tom found me."

They sat in silence, Chantal assimilating Sam's story. A gentle tap on the door broke Chantal's trance, signalling Tom's return.

Moonlight seeped into the room, as the door opened. Tom's figure outlined against the backdrop. "Only me," he spoke gently. "It's almost ten o'clock and I need to get home."

Momentarily, Chantal felt deflated as if the bubble she'd been in for the last hour had burst. She lifted her head from Sam's chest and made to stand up, but Sam pulled her back and whispered in her ear.

"Stay...please...Chantal."

She looked at Tom in the dim lamp light. "I ...I... don't know," she began.

Tom cleared his throat.

"I can return for you first thing in the morning, Chantal, if that's what you wish. I know Sam leaves early... shall I see you about seven o'clock?" Chantal nodded. "Goodnight," Tom added, turned and left.

Chantal sat back. Was she dreaming? This was unbelievable. After all these years, after all her strong feelings...here she was sitting beside the man she adored.

Sam reached out cradling her in his arms. "I love you, Chantal," he uttered and kissed her forehead, "but my life...everything... is such a mess."

Chantal trembled again, reality tweaking at the corners of her brain. "Tell me Sam," she urged.

She settled her head on his lap.

"I wasn't honest with you, my darling, and it's a bitter regret. Tom told me you know I am married. I did try to tell you in my last letter...but as I was about to place it in the envelope, I removed the sheet giving you the facts concerning my marriage. I figured if I didn't survive the war...it was better for you to remember our love, without that blight."

"But why did you withhold the truth from me during our time together?" she pleaded.

"Because the marriage was dead – it was a marriage of convenience, it meant nothing to me. Evelyn and I were thrown together as teenagers – she was the daughter of my mother's friend. She was attractive, but I didn't love her. I was a young student, taking hold of life and all it had to offer. Evelyn was devious and manipulative, tricking me by her pregnancy into an early marriage." He wiped his brow. "I was in my last year of medical school, and we lived with my parents – arguing constantly. One night after a dreadful row, she laughed at me scornfully and told me I wasn't even the father of our daughter."

Chantal gasped.

"I could take no more. I moved out of our room and told her I was seeking a position away from Edinburgh, when I qualified. It was a relief when I secured a job in Newcastle. Sadly, I was Francesca's father on paper and was expected to play 'happy families' for the sake of our parents, during Christmas and summer. It was the price I had to pay for a misguided decision as a young student. When I met you, Chantal, I discovered what it meant to be in love."

Chantal gazed into Sam's eyes. The eyes of the only man she'd ever loved.

"But why didn't you divorce her, surely she wanted to be with the father of her child?"

Sam laughed. "Oh, that was never going to happen – he was a married man when he fathered the child and our families are Roman Catholics, so divorce was not an option." Sam stopped talking and caressed Chantal's face, then kissed her lovingly. She felt a warm glow radiating throughout her being at the depth of his embrace. He ran his fingers through her hair, pulling her tighter.

"Staying here, in this shack, I felt so close to you. Visions of the time we spent here thrilled me...so I kept returning." Gently he brought his lips to hers again, his kisses were potent. They were locked in a capsule of relief...an expression of love and serenity.

"Oh, Chantal, I'm at a crossroads…I'm a dead man walking. I should have gone to Edinburgh and revealed myself…but I didn't… and now Tom tells me I am officially dead. Part of me sees this as a solution to be free from Evelyn for good… and I'm surviving. But my goal was to find you, then return to Edinburgh and face the consequences. I have no idea what will transpire."

They sat in companiable silence.

"I have nothing to offer you, Chantal… nothing, but can I ask… can we enjoy… one more night of love?"

The smile on Chantal's face spoke a thousand words. The bliss, rapture and ecstasy which followed was far more than words could articulate.

Chapter 22

News of Sam's 'return from the dead' brought great jubilation to the residents of Meckleridge House over the coming days. Astounding...amazing... incredulous...unbelievable – the words tripped off everyone's lips as his story gradually sunk in. For Sam and Chantal, a false sense of *'joie de vivre'* filled their days and a blissful euphoria filled their nights, which Chantal spent at The Bungalow, with Tom offering Chantal the use of his car. But the end of August was looming, and Chantal knew she must return to France. Discussions concerning their future surfaced from time to time. Pierre brought his wisdom into the situation. Sam was advised to seek legal advice as soon as Chantal returned home. Tom offered to assist.

"Will he face a criminal charge?" asked Peg, one evening towards the end of the holiday. Pierre exhaled.

"I would like to think his circumstances will speak in his favour. There will be questions as to why he was back in this country for so long, before he sought legal advice, but his state of memory may help. Legally, it will be a steep hill to climb, but he's one of hundreds, if not thousands of displaced people. The courts are slowly working through many similar cases."

The assembled group listened to Pierre's words.

"Chantal is determined to leave her job, return to England and seek work here," commented Rachel. "It makes sense…who can blame her, they have been separated for ten long years. If she is living here, she can support and encourage him whatever he faces. It's certainly a cause for celebration – to witness their joy is so heartwarming."

Tom was thoughtful. "Celebration on one hand, yes… but on the other hand – it's unlikely Sam's wife will agree to a divorce, even though the daughter is over twenty-one now, and is no longer a dependant. It will be a tough call for them to overlook the expectations of society. They will require great determination to overcome the obstacles which lie ahead.

In the corner of the room, Jonty, Josh and Henri were playing cards, but Henri was listening to the other's conversation. Like everyone else he'd welcomed Sam Carter – until recently only a name, but a name which symbolised 'hope' for Chantal. He'd spent hours walking the suburbs of Edinburgh, helping Darcy on her mission to uncover the man's background. He'd also shared Darcy's opinion regarding Chantal – hiding behind this 'hope' thing avoided facing up to the facts. Yet, all the time Chantal's gut feeling was correct.

"I win!" shouted Jonty, slamming down his final card.

The three lads laughed and one by one left the room. Henri ambled into the kitchen to get a glass of water. It was a tactic he'd adopted – to avoid watching Josh and Jonty taking the stairs two at a time. It hurt him mentally to observe their agility. Was he avoiding facing the facts? He'd postponed his initial idea to return to France with his family, after Tom cornered him a couple of weeks ago.

"Henri, please reconsider," he'd pleaded, "I need your help. All your record keeping will be wasted – how can I find the time to make detailed progress notes? Your ideas have been invaluable. Please stay until we see the results of these current experiments, and then return."

So, he was staying at Meckleridge House until November. But what about Darcy? Jonty's rationale, the week after they arrived, was at the forefront of his mind every day. His cousin had advised him to reconsider his relationship with Darcy – together they could be strong. Aunt Peg had tackled him last week. "You're good at this," she remarked, seeking him out in the greenhouse. "My brother tells me you have flair for this horticultural work. Think carefully, Henri – do you want to turn your back on this golden opportunity to be an apprentice in this area? What kind of work would give you this sense of achievement? Can you think of a comparative occupation in Lyon? Your medical condition will bring restraints, we all know that, but it doesn't have to be a sledgehammer through your life. You still have a brain. You have a rewarding occupation. You have an employer who understands your needs and will accommodate medical appointments and periods of absence, should they arise."

Uncle Pierre added his views. "You talk about returning to live in Lyon, Henri. You are always welcome to stay with us – but consider the practicalities. We live in a first-floor apartment – even if you seek your own apartment, climbing stairs will be a regular feature. Should your condition worsen, city living will prove challenging. Remember your mother in her wheelchair – she rarely left your apartment...is that what you want? Staying at Meckleridge will give you a better environment in which to live."

Henri climbed the stairs to go to bed, in his slow but pain-free fashion. Staying at Meckleridge was the best solution for his work, his accommodation and his medical care...but what about Darcy?

* * *

The night before the French visitors' departure was painful. After enjoying a celebration meal, courtesy of Rachel, Sam and Chantal returned to The Bungalow. As they sat in the faint glow of the paraffin lamp, Chantal stroked Sam's rough, gnarled hands. "Will these hands bring care and healing to injured, sick bodies again, my darling?"

Sam shook his head. "It's a dream, Chantal. I'm not a natural manual worker. I see young Henri and his orthopaedic problems – reminding me I used to assist men with the same condition. The medical advancements in the ten years I've been away, will have progressed and will continue to do so every day. He must not give up on a medical solution. But will I be given the chance to use my expertise again? It's a cherished hope, Chantal... maybe one day I can retrain, and use my medical skills once more." He placed his arm around his beloved and kissed her tenderly.

"How do you think your family will react?" Chantal enquired. She'd asked probing questions about his family since their reunion, but he was always reluctant to divulge details. He was silent for a few minutes.

"I think they will welcome me back, but the financial side of things will take some sorting. I was their sole heir. My mother inherited Matthison Hall on my grandfather's death – she was his only child. He made his money in a shipping company, which was sold when I was a youngster. The property plus the financial resources will be substantial. I expect Francesca and Evelyn will be set to inherit the Matthison assets, because it's their home. I am still Francesca's father...on paper." Sam shook his head. "I hope it can all be resolved. My return will certainly 'muddy the waters'." He bent over and caressed his dear one's face.

Chantal smiled. "Something else to hope for, Sam. I think I would be lost if hope wasn't present in my life!"

Sam tilted her head and gazed adoringly into her eyes. "Hope for a smooth process over my legal affairs; hope that Evelyn will grant me a divorce; and hope in resuming my medical career."

"But the miracle of it all, Sam, was the hope fulfilled in being reunited with you. I am so grateful we found each other again."

The early morning parting was brief – they spent their last night together, savouring the love they shared, but the final embrace took place. How long would it be before they met again? The future was uncertain, but at least they could communicate via letter and telephone. Chantal waved Sam out of sight as he rode his bike into the distance. Then collecting her belongings and locking The Bungalow, she drove Tom's car back to Meckleridge House.

Frenzied farewells resounded in the hallway, as the French visitors prepared to leave. Henri and Darcy were standing at the foot of the stairs, watching the proceedings. Rachel and Chantal were deep in conversation out on the driveway. Chantal and Darcy had said their parting words after breakfast.

"I've left my jacket on the bedroom door," yelled Sylvie, flying up the stairs to fetch it. Jonty and Josh were sharing some last-minute joke.

"Thank you, again, Rachel." Peg was hugging her sister-in-law. "It's been a memorable holiday. We're expecting to see you all in Lyon next summer." Bennie the farm manager was driving the visitors to the station along with Tom, so Rachel was staying behind.

Pierre walked over to Henri and hugged his nephew. "Stay positive, young man. Fight it!"

Henri nodded. "I will, it's been good to see you and share my problems," he added.

Darcy raised her eyebrows at the comment.

"Challenges, Henri...not problems," remarked Peg, hearing her husband's words and pulling her nephew into a farewell embrace. "You're made of strong stuff, young man – be an overcomer," she added.

Eventually, the cars drove away. Rachel asked Darcy for help stripping the beds and Henri bent over to stroke the dog. Darcy couldn't resist a comment as she walked past Henri to follow her mother upstairs.

"Stay positive...fight it...be an overcomer! Your family believe you have the ability; I believe you have the ability, Henri Dukas – you've the one who won't believe it! Oh, and for your information, I have a date tonight with Fred, the boy I danced with at the jamboree. I'm not sure why I'm telling you, but after six weeks I've decided to accept his invitation, before he goes to university." She turned and stomped up the stairs.

It felt like a stab in the back. Darcy was going on a date. He remembered the lad on the dance floor that night. So, this Fred asked her out...yet she'd waited to accept his invitation. Henri swallowed. Perhaps she'd postponed it... in case things resumed between them? He stood up and left the house.

The usual absorption in his work was elusive that day. Henri couldn't concentrate – he was in danger of making a mistake, so he walked out of the glasshouse and wandered across the lawn. His mind was in turmoil. The thoughts of his Darcy...his beloved Darcy, in the arms of another man was unbearable. He loved her with a passion he didn't think he could experience.

These weeks of self-inflicted separation had been torturous. He allowed himself to recall the feel of his lips on hers. She was his everything. Life held no purpose without her. He was a fool for throwing her into the clutches of another. If it had been that Grady Forrester, his old adversary, he'd have...have...punched him and sent him packing! She was his Darcy...this lad Fred didn't deserve her.

He ambled around the grounds, considering the advice he'd been given by his family. He recalled the looks of adoration he'd noticed on Sam and Chantal's faces – the way they held hands, entwining their fingers; Sam's arm around Chantal's shoulder, gazing lovingly into her eyes – it was love and he was throwing his love away. He looked up, a wave of decisiveness swept over him, and he walked back into the house with purpose.

* * *

"Where's Darcy?" asked Josh flying into the kitchen and sitting down at the supper table.

"Out on a date with Fred Morrison," replied Rachel.

The knot in Henri's stomach twisted, as he stared into his bowl of tomato soup. Rachel had already spoken about the 'nice young man', Fred Morrison, whom she used to tutor a couple of years ago.

"Where have they gone?" enquired Josh, piling onto Henri's anguish.

"Newcastle. They are going for a meal, then to see a film and getting a train home about nine o'clock," Rachel replied, collecting the soup dishes. It was cosy eating in the kitchen after four weeks of using the formal dining room.

Josh was looking reflective and stared at Henri. "So, are things over between you two?" he asked bluntly.

"Josh," reprimanded his mother, "that's none of your business."

Josh pulled a face and mouthed 'sorry' to the Frenchman. After finishing his meal, Henri excused himself and Rachel buttonholed her son.

"Josh, Henri and Darcy's friendship is going through a sticky phase. It's best not to mention it in general conversation, I sincerely hope they can overcome their difficulties. Darcy is free to date other young men during this time."

Josh pulled a face again, feeling put in his place over the subject.

"I telephoned the solicitor when I got back from the station," remarked Tom to Rachel. "I've got an appointment on Friday." Tom was hoping to make anonymous enquiries regarding Sam, when he visited their family solicitor.

Rachel sighed as she washed the dishes. One lot of issues solved... and another lot of issues were waiting in the wings. It was life...and life was filled with ups, downs, twists and turns.

Henri was sitting at his desk, studying. He was also watching the time. Just before nine-thirty he closed his textbook and walked over to his bedside drawer. He picked out a tin containing an assortment of odds and ends. Rummaging around he found the object of his search. He donned his jacket, suspecting there would be a chill in the air, and placing the item in his pocket, left the room.

He walked along the landing, and quietly descended the stairs. Thankfully, no one was around as he slipped out of the front door, gently closing it behind him. He made his way down the driveway then stood behind some laurel bushes to wait. He was unsure of the exact timing but was guessing his wait should be rewarded within thirty minutes.

The minutes ticked by, and Henri was feeling cold. A late summer chill surrounded him – he'd been wise to fetch his jacket. Just after ten o'clock, he heard a crunching noise on the gravel driveway, followed by low voices. He stayed still, then peeped out as the two figures walked onwards up the winding drive. Judging a suitable distance, Henri stepped out onto the path and followed Darcy and her companion as they approached the front door of Meckleridge House.

He kicked at the gravel to herald his approach, deliberately keeping his head down.

"Henri," called Darcy, turning and looking startled. "What are you doing out here?"

Henri stopped in front of the couple. "Oh, I was taking a walk to clear my head, I've been studying," he explained. Darcy introduced her friend to Henri. Then moving towards the door he added, "Darcy, can I speak to you when you come in, I'll wait in the hall." Henri opened the front door and stepped inside the house – his plan was working... so far. He sat on a chair, hoping the family were elsewhere. In less than two minutes, Darcy entered the hallway and Henri stood up. Darcy removed her coat, hanging it on the coat stand then walked over to the young Frenchman.

"Did you do that deliberately, Henri Dukas?" she asked mischievously. A slow smile tweaked at the corners of Henri's lips, as he dropped his eyes to stare at the floor. "That's the sort of antics I would expect from my father, not my ex-boyfriend," she chortled.

Henri lifted his head. "Can we talk...in private?" he asked.

Darcy smiled and led the way across the hall to a small room, rarely used. She switched on the light. The room smelt musty. Henri had been in this room before – it was the library – a throwback to the hotel days, but mostly neglected now.

"Gosh, this place could do with sorting," Darcy remarked, walking into the centre of the room and turning to face Henri who closed the door. "Well, monsieur – what's on your mind?" she asked, smirking, and hoping her plan had worked.

Henri leaned against the dresser. "Two things. Firstly, I want to apologise for my behaviour towards you since my diagnosis. I confess I've been self-centred, and rejecting you appeared the only way to handle things." He paused and Darcy started to tap her foot impatiently.

"Get on with it, Henri – say what's on your mind without giving me a speech!" she exclaimed.

Typical Darcy, thought Henri – he'd spent all afternoon preparing his words of apology.

"Okay, so you don't want the speech…I'll move on. Secondly," he coughed; Darcy burst out laughing. "Right, little miss…. Here it is… up front and in your face." Henri Dukas stepped across the room and placed his hands on Darcy's shoulders. He towered above her. She lifted her head, and their eyes met, closely followed by their lips. His kiss was deep and demanding – he was a man on a mission…a mission to convince the woman he loved how much she meant to him. Darcy enjoyed the thrill and the excitement of his actions, responding to his obvious hunger. He pulled back.

"They say actions speak louder than messages – have you got my message, Miss Smallwood?" he asked with a cheeky grin on his face.

Darcy chuckled. "It's words, Henri, not messages... and in response – yes, your message is loud and clear! Now, monsieur...what is your second thing?" Henri reached into his pocket and retrieved the item he'd placed there earlier. He held up a tiny ring. Darcy stared, almost going cross eyed, it was so close. The ring was small and delicate, consisting of a garnet stone and two tiny diamonds. She gasped wide-eyed.

"Secondly, I can't get down on one knee and I've already done the romantic location bit. So, here's my second time proposal. It's plain and simple, no flowery language. Will you, Darcy Smallwood, knowing everything that's against us, be willing to bind yourself to me, on a rocky path called marriage?"

"Oooo, Henri Dukas, you have such a way with words. That's probably one of the most unromantic proposals a man could make...but it suits me fine and the answer is... YES!" she yelled the final word.

Henri placed the little ring on her finger. "It belonged to my mother – it's been in an old tin box for years. If you don't like it, I can buy a new one."

Darcy flung her arms around Henri's neck. "I love it, Henri, and I love, love, love you! Don't you go all self-centred and resigned on me again. No more 'pity parties', do you understand me? We're in this together and I adore the ring, I wouldn't change it for anything. Now there's one small detail you might have overlooked...my dad!"

Henri lifted his eyebrows.

"Yes, I know...he'll want you to wait until you are twenty-one – that's over two years away. I'm not sure we can wait that long. I mean, to put it bluntly – will I be agile enough by then?"

Darcy blushed. "Henri Dukas, fancy having those kinds of thoughts," she commented, as the library door opened.

Tom stood in the doorway. "I thought I heard voices, is everything alright, I thought you'd been out with Fred Morrison, Darcy?" Tom asked, slightly bewildered.

"Yes, Dad, I had a pleasant evening with Fred and my little plan worked. I set a trap for Monsieur Dukas, and he walked straight into it. I think it's called applying feminine wiles!" Henri looked perplexed. "I'll explain later, Henri. Anyway, Dad...look at this." She wafted her pretty engagement ring in front of her father.

Tom was dumbfounded. He looked at Henri.

"I'm sorry, Tom. I should have spoken to you first... but circumstances took over. Can I arrange to chat with you tomorrow?"

Tom sighed and wrapped one arm around his daughter and one arm around the young Frenchman.

"Congratulations and God bless you both. You've got a struggle ahead, but I think you'll cope." Raising his voice he yelled, loudly, "Rachel, can you come in here please?"

Within seconds, Rachel came hurtling through the door. "Yes, where's the fire?" Rachel asked, panicking.

Tom reached forward and lifted Darcy's hand, showing his wife the ring. Rachel stared in astonishment, clasping a hand to her mouth.

"The only fire around here is the one that's burning inside these two," Tom chuckled. "We'll talk... at length tomorrow, Henri," he declared. "After breakfast in my office."

Rachel embraced the young couple, adding her congratulations.

"What's going on?" asked Josh, entering the library, followed by the dog.

"Your sister and Henri are engaged, Josh, congratulate them," she announced, smiling.

Josh was puzzled. "But I thought things were over between you two, and you went out on a date with Fred Thingy," Josh queried his sister, admiring the dainty ring.

"It's called strategy, Josh, female strategy...and it worked!" Darcy declared, taking her fiancé by the hand and leaving the library. "Come on, Henri – we have much to discuss." They walked through to the lounge, a room on the side of the house overlooking the greenhouses.

"This room is pleasant, but your family don't use it much – is there a reason?" Henri enquired.

Darcy shrugged. "It used to be used all the time when the house was a hotel. But since the war ended, Mother and Dad prefer the conservatory, because it benefits from the sun all day."

Henri sat down and hugged Darcy. "Now, *ma chérie*, what were these 'feminine wiles' you spoke about earlier?" he queried, grinning.

Darcy tried to look completely innocent but could not contain her laughter. She draped her arms around Henri's neck and pulled him into a lingering embrace.

"Let's just say it was worth enduring an evening with the bombastic Fred Morrison, to achieve this staggering result," she chortled, wafting her engagement ring in front of Henri.

He cupped her face. "You, Darcy Smallwood, are a devious little tease, but I wouldn't have you any other way."

Chapter 23

Henri fidgeted with his hands as he sat in Tom's office the following day. Tom was on the phone. In the cold light of morning, his actions the previous night appeared hasty and rash – but satisfying. The bleakness of his future was transformed. From the day he'd received news of his condition until last night, he'd walked a troubled path, seeing negatives everywhere. He'd been in a long, dark tunnel of resignation and self-pity, which felt like two years instead of two months.

He straightened in his chair as Tom lifted one finger – Henri assumed the call would terminate in one minute. He glanced out of the window – the murky, morning mist was lifting. Sunlight was tinkering around the edges, hinting at the promise of a fine autumnal day. Sunrise, sunlight, sunset and moonlight, the four light stages of the day, each brought their beauty and with Darcy at his side they would walk through those days together.

"Sorry about that, Henri," remarked Tom, replacing the receiver. "Now, young man…last night?"

Henri had spent a restless night trying to guess how this chat with Tom would proceed.

"Tom, I'm sorry if I did things the wrong way round. It was not my intention to overlook the protocols of seeking your approval for my engagement to your beautiful daughter. However, circumstances took over and I knew I needed to be proactive, hence my actions." Henri was aware he was blabbering, so unlike his usual controlled mode of conversation.

Tom sat with his arms resting on the chair, his fingers steepled, his face serious.

"I may as well say what's on my mind, Tom. I love your daughter, deeply. Before my diagnosis I had asked her to marry me, and she accepted. Of course, we knew it would remain unofficial and guessed you would advise us to wait until Darcy reached an appropriate age." Henri paused, recalling how their future was so bright at that point.

"Then this happened–" he slapped his thigh– "and all my expectations tumbled around me. The last two months have been a nightmare. I terminated my romance with Darcy the next day, hoping we could remain good friends, which we did... but it was becoming increasingly difficult. I've wept, rationalised, analysed and tried to justify my reasons to turn my back on Darcy, but I've failed. I need her in my life, Tom." He broke off, trying to formulate his next words.

"Things seemed to come to a head yesterday and I acted on an impulse – but it was genuine. I adore your daughter, Tom, and will do everything in my power to make her happy. I need her by my side – together we can be strong. It's a big step and a gigantic leap into an unknown future. Am I being selfish? I've asked myself this question countless times, but I can't envisage a way forward without Darcy in my life." Henri stopped – there was one more thing he needed to say.

"So, in conclusion, I'm asking for your approval on what may seem a reckless request. I would like to marry Darcy as soon as possible, because I want to be a proper husband to her. The physical implications of my condition are unknown, but I want us to experience a few years of normal married life. She wants our marriage as much as I do, so I'm not speaking out of turn. However, we will abide by your decision." Henri exhaled, relieved to have ended his discourse.

Tom rubbed his jaw. As Darcy's father he of course desired the best for his daughter. From first holding her as a baby in his arms, he'd wanted her to fulfil her potential in life. As she grew and her feisty, determined attitude developed, he'd always hoped she would make her mark in the world. The world war had robbed young people of their ambitions, but thankfully, his daughter had escaped those harsh realities. Even with this scatterbrained notion to become a journalist, Tom knew he would support her... and now this young Frenchman had worked his way into her affections.

He admired Henri Dukas. He'd proved himself to be a keen learner and was showing great aptitude in the study of horticulture. He'd displayed fortitude handling his difficult upbringing. Circumstances had accelerated his maturity into a sensible young man. Tom faced a dilemma. There was no doubt the young couple were in love...but would it stand the test of time? He was happy to approve their engagement ...it was a *fait accompli*. But what would happen if Henri's condition worsened? Envisaging his beautiful young daughter, bound in marriage to a dependent husband...the prospect troubled him...so, he must convey his concerns.

"Henri," Tom responded, "I understand your reasoning. As indicated last night you have my wife's and my own congratulations on your surprising engagement. I could have wished for a more conventional approach, but knowing Darcy – I doubt that was ever going to happen. However, I must ask you to wait to marry. She will be twenty-one in just over two years' time. Give her a chance to pursue this journalism idea... and grow up. Two years will help you to get to know each other better and to avoid a hasty marriage. I'm sorry if this is not the response you were looking for today, but I trust you will understand my caution." Tom stood – what more could he say? They shook hands and Henri left Tom's office.

The young couple were disappointed... but not surprised.

"I start my secretarial course next week," Darcy informed Henri. "I'll be travelling into Newcastle each day, so it will keep me busy. Let's remain hopeful – hopeful for a medical solution to your condition, hopeful for our marriage to be sooner than expected, and hope for my journalistic career to begin properly. It's *hope on hope*, Henri!"

* * *

Tom Smallwood and Sam Carter stood outside the solicitor's office in Malhaven. It was a place Tom had frequented many times in his lifetime, for a variety of reasons. Today's visit was somewhat unusual. A brief appointment with Hugh Porter, a long-time associate of Tom's, the previous week, had led to this crucial meeting today. Beside Tom stood a man who legally did not exist. Tall, erect, a little ruddy in complexion but cleanly shaved and smartly attired. Two days earlier Sam had undergone a transformation back to civilisation. He had left his job on the farm he'd worked at for many months, the farmer sad to hear he was moving on. He collected his belongings from The Bungalow and took up residence in a former hotel bedroom in Meckleridge House. Bennie the farm manager was happy to accommodate a new worker on the farm.

After visiting Tom's barber, Sam's face and hair were refashioned. Tom's tailor in Malsett continued the makeover – a new wardrobe of clothes, shoes and accessories were purchased. An appointment at Tom's dentist was somewhat uncomfortable, but necessary. In the space of two days, the 'vagrant' from Trespershields resembled a man befitting of his former status.

The family applauded the new look Sam. "A photograph," declared Rachel, running to the bureau to retrieve her old box Brownie camera. "We must send a photograph to Chantal to showcase the recreation of Sam Carter." But the process of returning to civilisation required more than a renewed appearance.

"Good morning, Mr Carter, I am pleased to make your acquaintance," greeted the solicitor, looking much older than the young man who had represented Tom many years ago. After taking their seats Hugh Porter addressed Sam.

"Tom has apprised me of your unfortunate wartime experience, Mr Carter. Personally, I have not handled a matter of this nature before, but I am aware of professional colleagues who have encountered similar circumstances. I have obtained the necessary forms to counteract your 'death certificate', but I must inform you it is inevitable the police will become involved, and each case is individual. It is a legal process, and it will take many months or even longer to conclude. But, Mr Carter, you have taken the first step today – so your journey back from the dead has begun!" Hugh Porter smiled, but it did little to quell the panic rising within Sam. A long trail lay ahead.

* * *

Epilogue

JANUARY 1950

'Happy birthday to you
Happy birthday to you.
Happy birthday, dear Darcy,
Happy birthday to you!'

Rachel was standing beside Darcy's bed holding a breakfast tray. It was laid with an embroidered tray cloth and rose patterned crockery. She placed it carefully on the bedside table as the birthday girl sat up. Darcy rubbed her sleepy eyes and looked at the clock.

"Mother it's only six o'clock, what are you doing up at this hour?" Normally, it was Darcy who graced the early morning hours, but today Rachel had made a special effort.

"Well, considering it's your last morning as Miss Darcy Smallwood I thought I'd make the effort and present you with breakfast in bed. Happy birthday, darling, and happy wedding day!"

Darcy sipped her tea and cracked the shell on her soft-boiled egg. "Oh, mother – 'dippy soldiers'," she squealed in delight, as she placed the teaspoon into the egg, sitting proudly in its bone-china egg cup. A volcanic eruption of runny yolk oozed out of the shell as Darcy poked her brown bread soldier into the yellow lava. "Just the way I like it," she enthused.

Rachel sat on the bed watching her twenty-year-old daughter delve into her breakfast, with no evidence of wedding nervousness. Twenty years…how was it possible? Where had the years gone? Since Henri and Darcy became engaged in August 1948 this day had been eagerly anticipated.

The young couple accepted Tom's insistence they should wait until Darcy's twenty-first birthday before marrying. They both settled into their work routines as an engaged couple. Darcy's days were busy, first with her secretarial course at a college in Newcastle and then a year ago she had taken up a position with a small weekly newspaper – The Malsett Guardian, at their offices in the town.

Henri bought a car, and she drove herself to work each day. 'Journalist' was hardly the correct description for her role, but her typing and shorthand skills were used, and she was hopeful it was the first rung on the ladder. She frequently wrote articles for magazines and newspapers, submitting them regularly. So far, she'd been successful, with one article published in The Newcastle Journal.

Last August, a year after the engagement, when Peg and family were visiting for their annual holiday, Tom made a surprise announcement as they were finishing supper in the dining room. He rattled his glass with a spoon and stood up.

"I have two announcements to make, and both require a toast. So, Rachel, would you supply everyone with glasses, while I collect some bottles from the pantry."

Rachel and Peg hastily brought out the flutes, from the sideboard as Tom walked back into the room carrying bottles of champagne. Everyone looked excited and at the same time perplexed.

Chink! Chink! Chink! Tom tapped the side of his glass as a signal for the first announcement.

"My dear family...as you are all aware, I have held a dream for many years of developing a new species of rose. Yesterday, I received an important letter. I'll spare you all the boring technicalities and it is only a first step. But, with the help of my wonderful assistant, Henri, we have cultivated a new species of pink rose, with a somewhat 'fruity' fragrance." Cheers resounded around the table, as a beaming Tom lifted his hand for them to pause. "As was required, we were asked to supply a name. for our creation and we are delighted to inform you the name of our new rose will be… 'Darcy'!"

Hoots of delight, handclapping and backslapping erupted from the assembled guests. An animated Tom continued. "And the name has been approved." With whoops of praise, glasses were clinked, and a chorus of 'well done' resonated around the room.

"I confess when we named our firstborn child Darcy Rose, I must have been prophetic."

Everyone laughed, and an outburst of applause followed, although many of the assembled group were unaware of Darcy's middle name.

"Have you been keeping secrets from me, Henri Dukas," whispered Darcy to her fiancé.

Henri squeezed her leg under the table. "Sorry, but I couldn't steal your father's moment of glory!"

"You said two announcements, dear brother," Peg reminded Tom.

"Aah, yes. Well, as you all know Henri and Darcy have been engaged to be married for almost a year now. I confess to being the 'stumbling block'; the one who wanted them to wait; I was cautious of their youthful romance, thinking time would help them to be sure... but as I have observed their love and devotion to each other...I cannot deny them any longer. So, I'd like to announce I will give my blessing to their marriage on Darcy's twentieth birthday – 30th January 1950!"

Darcy almost choked on her champagne. "Henri Dukas, have you been keeping another secret from me?"

> *Henri squeezed her leg again. "Not this time, I knew nothing of your father's decision," he admitted, chuckling.*
>
> *The glasses were raised a second time. "To the marriage of Henri and Darcy!" everyone cheered.*

Rachel blinked as her daughter finished her breakfast with a flourish. "I can't believe it, Mother. Today I will become Madame Dukas."

Tears flowed down Rachel's face – it was sadness and joy mingled together. She reflected on the 'mishap' Henri had sustained in the greenhouse last autumn. He had stumbled, badly. It was over an hour before Tom found him in agony on the cold concrete floor. It took two weeks of bedrest before he recovered and a further two weeks using his crutches. It was inevitable there would be further occurrences of this nature.

So much uncertainty awaited the young couple… but then, wasn't uncertainty a part of life? Her daughter and future son-in-law possessed a steadfast hope for their future, and surrounded by a loving family she was sure they would make it.

Meckleridge House was no longer a hotel, but it was almost back to its former use. It would now provide accommodation for three families…The Smallwoods – Tom, Rachel and Josh; Monsieur and Madame Dukas; and the Carters – Sam, Chantal (still Martin) and their eight-month-old twins, Conrad and Hope. Sam's family had welcomed his 'return from the dead', but Eveyln held on to her determination, refusing to agree to a divorce. The legalities of his parents' will were still being processed.

The bride looked radiant as Tom led her down the aisle of St. Cuthbert's Church in Malhaven. Rachel had spent hours creating a stunning bridal gown. Henri's joy was overflowing as he took his beautiful bride's hand and gazed adoringly into her pale blue eyes. Chantal and Sylvie were bridesmaids and Jonty and Josh were best man and groomsman respectively. As the young couple took their vows, there was a strong emphasis in Darcy's tone as she pronounced the words...*'in sickness and in health'*.

The wedding breakfast was held in the hall adjacent to the church and afterwards the family returned to Meckleridge House to wave the newlyweds off on their honeymoon in the Lake District. The day was cold but dry. Jonty and Josh were gainfully employed attaching tin cans, bound together with string, to the rear bumper of Henri's MG sports car, when Sylvie appeared.

"My sister will be furious," laughed Josh, as Sylvie liberally adorned the inside of the car with coloured paper confetti. Minutes later the happy couple emerged from the house, followed by the rest of the family. Darcy and Henri stared at the decorated red car in amusement.

"Oh, no – I might have guessed. Just wait until it's your turn...I'll remember this send off!" chuckled Darcy. The cans clanked and rattled as Henri drove away and they waved farewell to their loved ones.

Sam and Chantal took their place alongside the others, Sam holding baby Conrad, and Chantal holding baby Hope.

Sam whispered in Chantal's ear. "One day, my darling, it will be our turn... our hope to marry will be rewarded!"

Two months previously, Sam was officially informed he was 'alive' and next month he was to begin his retraining programme to become a registered doctor again. "Two 'hopes' achieved, Chantal... and one more to go," he remarked.

Chantal smiled, twisting her fake wedding ring, as baby Hope gurgled. "Let's keep building, Sam... *hope on hope!*"

Author's Note

HOPE ON HOPE is the sequel to BLOSSOMING OF TRUTH, Tom and Rachel's story.

Originally, BLOSSOMING OF TRUTH was meant to be a 'standalone novel', but after living with the characters for many months, Tom 'got under my skin'. I felt compelled to continue Tom and Rachel's story – HOPE ON HOPE is the result. Although he is not the main character, Tom's role is significant, and I trust you have enjoyed Tom and Rachel's participation as they navigate the traumas of family life.

Of course, I needed to leave the days of the 1920s behind, but I found post-war Britain was an equally intriguing era in which to set a novel.

The Bungalow is modelled on a country retreat owned by my grandparents. It was demolished, along with other properties, to make way for a local reservoir, constructed in the 1960s. Childhood memories shaped the setting, and I evoked reminiscences among family and friends who could still recall the country shack.

Susan Gray

* * *

If you have enjoyed reading HOPE ON HOPE

Please leave a review on Amazon or Goodreads.

Please follow me on:

- *www.facebook.com/susangrayauthor*
- *www.instagram.com/susangrayauthor*
- *www.x.com/susangray275384*
- *www.tiktok.com/@susangrayauthor*

* * *

Acknowledgements

Firstly, to my readers…a big thank you. When I first put pen to paper in 2020, I could not have envisaged publishing three books. The encouragement and support I have received via reviews, messages, personal notes and conversations have inspired me to keep on writing.

I am indebted to my dear husband, Vic, for his continued support and encouragement. He always provides a listening ear, helps with research and offers advice when needed and I greatly appreciate his 'chef skills'.

Once again, I wish to thank my friend and cousin, Ruth. We enjoy countless 'coffee and chat' sessions as the plot lines unfold. The extra pair of eyes and ears to scrutinize the development; the ability to stand back and view the whole storyline from afar; the pertinent suggestions she makes, have all proved invaluable. I am grateful for her artistic skills as she brought *The Bungalow* to life, based on our combined childhood memories.

I want to add a note of appreciation to my other 'draft' readers. Also, to the authors I have connected with on social media – it's good to share experiences.

Finally, my thanks go to UK BOOK PUBLISHING for working with me on this third publication.

About the Author

After celebrating a significant birthday, Susan Gray picked up her pen and began writing novels. When asked 'why?'…she replied, 'why not, you are never too old to follow your dreams'!

To date she has written seven novels and three are published – SPANISH HOUSE SECRETS, BLOSSOMING OF TRUTH and HOPE ON HOPE. They are all romantic mysteries set in the first half of the Twentieth Century.

She lives in northeast England with her husband and has a daughter and son, both married, two granddaughters and a grand dog. In addition to writing, she enjoys reading, crafting, puzzling, catching up with friends over a coffee and travelling.

She sets her books in the rolling hills and valleys of northwest Durham and tries to include many of the places she has visited in her writing.